Garden of Stones

by

Jody Offen

PublishAmerica

Baltimore

First printing

ISBN: 1-4137-2115-X
PUBLISHED BY PUBLISHAMERICA, LLLP
www.publishamerica.com
Baltimore

Printed in the United States of America

I dedicate this book to some of the most important people in my life. To my mom and my husband Rich for always believing in me. To my sister-in-law Cathie Fisher, and long-time friends Kelley Sullivan and Nancy Klinefelter for always being there when I needed someone.

I need to give special thanks to Kelley Sullivan. If it weren't for her constant encouragement, great sense of humor and belief in me, I may never have attempted to publish this story.

CHAPTER 1

He felt it again, feather light, brushing at the back of his mind. They were feelings not his own. Sorrow, anguish, despair. Focusing on the intruding emotions he waited…as gentle as a caress it came, a whisper: "Are you out there?" It was a voice so pure, so beautiful he couldn't comprehend the very thought of it. So filled with grief yet so disturbingly enchanting it touched his dark soul. He closed his eyes. He saw a cemetery filled with old growth trees. He could smell them. Cedar, pine, fir, they grew scattered amongst the headstones. Old headstones. Not as ancient as the stones of his homeland. The cemetery rested near a cliff overlooking the ocean? Yes, it was an ocean. He could smell and taste the salt in the moist night air. He saw the back of a female as she stood looking out over the vastness of the waters. She was dressed simply in blue jeans and a gray sweatshirt. He could not see her face. Long honey-colored hair spilled down her back and blew restlessly in the ocean breeze. Even in the light of the partial moon it glistened as if kissed by the sun, a sun he had not seen in over 500 years. Then it was gone.

He ran his hands through his dark thick hair before reaching out to switch on the computer. The screen instantly burst to life turning from black to the blue sky and white clouds screen saver that came pre-installed. Each time it came on he thought about changing it to something more personable, something more realistically suited to him. He sighed, there was no hurry. Time was the one thing he had plenty of. Leaning back in his favorite brushed leather chair, he put his hands behind his head and pondered the vision he had just experienced. He had felt the other's emotions on two separate occasions over the last few days, but had not experienced visualization until now. He was quite capable of communicating telepathically with his own kind or to read humans, as well as plant thoughts or images in their minds, but never had a human connected in this fashion to him. Was she one of them? He dismissed the idea and chastised himself for even allowing the thought to enter his mind. If she were of their kind he would know it. Who was this girl and where was she? Such raw, painful emotions she conveyed…the loneliness, a feeling he was no stranger to. An overwhelming urge to reach out to her possessed him. Channeling his thoughts along the mental pathway in which he had received her he responded, "I am here. Talk to me."

As he replayed the images in his mind, hearing her words again, he reveled in the feelings her voice alone produced in him. It had been centuries since he felt the emotions she unknowingly triggered within him. It stirred, touched, and tantalized him. He could smell the salt in her tears mingling with the perfumed fragrance of her hair as it danced ever so softly upon the wind. He could hear her heart beat. He was overcome with intense need, followed closely by desire. A longing to touch, possess and control her, to have her, to claim her. He groaned with the wanting of her. Fangs burst forth in his mouth.

Jamie wiped at her puffy, swollen eyes for all the good that was doing. At this point in her crying jag it was all but pointless to try and staunch the flow of tears that still had yet to come, she was nowhere near finished. Having that realization she wiped at her nose instead and let the tears run freely. She was a mess. Looking out at the water was as pointless as wiping her eyes because she couldn't see anything through all the tears anyway.

She sat down on the outcropping of rock and let her bare feet dangle recklessly over the edge. It wasn't a long way down, but if she were to fall she would surely suffer a broken bone or two at the very least. Right now she didn't much care one way or the other. She gazed up at the moon, which was not quite full yet, but provided enough light to see by. Its beam cast a long glowing line that shimmered like a path of silver out over the cold black water. The moon would be full tomorrow and she thought how unfair it was that Payton wouldn't be there to share it with her. She had buried him three days ago. The gut wrenching feeling of grief and loneliness enveloped her entire being. Did he suffer great pain? Will she ever see him again? The questions poured forth, as did her tears.

The cemetery had been closed to the general public for years now. It was an old family plot and all the family was gone now. She was truly alone. Alone and crying like when she was seven years old and had fallen off her bike skinning her knees. She took a ragged breath and thought of her family. The McPhersons were a pioneering lot. Strong Scottish roots that first stepped foot on American soil in the mid 1600s. They were of the few pioneers that forged into the wilderness, making the roads that other settlers used to migrate west. Her direct line of ancestors kept moving west till they ran out of land, coming face to face with the great Pacific Ocean. That is where they built their home, raised their families, lived, worked, and loved, as well as died. They were woodsmen, loggers and fishermen by trade but that was in the early years. As times changed and the forests shrank so did the size of their families. They used to have an average of seven to ten children back then and now most only had one or two. Where did they all go? She looked around at scattered grave markers belonging to her ancestors. Twice she tried to get special permission to bury a loved one here and twice the county officials denied her. The first time was seven years ago when her parents were killed while driving home in a rainstorm. She was sixteen years old. The only things that kept her going were her brother Jim, her paintings and craft work, and of course Payton, but that all changed a little over a year ago. Serving as a deputy sheriff Jim was shot and killed in the line of duty during a domestic violence call. That was when Jamie's world shattered.

She looked over at the still fresh grave where Payton lay. The moonlight bathed the small wooden cross she had lovingly made herself. Payton had been her friend, confidant and partner in life as well as grief. He was her rock. Payton made it possible to go on. Payton was gone now. Fresh tears seeped through her lashes. Payton knew how truly lonely he was. He knew because she told him. She told him everything, her thoughts, her fears and most importantly her dreams. Together they would sit on this very rock cliff. She would tell him all about her doubts as to whether or not she would ever meet anyone who felt right -- that special someone, the hero young girls dream about rescuing them from some dreadful catastrophic event. Where was her hero now when she needed him the most?

Still sobbing Jamie stood up, knowing that she needed to go home. She was so tired. The fine, cool, salty mist blowing in off the ocean breeze cooled her flushed skin, but did nothing to stop the sting of tears that still fell freely from her swollen eyes. She looked out over the waves, hearing their constant tumultuous roar as they crashed onto the log-strewn beach. Raising her arms to the heavens she called out with all her heart, with all that she was, with all that she was to be…"Are you out there?"

"I am here…talk to me."

With a start she whirled around only to find herself alone. Fear overwhelmed her as she scanned the shadows of the desolate cemetery. Reality made her look cautiously about, but the realization, which was slow in coming, was that she heard the words spoken in her head. Gasping for a breath she had forgotten to take she started walking. With a shaking hand she ran her fingers through her hair as she let out a nervous laugh, "Okay I'm hearing voices. I have totally lost it." She kept looking around, anxiety building within as she made her way back through the cemetery. She let out a start as she almost tripped over a tree root. "Of course I have lost it, I'm in a cemetery in the middle of the night. What am I doing out here in the dark?" She started to question her own sanity. "I didn't really hear voices I heard a voice. One voice, a male voice. It was the voice of my hero." She hiccupped. Was she babbling to herself? Of course she was, perhaps she was losing it. "Okay, calm down. I'm mentally and physically exhausted. I just need some sleep. I need to go home." She stubbed her toe and winced. "No… I'm really losing it." She almost fell over Grandpa Granville's marker. Damn, she should have brought a flashlight. Better yet she should have worn her shoes. *But people who hear voices in their heads don't do sane things like bring flashlights (or wear their shoes) to graveyards in the middle of the night, now do they?* she thought. Out loud she continued to ramble on to herself. "What am I doing out here? I'll tell you what I'm doing here. I'm talking to dead people. I'm not only talking to dead people, I'm talking to hero's that don't even exist," another nervous laugh, "and they're answering me." She groaned, "Oh God, please don't let me be going crazy." Under her breath she added, "please don't you answer me too."

Jamie all but ran up the dirt path the short distance to her house. Once inside she went straight to the cabinet above the cook stove dragging one of the old wooden kitchen chairs with her. Climbing up onto the chair she reached to the back of the cupboard. With a sigh of relief she removed a dust covered bottle of whiskey that had belonged to her father. *Now*, she thought, *just might be a good time to have a drink.*

"Aerik, calm down. You are making way too much out of this," Trayvon said, as he watched his friend continue to pace the floor, as he had been for the last half hour.

"I'm telling you I connected with her. How is that possible? She is a human." Aerik threw his hands up in the age-old cocky gesture of 'well, explain that.'

Trayvon could not help but grin. Aerik was most definitely not himself. It had been a very long time since he had seen his friend at a loss for an answer. Usually it was quite the opposite. Aerik had an answer for everything. Others actually sought him out for advice, yet here he was wearing a path through a two-hundred-year-old fine Persian rug. Over a vision of the back, back! mind you of a human woman as she wallowed in misery. It wasn't that he was totally cold-hearted, (well maybe he was but that was beside the point). Aerik didn't know this girl and she appeared to have no connection to anyone they knew. She didn't carry the essence of their kind, meaning she hadn't been marked.

Aerik continued on, knowing full well that Tray wasn't going to have an explanation, and if he did it probably would only be something he had already thought of himself.

"If this human girl is so under your skin I suggest you go find her, perhaps it is her destiny to be turned," he offered. "Where is she?" He couldn't help it. He knew Aerik didn't know exactly where she was, but he hadn't sparred with his friend in quite some time. It felt good.

Aerik pointed his finger at his best friend and said, "Wipe that grin off your face before I do it for you." All the muscles in his corded arm rippled as he moved. He was a large man and his shear size alone was enough to intimidate most.

Tray took a playful boxing stance. "Aerik, do you need to burn off some of that nervous energy?" he backed off and asked more seriously. "Have you fed lately?"

"I have fed, that is not the problem." Realizing that he was indeed acting like a nervous dolt Aerik sat down on the edge of his desk. "I know she is in America, most likely on the coast in the states of Washington or Oregon. She was surrounded by old growth forest. I could smell the trees, the soil; I could see the ocean." He crossed his arms over his massive chest and exhaled heavily.

"Do you think these connections will continue?" Trayvon inquired.

"I don't know but I cannot continue to sit around just waiting for them to happen. I feel that if I'm closer to the source that I may be able to find her and strengthen the connection between us. Help her some how." He shook his head. "The feelings I felt for her were," he struggled for the right words, "I shall just say they were quite intense, to say the least." He looked back at his friend. "I will find her. Perhaps then I will be able to find out why we have mentally linked."

Trayvon studied his friend. After a long silence he said, "Aerik, if you fall in love with this girl you will want to turn her. We both know that's not a choice to be taken lightly. If you fall in love and don't turn her, you may watch her grow old and die. Be careful that you don't end up being the one who's grieving." He held out his hand and a set of keys appeared from out of thin air. He dangled them like candy to a baby. "You may stay at the house I keep in Seattle."

Aerik squinted his eyes and questioned, "Since when do I need keys?"

"You don't," Tray shrugged nonchalantly, "but they do look good when you're opening the door to things like a house or car. There's a Jag in the garage." He smiled as Aerik took the keys. "Remember, my friend, first impressions are everything."

Jamie grabbed at another weed and yanked. The leaves broke off in her hand leaving the root still embedded in the ground. "No you don't." She grabbed her little garden claw and whacked at the dirt, ripping at the root that refused to give up its little bit of earth. "You're out of here." She took a firm hold of the annoying dandelion root and pulled with all her might. As if trying to get even for being torn from its home the root came loose suddenly, sending Jamie backwards, landing on her bottom. "Damn weeds." She looked at the root still in her hand. "You must have been the real cause for the term 'root of all evil' and some poor bastard decided to turn it into a money thing." Picking herself up off the ground she tossed the offensive weed into the pile of other just as offensive weeds that she had started about an hour before. She walked up and down the flowerbed along the front of the old farmhouse porch. Except for a few weeds she missed behind the rhododendron bush, she thought it looked pretty good. She went up to the porch to get a drink of soda before attacking those last few.

Her great grandfather had built the house where she grew up. Each generation to follow had added on to it making the home what Jamie thought of as a human puzzle. The wraparound porch was her favorite part of the house. Once painted white it was now a light shade of gray. She planned on painting the house this summer. Though weather beaten, it still held a strong homey charm. It would have made a great bed and breakfast but Jamie cherished her privacy too much to open her home to strangers.

She enjoyed sitting on the porch and looking out over the ocean. Jamie ran her hand reminiscently along the banister, over the spot where her mom used to always sit her cup. In the summer she would have tea after dinner, in the fall hot cocoa, and on New Year's Eve – hot buttered rum. Tears started to well up in her eyes. Removing her hand from the banister she quickly went down the few steps back to the yard. Taking a deep breath she decided to attack the last of the weeds then get busy spreading beauty bark. If she could just keep busy then she wouldn't have to think. If she didn't have to think then she wouldn't have to feel. If she didn't have to feel she wouldn't hurt. Keep working. The sun would be down soon and she would have made it through another day. She crawled back behind the rhody. The rhododendron shrub had leaves that stayed green year round and bloomed large pink flowers. It was protected by law as the state flower. Her mom said it was more important to them because they had a family story about the rhododendron. Her great-great grandmother was Elizabeth McPherson. The family lore was that she was a little sprite of a woman; very opinionated for the times and didn't take guff from anyone. She told you exactly what she thought whether you wanted to hear it or not. Well, Elizabeth's husband had told her that she would never see the day that a woman would vote, and come hell or high water his wife would never go to the polls. One day in 1892 the state of Washington set up voting booths for the women to choose the state flower for the up coming 1893 World's Fair to be held in Chicago. The story has it that Elizabeth marched herself to the voting booth wearing her Sunday best. She was also carrying a big stick just in case someone tried to stop her from casting her vote.

When the last of the weeds were pulled Jamie stopped long enough to grab her glass of soda and start back to spread the bark. As she stepped off the last step of the porch she tripped. Reaching out to break her fall she landed hard against the ground. The soda glass still clutched tightly within her grasp shattered upon impact slicing deeply into her hand. The pain was sharp and intense, burning like liquid fire. Retreating to the house she realized that this was no small cut. The blood was running down her arm dripping onto the floor as she made her way to the kitchen. Dirt and blood mingled in the bottom of the sink mixing with the running water. Jamie began to feel a little nauseous and dizzy. Putting her head down slightly she prayed that she wouldn't be sick. She silently scolded herself for being so weak. She was a McPherson. What would her Grandma Elizabeth do? She laughed a painful nervous laugh to herself as she thought in a panic. Probably get out her darning needle and sew herself up between fixin' supper for ten kids and chopping wood for the cook stove. Jamie quickly wrapped her hand in a kitchen towel and grabbed the keys to the truck off the wall by the door. She briefly wondered if the keys had hung in that same spot since they gave up their horse and wagon for a pick-up truck.

Jamie climbed into the big black Dodge Ram truck that had belonged to her brother. Blood was already seeping through the towel but she was sure she could make the ten miles into town. Thank goodness the truck wasn't a stick shift. Looking down at the blood-soaked towel she wondered how much blood loss was too much. She was hoping it wasn't shock she was feeling as a wave of nausea over came her. She felt weak and cold. She wished she had been wearing a sweatshirt instead of the Mickey Mouse tee shirt she had on.

The driveway was long and full of ruts. The truck bounced unmercifully. Wincing, Jamie reached out turning on the heater. She was shaking…cold or shock? The towel fell from her hand and she bled freely onto the truck seat. "I'm bleeding too much, this isn't good," she said aloud. She started to sob from fear as much from the pain. The main road was in less than a mile. She stopped long enough to re-wrap her hand. She was shaking so badly. Even her teeth were chattering. Questions pounded at her mind – Am I going into shock? I must have cut a vein. Maybe I won't make it town after all, if only I would have called someone first. Maybe I can make it to the store. Jamie started to panic and prayed for help. Suddenly she felt a little at ease, the pain and fear had lessened, almost as if something was shielding her from the hurt. The main road was close but she was getting light headed. It was at that moment that she realized she might not make it. Fear once again took over, gripping, choking her. She became angry with herself for making the wrong decision to drive into town. She didn't know why, perhaps it was in anger or just pure desperation, she called out in a half cry, "I know you're out there…I heard you." She said it almost as an accusation. She sobbed, feeling the weakness take possession of her body, robbing it of all her strength. "Please help me," she pleaded to whom, or what…ever it was she had been feeling and hearing in her mind.

"I'm coming." His voice was in her mind, strong, calming, reassuring.

"Hurry," she whispered. Her last thought before passing out was that she was so cold, so very cold. The truck coasted off the side of the road and bumped gently into an old tree stump, ten feet from the main road.

Minutes later, as the last rays of the sun disappeared on the horizon, Aerik burst forth from the earth where he had taken refuge just before dawn. He knew where she was now. His mental bond with her sharpened now that he was closer to her. He heard her prayer for help and knew she was dying. He had tried to ease her suffering by taking the brunt of the pain into himself, but he wasn't at full strength yet and was unable to transfer all her fear. Now that the sun was no longer in the sky he felt rejuvenated, at full strength, he moved quickly. He was at her side almost instantaneously.

The sight of her lying on the truck seat covered in her own blood gave him mixed emotions. He knew if he didn't act quickly that she would pass from this world and be forever lost to him. Was it fate? Was it her time or was he meant to find her to help her, to have her? As he fought the war within himself, over the right and wrongs of humanity and his destiny in it all, he slashed his wrist and held it to her mouth. He commanded her to "Drink." He sent the compulsion to her so strongly that she had no choice but to obey. He mentally forced her to take his life-giving fluid, knowing that with out his blood she would not survive. He also sent her sensations, feelings of comfort and reassurance that she was being cared for. He knew that if she did indeed survive this night they would be irrevocably bound for all eternity. With the taking of his blood he marked her. There would be nowhere she could go that he could not find her.

He bent over her small frame as his incisors lengthened just long enough to produce a small clear ball of fluid that dripped into her cut then retracted. Using his tongue he spread the precious healing liquid across the ragged wound on her hand. The nasty cut wrapped from the bottom of her pinky to the middle of her palm and was quite deep. She had severed many small blood vessels, the cause of all the bleeding. With the touch of his healing fluids he sealed the bleeders on her raggedly torn hand.

The taste of her blood slammed into him with such force it took his very breath away. Feelings and emotions swirled through him like a current of raw electricity. He snapped his head back needing even that smallest of distance between himself and her precious blood. Still he could not stop the fangs that exploded in his mouth. His eyes glowed crimson with need. Never had he tasted blood so sweet, so pleasurable to his senses, so totally intense it rocked his very soul. Exhaling slowly, he struggled to take control of his emotions. Never had he been so close to losing control of himself as he was at this very moment. The only thing that saved him from taking of her right now was her weakness and he would not jeopardize losing her.

As Jamie started to come to she was horrified and confused at what was happening to her. She could not stop drinking the precious life-giving fluid being offered to her, yet it repulsed her at the same time. She could only stare wide-eyed up at the beautiful stranger that held her so gently in his arms. His wrist pressed intimately to her mouth.

He felt her confusion, saw the terror in her eyes, smelled her fear. "I will not hurt you," he said aloud and in her mind simultaneously. "If you do not take what I offer you will die."

He wouldn't hurt her…she felt it, knew it, believed it. He was emitting a sense of calm. It flowed from him and engulfed her very being. She knew what he said was true. She didn't know how she knew, she just did. He was giving her life. She focused on his eyes, drawn to them. They held her captive almost as if by force. They were mesmerizing, deep dark pools that appeared to be bottomless; so dark they could almost be black. She felt as if he could see right through to her very soul. She felt intimately connected to this dark stranger. How could that be?

"Enough," he whispered in her mind. He removed his wrist the gash he had created sealed itself as if by magic. He wiped the blood from her lips. "Someone is coming, I must go." He brushed her hair back from her face looking at her perfection with awe. She was beautiful beyond description. "I have stopped the bleeders in your hand so you will be okay until she gets you to a doctor."

Jamie heard what he was saying; yet all she could really hear and feel was that he was leaving her. He saved her life. She knew it, like she knew the sun would rise tomorrow with or without her, and he was leaving. Panic rose swiftly, she did not want him to go. She needed him. "Don't leave me," she pleaded, but when she reached out to him he faded into a fine mist before her very eyes, then disappeared. In her mind she heard him speak. "Don't fear, little one. I will be watching over you. You only need to think what you want to say to me, I will hear it, we are connected."

The next thing she knew someone was opening the door to the truck gasping at the sight of her. "Oh my lord, honey, hold on." It was a voice she recognized. Looking up at her Jamie recognized Clare, who managed the little quick stop on the edge of town.

CHAPTER 2

Jamie sat on the hospital bed watching as the young intern with the goatee stitched her hand. A million questions buzzed in her mind like a swarm of bees. She felt utter horror and disgust at the thought of consuming a stranger's blood. It saved her life. How could his blood save her life? How did he know to give her his blood? She could hear him in her mind and he clearly heard her. What was he? *Vampire*...the word jumped out at her, causing her to gasp as the reality of the situation hit home. The intern looked up at her and apologized; he just assumed that he had hurt her. *It couldn't be*, her mind screamed out. *Vampire's don't exist, they're stories made up over the centuries to scare people...weren't they?* She drank his blood. She felt her stomach roll at the mere thought of it. She could still taste his blood, coppery, spicy, metallic. Through his transfusion she had felt so stimulated, so alive. She could actually feel her energy returning to her, a complete repletion. There must be something special about his blood that restored her, saved her. She had called to him and he came. They had a psychic bond; that she was sure of. He frightened and intrigued her. She wanted to talk to him. He said he could hear her thoughts to him.

Raised voices caught her attention. She strained to hear the conversation going on behind the closed curtain in the adjoining hallway.

"Clare, do you know how crazy that sounds?"

"I know, Doc, but you and I both know that I'm not off my rocker...not yet anyway. I'm telling you it was a big black wolf!"

"Perhaps it was a large dog. Hell it was probably one of those foreign breeds we don't see around here much," the doctor said.

"Well it didn't look like any damn dog I've ever seen. I swear it was inside the truck with her, then went out the window and just

17

disappeared…like it never existed."

"Perhaps the dog just smelled the blood and came to investigate." He cleared his throat. "Calm down and go on home, Clare. I'll see that she gets home safely."

Clare shook her head. "I don't know, I think I should stay with her."

"You'll do no such thing. It's getting late, go on home. I'll have Nancy Edgewood send her son Jeff over to take Jamie home and see to the truck. They've been dating since high school. She'll be fine." He used his 'doctor knows best' voice hoping it would help calm Clare down. She seemed more traumatized over this event than poor Jamie who was receiving all the stitches in the next room.

Jamie groaned when she heard the doctor mention Jeff Edgewood. He was the last person she wanted to see tonight, let alone helping her home.

"Did that hurt?" the intern asked, assuming the groan was due to his lack of experience.

Jamie shook her head. "I'm okay," she told him. She wondered to herself if that was a lie. Everything still seemed foggy. The peaceful feeling that surrounded her didn't seem right, like it was induced some how. Was it him? He said he could hear her. "Are you there?" she tested.

"I am closer than you think." His voice was clear, confident, it felt good, it felt right. She had the feeling that she had just received a hug. She looked around trying to see him.

"Hold still," Aerik ordered, in a voice that would only accept compliance. "The man has a needle in your flesh."

That voice! It internally caressed her. She could listen to that voice all night and not tire of it. Did it feel so good because he was speaking to her telepathically?

"Who is this Jeff that disturbs you?" he questioned. If she were thinking of him it would be easier to sift through her thoughts and memories surrounding him.

Jamie didn't know where to begin. She was so confused. What was happening to her? She didn't want to think about her relationship with Jeff. "Ow!" The intern had hit a nerve. She jerked her hand.

"Sorry," he apologized, for the third time. "Almost done. I just need to tie this off. There, we're done. I'll put these things away and I'll be back in a few minutes with your medication. I'll let Doctor Shepherd know that were finished in here."

Aerik had read enough of her mind to know that he was not going to let this Jeff take her anywhere. He wanted a relationship with her that she did not want.

"I will take you home." He said it more as a statement, than an option she could choose from. As his words sunk in, he felt her fear of the unknown, of him. "When I come for you do not fear leaving with me." He gave her subconscious a gentle command to obey him. It wasn't strong enough to demand complete obedience. If she truly did not want to go with him she would be able to override his persuasive suggestion.

The doctor entered briskly like he was in a hurry. Jamie wondered why he would be in such a hurry since she appeared to be their only patient. Maybe he had a late dinner waiting in the lounge. He looked over the job "Mr. Goatee" had done on her hand, nodding his approval of the intern's work. "So you cut your hand falling onto a drinking glass?" he asked yet he wasn't really asking. "I'm sure you'll be more careful in the future while walking with a glass in your hand. You're very lucky, a little deeper and you would have been in serious trouble." He began wrapping it up while making small talk.

"I guess I just didn't come down off that last step very well. To be honest I can't actually say I even tripped, I think I may have just placed my foot down too close to the edge of the step," Jamie told him.

"Your blood count is a little low, but from how Clare described the inside of your truck I'm surprised you have a blood count at all." He looked up at her and smiled before he went back to carefully wrapping her hand. "How's the pain? Is the shot we gave you for pain working?"

Jamie nodded.

"How have you been, Jamie? Are you doing all right out there in that big old house by yourself?"

Jamie remembered the last time they had talked was when her brother was murdered. Doctor Shepherd was a kind man, but even then, all the proper words delivered at just the right time wasn't enough to console her. "I'm doing okay," she lied.

"I saw one of your paintings on display at the lodge in Port Angeles about a month ago. Real fine work, real fine." He finished and laid her hand down gently. "Ah, just in time, Jasper," Doctor Shepherd got up. "These pills will help with the pain." He went on filling her in on the medications he was prescribing, and the post care of her injured hand. Before he left the room he added, "I called Nancy Edgewood and she's sending Jeff down to give you a ride home and see to your truck. I hope that was alright?"

"I already have someone coming to get me," she told him looking over at the phone, hoping not only that it worked but also trying to give the impression that she used it to call for a ride. She was a terrible liar and felt guilty over trying to be deceptive.

"Well I think it's probably too late to stop Jeff from coming but we can explain the mixup when he gets here," Doctor Shepherd told her. "Would you like to sit out here and have some coffee while you wait?" He pulled back the privacy curtain. "At least you won't feel so isolated."

"Thank you, I'd like that." Jamie really liked him. He certainly chose the right profession, caring for people seemed to come naturally for him. She followed the doctor out of the little cubicle into the main waiting area. *Much better*, she thought, just as empty but better just the same. She could actually see more than a pale white wall and a blue curtain. The pain medication was making her woozy and groggy, feeling as if she were living some horrible dream. *Am I dreaming?* That would sure make things much easier.

Jeff Edgewood in all his glory came bursting in through the emergency room doors. He still looked like the high school jock she remembered him being, not that it had been a long time, that would only be wishful thinking on her part. He was the all-American good looking boy, and he knew it. You could tell what season it was by the clothes he wore. He was dressed in blue jeans and a baseball jersey. Jamie almost wanted to laugh but it wasn't funny.

She had broken up with him shortly after Jim died. They had dated a few times during their high school years. It was after high school that the relationship became more serious and they only dated each other exclusively. She just always felt like something was missing, that he didn't truly love her. She believed from the bottom of her heart that if she were in true love she would know it without question. She would feel something so special inside that nothing on earth would matter but that one person and herself. She just didn't feel that way with Jeff. Then he started pressuring her to get married. When Jimmy died she just couldn't deal with the pressure anymore and broke it off. Jeff's reaction to that breakup told her that she had done the right thing. She will never forget his bitter words of anger. "You mark my words, Jamie McPherson, you'll never make it without me!" Jeff had yelled as he stormed off to his truck. "Don't you know what you're sitting on here? My parents could get us started and we could have it all!" Of course days later he apologized and tried to get back into her good graces but to no avail. The more he pushed her the more she distanced herself. She was even staying away from town just to avoid Jeff and his family. The last time she went to the hardware store Jeff's father, Connor Edgewood, cornered her asking why she dumped his son. Two days later Nancy, his wife, came to the house for coffee and a little "girl to girl" chat as she called it. Jamie basically spent the next hour listening to why she should be forgiving, (since it would be the right thing to do,) and give Jeff a second chance. Jamie felt like it was more important to Mr. and Mrs. Edgewood that they get married than it was to Jeff, which just didn't make sense since it would end up costing them money. Jeff's great plan was to get married and borrow money from his parents to develop Jamie's oceanfront property for a lodge or bed and breakfast similar to the one his mother already owned. It had only been seven months or so and Jamie had seen him with three different girls. Why she couldn't see it before the breakup was beyond her. It was now very obvious that he wanted her as a package deal and that package came with land. Yet here he was.

"Jamie, are you okay? Mom said you were in some kind of accident and needed a ride home. What's going on?" he questioned.

"I had a little accident while I was outside gardening." She held up her bandaged hand. She didn't want to explain to Jeff that she was clumsy and hoped that he wouldn't press her for more details, so she quickly added, "But I don't need a ride, Jeff. Doctor Shepherd didn't know that I already had someone coming to get me," she explained.

Jeff immediately looked irritated. "Who's picking you up?" he asked.

"I am." Aerik walked up like a breath of fresh air. His voice sounded like a musical instrument, it commanded attention. He came to a stop beside Jeff and reached out for Jamie's hand like a knight would a lady. Jeff moved over, intimidated not only by Aerik's size, (which was making him look puny and insignificant), but by his imposing manner. The man was down right massive!

"Jamie, who is this?" Jeff stammered, clearly at a loss for words.

Aerik turned immediately to face Jeff. His muscles flexed and rippled beneath his black shirt as he moved. "Allow me to introduce myself," he said in a voice that sounded almost hypnotic. He took Jeff's hand in his and gave it a firm quick shake. "I am Aerik Wolfe."

Jeff tried not to visibly wince. The strength of Aerik's grip was bone crushing. Who the hell was this arrogant bastard, and where did he come from?

Aerik smiled, "And you are?"

Jeff tried to stand taller, he wasn't used to being intimidated by anyone, and he didn't much like the feeling. "I'm Jeff Edgewood. I'm Jamie's boyfriend," he said with as much confidence as he could muster.

Aerik leaned down from his six-foot-four height to look Jeff right in the eye. "I'm sure you are confused. Jamie is with me, do you understand?" He spoke in a low, clear, authoritative voice.

"Yes," Jeff answered as he stared into Aerik's eyes. He felt as if he couldn't look away, held there by some spell. Those black eyes drew him in, pulled at him. He swore he saw a vision of a wolf ripping his throat open before they turned crimson red. He gasped and jumped back. All the hairs on the back of his neck and arms was standing on end. Never had fear so overwhelmed him.

"Jeff, are you okay?" Jamie asked.

Jeff's hand briefly touched his own throat then he brushed at his arms as if he were cold. "Are you sure you want him taking you home? Where did you meet this guy, Jamie?" His skin was literally crawling from fear.

Aerik wrapped his arm around Jamie possessively. He made it very obvious that he was more than just a friend. Mentally he spoke to Jamie. "Tell him I'm an old friend of your brother's."

"He's an old friend of Jimmy's," she said. "I'll be fine. I want to thank you for coming down, Jeff. I'm sorry about taking up your time," she added.

"Babe," Aerik called her, "let me take you home now. I have the car parked right outside." Aerik swept her around Jeff, leaving him to follow behind as they left the hospital. There was something he didn't like about Jeff, besides Jamie's ill feelings towards him. It was something he felt briefly when he shook his hand, a corruption of some kind. Probably in character from what he saw of Jamie's memories of him. He was glad that he would not be the one escorting Jamie home.

Jeff followed, but not too closely. He didn't like this Aerik Wolfe at all. He felt intense jealousy as well as dislike when he saw Aerik help Jamie into a mint colored Jaguar. Jeff seethed with envy, not so much that Jamie was with this man, but that he owned a car he could only dream about. Nobody around these parts drove a Jag. Who was he and where did he come from? Did he really see what he thought he saw, or did his last name plant the image in his mind? And what did he want with Jamie? The bottom line was that he didn't like this at all.

They rode in silence to the house, Aerik wanted to give her time to get used to him. He could still feel her fear of him. He couldn't blame her, he could be overbearing at times. He could validate all the thoughts and questions that were running around in her head, and there were a lot. He couldn't help but smile at one in particular; she thought he was sinfully handsome. She also liked the way she felt when he called her Babe. That he would remember for future use.

He followed her up onto the wraparound porch. "It is beautiful here." He watched her lean on the banister looking out at the Pacific Ocean. The cool breeze that swept over them rustled through the silky strands of her hair, allowing it to billow out behind her. He marveled at the sheer beauty of it. She subconsciously rubbed her good hand over the spot where her mother used to sit her cup. She was the most beautiful woman he had ever seen. His darker side wanted nothing more than to tear the offending clothing from her body, and take her where she stood. In all his years no woman ever made him feel this strongly.

Jamie turned to face him. She didn't bother to turn on the outside lights. The light from the full moon was plenty enough to see that he was the most handsome man she had ever laid eyes on. What was he? It didn't matter what he was, he felt right.

"You know what I am," he spoke to her – silently in her mind. Aloud he said, "but I'm not like the stories you heard as a child. I do not kill to feed."

"Will you feed on me?" she asked.

Aerik suppressed a groan. The mere thought of it was almost more than he could bear. "Only if you wish it," he said in a controlled voice. "I believe you are my soul mate and I would never take from you without your permission, you would have to offer it to me of your own free will." He could feel her heartbeat quicken at his words, smell the satisfying aroma of her blood as it rushed like liquid candy through her veins, every beat was music to his ears.

Jamie thought for a moment about his words, she hoped that they were true.

"You know they are," he spoke softly in her head. His eyes looked over her, holding her like she was a precious flower.

"I want to ask you so many things, I don't know where to begin." She said in frustration, "I think the shot they gave me is making it hard for me to focus." She rubbed her forehead as if it would help her think more clearly.

Aerik came to her side in one smooth motion almost as if he glided to her. He lifted her chin so their eyes connected. "Jamie, you need to lie down first. Let me put you to bed, and then I will sit with you and answer some of your questions."

She could spend all of eternity looking into those dark brown eyes and listening to his magical voice. How could she be so attracted to someone she was so afraid of? In her mind she heard him answer, "It's not me you're afraid of...it's what I am that frightens you."

"You're my guardian angel, my hero," she said without reserve.

Aerik tossed his head back and laughed deeply, it sounded husky, seductive. "I'm no angel, but I think you already know that."

Jamie moved away opening the door. "Can you read all my thoughts?" she asked.

He hesitated before answering. "Yes, but I'm not intrusive to your memories unless I need to be or you wish it," he said matter-of-factly.

"You're arrogant," she commented while studying his handsome face.

"I like to think of myself as proud."

"No, I think arrogant is more fitting." She held the door open. "Are you coming in?"

"Are you inviting me into your home?"

She looked him over thoughtfully while chewing on her bottom lip. "Should I not invite you in?" She thought of the *Lost Boys* vampire movie she watched years ago when the head vampire told the kids that they shouldn't have invited him into their house.

Aerik laughed. "I remember that movie," then added, "it's a choice only you can make, Jamie. What does your heart tell you?"

She stood there thinking. He was grinning at her because he already knew what she was thinking. "Get out of my head," she told him. His laugh that followed melted her insides. It wrapped around her like the red stripe on a candy-cane, and she loved candy-canes. "I'll tell you what I think. I think you're dangerous. I think that you are capable of committing great harm at your will, but I also believe *in my heart*," she emphasized, "that you won't hurt me. So...I'm inviting you into my home. Besides," she added, "I have lots of things to ask you." She yawned while turning on the lights. She really just didn't know how she felt about him leaving. For some reason she didn't want him to go. What did he do to her?

Jamie looked down at her blood-soaked clothes.

"You need to get cleaned up," Aerik said softly, "a shower and fresh clothing will help make you feel better. Would you like me to help you?" he asked.

"No, I'll be fine thank you," she said shyly.

"At least let me wrap your injured hand in something to keep it dry while you bathe."

Jamie nodded and he followed her into the kitchen where she produced tape and a plastic bag. When Aerik was finished Jamie left him to get into her pajamas. He was almost glad that she didn't want his help. Trying to keep himself in check was proving more difficult than he thought. Control was his middle name but she was definitely causing him to test his limits. He wanted to run his fingers through her long honeyed hair. It was almost unbearable to not reach out for it as she walked past him. It smelled so good. He wanted not only to run his fingers through each silky strand but to run them over every inch of her body as well, missing nothing. He wanted to know her mind, body and soul intimately. He wanted to taste her. He just wanted her.

He walked around the living room absorbing every detail. He missed nothing. It was beautiful yet simple. Country in design, which was fitting for such an old style farmhouse, not too elegant but tastefully decorated. The room literally glowed with the flare only an artist's work could produce. It was the painting over the fireplace that was totally unexpected and unusual. He could tell instantly that Jamie had painted it. He could feel her spirit encompass the work of art so much more strongly than the others throughout the room she had created. It was hauntingly beautiful, in shades of many colors, his colors, including gray, greens, browns, and deep blues. She had captured the image of a moonlit night, casting its glimmering rays across the sea to rest in an old cemetery. The trees looked as if they were alive, their limbs catching the lift of an incoming breeze. What was intriguing was the angle of the picture, from slightly above as if looking down onto the scene. It was so right, so perfect. He shivered from within; the realization of what he was seeing was so shocking he ceased to breathe. It was painted through his eyes. His vision. The only thing missing was Jamie on the edge of the cliff with her arms stretched out to the night sky calling to him.

He knew without a doubt that she was his soul mate. How was it possible that a human girl could be his perfect match, her pureness to his darkness, together creating a harmony so complete that they would be bound together for all eternity as one? She was human! It made no sense. She saw through his eyes? He felt as if the answer was within reach but he was failing to see it. Her life expectancy was but a breath in time compared to his.

Aerik moved from the painting that held him so entranced. He moved about the room carefully studying the other works of art that also carried her essence. He would have to do some research. In the meantime he wasn't quite sure what to do about Jamie. He didn't want to be away from her for any length of time, it would make protecting her more difficult. Not that she needed his protection it was an internal deep need he felt to shelter, to protect, to possess her. Even though he did not know this human girl, every fiber of his being wanted to claim her as his own. He wanted to take her as his mate without any knowledge of her past. All that mattered was that she remain in his life from this moment on. Again he questioned how this human girl could affect him so. It defied all logic. Never the less it was fact. She was his and he claimed her for as long as she drew breath. He would work out the details with time. He glanced at the ceiling as he heard the running water from her shower upstairs slowing then stop. He would probably not be able to convince her to leave with him. He needed someone to stay with her during the daylight hours when he could not physically be with her. He scanned the area for the right guardian. He connected to a nearby wolf, but he would not do, he had a mate and they were caring for a new litter of pups. It would not be right to take him from his mate. He sighed and continued his scan. There he was, a monster of a dog. *Perfect*, he thought. Aerik reached out to the beast with his mind. He was caged, uncared for, he howled his loneliness when Aerik connected with him. Giving him the comfort he ached for, Aerik communicated with the dog. He bombarded the poor creature with feelings of love and images of Jamie and himself.

Jamie appeared dressed in a long old-fashioned flannel gown that hung to her ankles. Aerik wanted to laugh, but it suited her. He removed the quilt from the back of the sofa and motioned for her to sit down. He then laid the quilt over her, watching as she tucked her feet up underneath the cover. He pulled up a side chair, wanting to be close but allowing for her to have her own space. He reached out briefly touching the end of her wet tresses, not trusting himself to touch her hair longer. Dark, wet, honeyed silk.

Jamie noticed how he dwarfed the chair. He was so large, masculine. When she ascended the stairs she had noticed how he moved about the room with a fluid grace, like that of an animal that was stalking his prey. Was she his prey? He was dark, dangerous, and handsome beyond compare. As his eyes settled on her she felt her stomach did a flip-flop. Was it fear, anticipation or both?

"Did you make this?" he asked picking up a miniature log cabin birdhouse from the end table. The instant he touched the piece he knew she had made it. He admired her attention to the fine detail in the piece.

"I had seen many different kinds at the various stores around here. I thought I would try making one of my own." She was happy with that particular piece and was pleased that he liked it.

Aerik sat the birdhouse back on the end table. He wanted to question her about the painting over the mantle but decided to wait for the proper moment. "How is your hand?"

"It's okay."

"It hurts you." He reached out for her hand. Jamie hesitated only a moment, before allowing him to take her injured hand into his own. When he touched her she experienced what she could only describe as a pleasant energy flowing over her body. It was like that first morning stretch upon awakening; how the sheets always felt so ethereal gliding over her body during the first wakeful movements.

Aerik took her hand gently and began unwrapping the outer protective bandage. "Jamie, you know I will not hurt you. I gave you my word." He looked up holding eye contact to emphasize that he meant what he said. "I did not have enough time earlier to properly heal your wound. I can speed up the healing process if you will let me."

"How?" she asked nervously, afraid of the unknown.

"We can heal cuts on others with a liquid that comes from within us. It is how we heal the puncture wounds after we feed," he explained. "Your wound is much larger and has already been doctored but I can still help it along. I can lessen the pain and quicken your cells' rejuvenation process." He touched her mind to see how open she was to the idea. He felt she was more curious than afraid. "Jamie, let me help ease the pain, it's my fault that you suffer so." He saw the questioning look in her eyes. "I could have healed you earlier if I had more time. I was so overwhelmed by your beauty that I failed to shield us to the eyes of others. My inattention to detail allowed the woman who came to you to see me giving you the nourishment you needed to live." He looked her in the eyes again then went on, "but do not worry, she will only remember the image of seeing a wolf." He sighed sincerely feeling that her pain was clearly his fault. Had he properly shielded them he would have healed her wound. Jamie would not have had to suffer through the healing arts of modern day witch doctors. "Please allow me to make amends."

Now she understood the conversation she overheard at the hospital about Clare seeing a wolf.

"Jamie, forgive me."

When he spoke her name she curled her toes. Nobody had a right to have a voice so enchanting, so pleasing to the ears. "Alright," she agreed smiling sheepishly, "I forgive you."

Aerik laid the outer bandage down and examined her hand. The cut was an angry red, swollen from irritation and the intrusion of the stitches. He looked up holding her eyes once again before speaking. "I am going to touch your wound with my tongue now, you will feel

29

it but it should not hurt." He assured her. When she nodded her acceptance, he kneeled down before her.

Taking her hand ever so gently into his own, he couldn't resist the temptation to first kiss her fingertips. He spoke in her mind, "You are the most beautiful woman I have ever had the pleasure of looking upon." He lowered his head to shield her from seeing his incisors lengthen long enough for him to drip the precious healing fluid he needed onto his own tongue. He could have applied it to his fingertip but in such a delicate spot the tongue seemed the most appropriate. Besides he would much rather touch her in this intimate way as opposed to merely running his finger over her wound. As he laved the skin on her hand he continued to communicate telepathically. He was whispering a healing chant in the ancient language of the Scottish Highlands. It was a chant that he had learned as a child, taught to him by his grandmother who was the village healer. As he did so, Jamie was delivered the curative properties that her skin so desperately needed.

Jamie thought she had died and gone to heaven. As he kissed her hand so intimately she experienced feelings within herself she didn't know were possible. This was pure pleasure. Never had she felt such strong emotions. She was experiencing a state of elated bliss. His words she didn't understand but she felt them working their magic. As his voice made her insides dance in delight, she saw in her mind the stars in the night sky. She had never seen them with such clarity; they were so beautiful, so crystal clear, so inspiring, she wanted to paint them. Then Aerik ran his tongue across her palm and between her fingers. It nearly took her breath away. When he sucked her finger into his mouth she felt something akin to a bolt of erotic electricity run through her body from top to bottom, settling in her pelvis a tingling fire burning out of control. A moan escaped her lips. It stopped. Everything stopped. Her eyes flew open as her mouth formed a protest but was caught in her throat as their eyes locked. She could feel his desire. She saw images of them, sexually, in her mind in short erotic flashes as if someone was showing very abbreviated clips from a movie. They were things he wanted to do to her. Graphic, sensual, heated with such intense sexual passion... things she had never thought of doing. She was so consumed with desire she just stared at him watching the images he placed in her mind. She gasped in fright at the vision of him taking her without caution, without restraint, it was almost feral, as he pinned her down piercing her skin with razor sharp teeth. The feeling that accompanied the vision sent not only fear but a burning need through to her very womanly core, leaving her wet with a desire she had never known was possible. Her reaction to the image implanted in her mind shocked and frightened her. Then again, it just stopped. Jamie couldn't even find her voice. She was so in shock over the experience she just let the feelings continue to wash over her trying to comprehend what had just happened to her.

Aerik stood quickly backing away from her, his muscles flexing under his skin as he moved. He turned from her and ran his hands through his hair taking a deep breath. "Jamie, I must leave." His voice sounded strained. "I made a promise to you, if I stay I won't be able to keep it."

"I don't want you to leave," she whispered to his back.

Aerik turned to face her, his eyes saying more than mere words could express. He looked like a predator, close to the edge, uncertain, dangerous. "You don't have any idea what you're asking," he paused before going on, "you're not safe with me right now, like this. I will not be far, we can still communicate, here." He tapped the side of his head then dissolved into a mist, then nothing, gone.

Jamie was sure she saw a flame burning in the depths of his eyes, or was she just imagining it? She looked around the living room knowing that she was alone but hoping just the same. She didn't know what to think. Getting up she hugged her arms to her body, shaking without being cold. What was happening to her? Never had she felt so...so turned on? So frightened? Was it possible to feel both simultaneously? It must be for she was certainly feeling both. She wasn't a virgin and knew the pleasure sex could provide yet...never had she been so intimately touched as Aerik touched her. But...he didn't touch her did he? How could this be possible? She looked down at her hand where it all started. Instead of red swollen skin she saw a whitish pink scar neatly sealed with blue thread running through it. She had stitches when she was younger and she could tell that at this stage of healing she could remove the stitches without fear. It was simply impossible. But then what wasn't this evening? She looked at the clock on the wall. It was late. Morning would be coming soon. Where did he go? Will he come back? Could he make her feel pleasure like this again?

"I could take you to heights you never thought possible, Cara Mia," he whispered in her mind. "You are meant to be mine. You *are* my soul mate."

Jamie continued to pace, circling the room. His voice even in her mind made her throb with passion. "How can that be if I'm not a vampire?" she questioned out loud, since she was more comfortable with that form of communication, besides, she figured, nobody was around to see her talking to the walls anyway.

"It's the expression of the word really. I personally believe that when you meet that one person meant for you and you alone that you will know it without question. I feel that way about you, thus…making you my soul mate. I know you feel it too."

She definitely felt it but did she want to accept it; he drank blood – ick! What he described – the knowing – was what was missing from her relationship with Jeff. The feeling of knowing it was right…complete was what she had been yearning and searching for. "Where are you?"

"I'm close enough."

"Where are you from? Where do you live?"

"I have many residences. I originally came from the highlands. I was once a great warrior." He sent images of him in his youth running the countryside in the highlands of Scotland. Then he sent bits of his memories of battles he had fought. Flodin Fields, Pinkie, and Sherriffmuir. He sent pictures of castles and estates, the rocky crags and rolling green fields, of his youth. "I am most recently from Europe." Images and visions of his home flooded her mind; it was old world, full of deep rich texture, colors and antiques of the past. She saw his library and it was stunning. If it weren't for the computer on the massive mahogany desk it could have been in another era. "I have an estate not far from London. Currently I am staying at an old friend's home in Seattle so I could better track you."

"Track me?" she made one more lap around the room turning down the lights, then went back to the sofa, curling up within the hand stitched quilt.

"I had an idea of where you were by the trees and ocean that surrounded you in my vision. I thought that if I was closer to you that the connection between us would become stronger. I was right about that. I was only in Seattle for one night and I knew exactly where you were. Do you have psychic ability that you are aware of?" It was his turn to ask a question.

"My mom said I was intuitive, but I wasn't aware of any psychic capabilities," she said then added, "and I don't suppose watching psychics on TV counts either?" She heard him chuckle softly.

"Jamie, I must sleep soon and I have something to discuss with you before you fall asleep."

"I can't help but listen, you're in my head," she said with a touch of sarcasm. As soon as the words left her mouth she winced inwardly wondering if being sarcastic to a vampire was maybe not such a great idea. She immediately saw an image of herself draped over his lap being spanked. "Oh very funny." It was her turn to laugh. "Okay, you have my complete attention." She could not believe that she was carrying on a conversation with someone inside her mind, and not just anyone a vampire! She was in serious need of a psychiatric evaluation.

"You're not losing your mind; I am very real. Give it time and you will feel that what I say is true." He coaxed her gently to give into the belief of his existence. When he felt her mind calm to a more rational thought process he continued. "I need to explain that when the sun is out I am at my weakest. If you need help at that time I will be all but useless to you. I want you to have a guardian during the daylight hours."

"What do you mean? Why would I need a guardian?"

"It's not that you need a guardian," he began, deciding that now wasn't the time to explain his vampire need to keep his mate safe at all times whether there is a threat or not. "I don't want you to be lonely when I can not be with you. There is a dog at the local pound. I want you to go when you awake this day and purchase him. If you do not go he will be put down near the close of the business day." He felt her mixed emotions. She was suffering over the loss of her beloved Payton. She felt that to get another dog would be disrespectful to Payton's memory. Loyalty lost.

"Jamie, you mustn't feel this way." He decided to resort to child psychology; it was imperative that she get the dog. He needed her to be protected from any intrusive situation, be it the unwanted advances of the exboyfriend or a wild animal that happened to wander onto the property. "Payton would want you to rescue this dog. He's lonely and his time is coming to a close because nobody cares about him. He needs you."

Jamie was quiet for a few minutes as she wrestled with her feelings. "He's truly lonely? You can feel that?"

"It is how I found him, almost like how I found you, except you reached out to me...I reached out to him."

"He's at the pound in town? How will I know him?"

"You will know." He sent her a picture of the dog and shared a little of the dog's loneliness with her. As soon as he shared the feelings he knew it was a mistake. It tore at her heart. She wanted to go to him now. "Jamie, you must sleep first."

"I can't sleep with him lying on that cold cement floor like that." She wanted to cry at her inability to help him, she knew the pound was closed and there was nothing she could do right now to ease the poor dog's suffering. Perhaps she could wake someone. That was it, she could drag someone out of bed to open the pound for her, but who? Her mind raced for a solution.

"Jamie, forgive me. I shouldn't have shared that with you." He subtlety calmed her. "You must calm down and sleep...or I will put you to sleep." He had her attention now.

"You can do that?" He had her attention now; she didn't know how she felt about that.

"You would be surprised at what I can do." He whispered in her mind his voice soft seductively teasing. "I can touch you physically. Do not be afraid."

Jamie felt as if his fingers gently ran the length of her cheek, running ever so softly downward encircling her neck with a feather-light touch before descending to run across the top of her chest. It felt soft and relaxing. It made her shiver at the impossibility of it. "Are you here just invisible?"

"I am not in the house."

"Mmmm," she moaned, "I like this."

"Will you sleep now?"

"Will you come tomorrow?"

He felt her growing anxious as he hesitated. "After the sun goes down, I will come to you."

"Good night, Aerik."

He moaned a sensual moan so softly she almost didn't hear it. She did however, feel the full body caress he gave her as a goodnight hug.

Without her knowledge he gave her a compulsion to sleep.

Jamie awoke slowly; she had been dreaming that a tall dark stranger had been making love to her. She felt good…her body was still being bombarded with pleasurable sensations. She stretched catlike, savoring the feelings. The silkiness of the quilt against her skin felt like she was wrapped in satin, as the sun shining through the window touched her face and arms with the warmth of the morning.

She didn't want to get up. She wanted to lie here feeling this way forever. That was when all the events of the previous day started to intrude on her pleasant awakening. For a fleeting moment she wondered if it had all been a dream. One quick look at the stitches in her impossibly healed hand said otherwise. When she remembered the dog waiting for her at the pound she looked at the clock on the wall. It was almost noon! She hurried and showered, dressing in a white tee shirt with a lightweight denim tank-top dress over it that buttoned up the front. Grabbing her white sneakers, she went out to the front porch steps to put them on, as was her habit. She was amazed at the healing that had taken place in her injured hand. All she felt was a soreness deep within as she manipulated her fingers while tying her shoes.

It was going to be a very nice day; it already felt like seventy-five, which was very warm for a day in May on the Pacific coast. The wind was calm as well, another rarity which undoubtedly contributed to the warmth. She took a deep, cleansing breath of the fresh ocean air. Nothing was more comforting to her then the smell of the sea except perhaps the smell of cedar. Jamie pulled her long golden brown hair back into a ponytail holding it in place with a white lacy scrunchie. This time as she descended the stairs into the yard she watched her feet. There wasn't going to be a repeat of the night before if she could help it.

As she walked across the yard she stopped at the mint jag shining in the early afternoon sun. It was confirmation that all was real and indeed happening in her life. It looked totally out of place parked at her old farmhouse. She noticed the keys were lying on the leather driver's seat. She smiled with the thought of driving the sports car through town, then frowned criticizing herself for wanting to show off at her age. She reached in, taking the keys off the seat and dropped them into her bag for safekeeping. Her truck was in the driveway, which surprised her. She expected it to still be up the long driveway resting against a stump. She was planning on having to take her Jeep Wrangler, which she kept parked in the garage so she didn't have to bother with putting the top on it. When she looked inside the truck window she saw that it was clean. No blood. Aerik must have taken care of it for her, after he left her last night. *When he said he was close, was this what he was doing?* she wondered.

All the way into town she kept running through the events of the night before. Life as she had known it had ceased to exist. Childhood fantasies, or should she say nightmares, were taking a serious turn into reality. If this man were a creature of the night, what the hell was she doing with him? She thought of cloves of garlic and holy water, crosses and mirrors. This was just nuts. Until twelve hours ago her world was fine, normal. It was exceptionally lonely, but it was acceptable by society's standards. She sighed heavily. Oh, who was she to fall into the norm of society anyway? This guy could be the devil himself for all she cared. He was sinfully handsome and touched her in a way that filled a void she had come to think of as never ending. Besides, she needed something more in her life. He intrigued her and she fully intended on learning as much about him as she could. After all, it's not like she didn't have anything better to do. She had no life. And...if for some reason she ended up being delusional and this was all in her mind, well, what a way to go, at least it was with an exceptionally creative character she conjured in her sick mind. Make that a handsome, intriguing, exceptional character. She smiled to herself as she flipped on the radio.

The humane society was a small, dingy brick building located on the other side of town. Since the population in their area was roughly two thousand or less there wasn't much need for warehousing unwanted dogs. There just weren't that many of them.

Jamie removed her sunglasses before entering the old building that once used to be the town's water department. She recognized the receptionist as a Wendy Brauna, a girl she went to school with. Wendy had her nose buried in a book till she heard the bell above the door tinkle Jamie's arrival. She seemed happy to be interrupted jumping up smiling. *The book she is reading must not be that good,* Jamie thought.

"Jamie McPherson. Why I haven't seen you face to face in years," Wendy greeted. "How are you?"

Jamie smiled back. *A little psychotic, hearing voices, in lust with a vampire other than that...* out loud she said, "I'm doing good, and you?"

Wendy turned sideways and stuck out her middle. "Five months pregnant with number four; if you can believe that." She giggled patting her expanding tummy.

"Wow, they must keep you busy."

Wendy gave her the "you better believe it" look. "So what can I do for you? Are you missing a pet?"

"No, I'm here to adopt one."

Wendy frowned. "Oh you'll probably want to drive into Port Angeles for that. We only have one dog available for adoption here and I doubt you're going to want him, he's pretty big."

"I want to see him." Jamie wasn't leaving with out that dog. Come hell or high water he was going home with her.

"He's an American Mastiff named Burl," Wendy told her as she walked her back to the kennels. "His owner wanted a big dog to guard their property but didn't think about the cost of food or the size of the droppings. So they brought him here when there was no response to their "for sale" adds they had placed for him." She wasn't going to tell Jamie that this was his last day. "He's dirty, smelly and absolutely huge. He does have one good quality, his specific breed doesn't drool." She looked back and smiled. "Since he was brought here he just lies there all day and howls at night, it's real sad, or creepy depending on how you look at it." She turned the corner pointing to the cage on the end that opened to the outside. "He weighs over two hundred pounds, he's going to eat a ton of food."

The massive golden dog with the black muzzle looked at Jamie and got up. He sauntered over to the fenced gate and sat down, resting his great weight against it. He raised his paw to her and whined.

Jamie's heart melted. "I want him, Wendy. Can you get the paperwork ready?"

"Are you sure?" Wendy thought she must be nuts to want a big dog like that. She herself loved animals but you had to draw the line somewhere, didn't you? "You know, that's the most I've ever seen him move. He must like you."

"I'm sure. How much is he?"

"Well let me call Mr. Paulson and ask, he may have been fixed which will make it cheaper." Wendy went back to the reception area leaving Jamie behind with the dog.

"Burl, do you want to come home with me?" she cooed to him, trying to pet him through the wire. He whined again waging his tail. Jamie took an exercise leash off the wall and brought him out to the reception area.

"He looks like he's going to take you for a walk." Wendy laughed. "Are you sure you're going to be able to handle him? He weighs twice as much as you do."

"I think so. He likes me." Burl sat down next to her.

"Well here's the deal," Wendy told her. "My boss says he's been fixed and he's current on his shots, so if you want him it's going to cost you ten bucks." (She lowered her voice as if someone would overhear them in the empty building). "He actually said we should pay you to take him."

Three hours and a yard bath later they were both dried off and hanging out on the porch together. Jamie had brought her easel out and was painting while Burl snoozed. The porch was her favorite place to paint on nice days. The ocean breeze diluted the smell of the paint, not that she minded the fumes she actually liked them. She assumed do to the fact that she associated them with something she thoroughly enjoyed doing. Her brother Jimmy however, wasn't as thrilled over the "toxic aroma" as he called it. One day she came home to find that he had moved her easel out onto the porch. At first she was angry with him. Two days later she thanked him.

Jamie took a drink of her soda and stared at the painting. It was a bed. It was the bed in her dream last night. The bed she was being made love to in. Intricately carved from birch it was massive, with tall heavy posts at each end supporting an equally elegant designed footboard. The headboard was of such tasteful beauty she couldn't help but admire it. It was a craftsman's masterpiece, totally exquisite. The deep burgundy bedspread was tousled, but to Jamie it gave the perfect effect. She didn't think that her replica did the bed justice. She just couldn't capture the true detail in the craftsman's handiwork. The posts on each side of the headboard were large carved trees true to form. The footboard was a very detailed scene of a forest. It was the headboard she truly admired for it was a work of art. A very skilled craftsman's labor of love, for nothing less would have created such intense perfection. The scene was also that of a forest with great mountain peaks and trees as the background, but this scene showed a wolf chasing down a large deer or perhaps it was an elk; Jamie couldn't differentiate between the two but the animal had an impressively large rack of horns.

Burl raised his head in the direction of the driveway and stood up. Seconds later Jamie heard a vehicle approaching with its radio blaring. She wasn't surprised when Jeff's forest green Toyota Tundra pull up. Not who she wanted to see. She hurried inside, grabbing up her gauze wrap the doctor put on her hand the night before. She quickly wrapped it up so Jeff wouldn't see that she had been healed. When she returned to the porch she saw that Burl wasn't going to let Jeff out of his truck. He stood like a two-hundred-and-thirty pound rock next to the truck door. He wasn't budging. Each time Jeff told him to "Get," Burl just curled up his lips and snarled low and deep.

Jeff yelled over to her as she made her way across the yard. "Jamie, what the hell is this? Where did this dog come from?"

Jamie walked up to the truck and gave Burl a pat on the head. "I got him at the pound today; he needed a home," she told him. "What's brought you out here?" she asked trying to be polite. What she really wanted to ask was "what do you want now?"

Jeff eyed the dog. "Are you sure he's not rabid?" he snarled himself, not waiting for her answer he continued, "What the hell made you want to get this dog?" Jeff looked over at the jag parked nearby knowing all to well who must have been behind it. The little green monster of jealousy was clearly sitting on his shoulder, and he wasn't just sitting on his shoulder he was jumping up and down as he looked over at the sports car.

"Why are you here, Jeff?" Jamie asked, not even trying to hide the irritation she felt. *To heck with being polite.*

"Well for starters you can tell me what's been going on around here. Christ, Jamie, you show up at the ER nearly bleeding to death, then some goliath of a guy picks you up in a Jaguar, Now you have Godzilla here for a pet, he won't even let me out of the flipping truck. Why don't YOU... tell ME... what's going on."

"You don't own me, Jeff. We broke up, remember?" She glared up at him for copping such an attitude.

"Well I didn't think you were serious. I just thought you needed your space till you were over your brother." He pulled a cigarette out of his flannel shirt pocket. He lit it with such determination you would think that his life depended on that first drag, which he blew a little to close to her face.

Jamie looked at him with disgust. "Get over my brother? I'll never get over my brother... Don't you get it, Jeff? It wasn't going to work out for us. The feelings weren't there. We tried it and it just didn't work out," she paused trying to keep her own temper from flaring. "Jeff, we were good friends and there just isn't any reason why we couldn't continue to be that...friends."

"Hell this didn't have anything to do with feelings that were or weren't there, or being just friends. Breaking up with me was just an excuse so you didn't have to tear down this old dump of a house. You wanted to back out of all the plans we had made for our future," he spit out vehemently. "You were afraid of hurting your precious dead family's feelings. This house is more important to you than I ever was." He stopped to take a breath or gain momentum, Jamie couldn't tell which. "Oh I know what you're up to... You went and found someone with more money. I get it. Mr. Gargantuan," he nodded over at the Jag before continuing, "he probably had bigger and better plans than we did. Is that how you work? You were just using me, weren't you?" He was trying to turn things around on her. He was just being mean. Mean and honest. He knew there wasn't ever going to be any "them" now. He had such grand plans. He was going to make a name for himself in this rinky-dink of a town just like his parents did. He wanted to be on top and without Jamie's oceanfront property it just wasn't going to happen. He was being left with no other choice but to continue riding his momma's apron stings.

"Are you done with your tantrum?" she asked. "Because I've heard enough, they were your plans, Jeff, not mine. I think you need to leave now."

"Just get rid of me for the sugar daddy?" Jeff snorted in anger. "Is that what you're saying, Jamie? That's it right?"

"That's it," she told him. The last thing she wanted to do was

41

provoke him, but she was fed up. If she was capable... what she really wanted to do was drag his sorry ass out of that pick-up truck his daddy bought him and knock him out. That's what she really wanted to do. "Go on, Jeff. Get out of here before I have to call your momma to come get you." She couldn't help it; he had pushed her buttons.

"You haven't seen the last of me, bitch." Jeff tossed his cigarette out he window directly at her. If Jamie hadn't jumped out of the way it would have hit her in the chest.

Burl, as if being contained by some invisible barrier, burst to life and jumped up on the side of the truck snapping and snarling. Jamie couldn't have pulled him off if she wanted to.

Jeff rolled the window up as fast as he could. Gunning the engine his truck took off fish-tailing down the gravel driveway, the tires kicked up rocks spraying Jamie and Burl as he left in a state of rage.

Jamie cried out in pain as a small rock caught her just under her right eye as the shower of gravel kicked up by his tires hit her full force. The material of her dress saved her legs from being cut up but her hands couldn't shield her face as well. "Damn it!" she cried out her eye watering from the pain. In her anger she didn't yell, she screamed after him at the top of her lungs. "Jeff! You're a spoilt rotten little bastard!" As an after thought she yelled, "Momma's boy!" she knew he wouldn't hear it but it made her feel better just the same. As she went into the house to look at her face she swore she heard Aerik chuckle softly in her mind.

There was a small cut under her eye that stung like the dickens but she would live. Looking at the clock she realized she was counting the hours till the sun went down. There were still a few hours of daylight left. It had been a long time since she looked forward to someone coming to the house. Just because her caller was a vampire shouldn't change much. Jamie wondered if Great-great Grandma Elizabeth was rolling over in her grave knowing that a vampire was coming to call in a kitchen built for her.

CHAPTER 3

For dinner Jamie made hamburgers and fries for herself and Burl. She had one burger with extra cheese and Burl had four without lettuce. She wandered around trying to keep busy. She was so anxious, pacing from room to room like a schoolgirl waiting for her first date to show up. After walking over to the window for the twentieth time, watching as the sun slowly faded on the horizon, she went to the next window then told herself to quit before she drove herself crazy. She moved her easel inside and decided to shower and change before Aerik came.

The shower was just what she needed. Hot water was always a good way to relax tense muscles. Now that she felt good she wanted to look good. After staring into her closet for about ten minutes she finally decided on a white soft cotton two- piece. The skirt hung perfectly, accentuating her slim hips. The shirt was one of those half shirts that showed off the midriff with the slightest of movement. It was probably more of a summer out fit, but due to the unnaturally warm weather today she decided it was perfect. She took her hair on the sides and pulled it up and back holding it in place with a hair clip. This way she could wear it down yet it was out of her way. Even pulled up, her long hair still hung to just above her waist. Looking at the clock on the wall, she sighed. She still had an hour or so till sundown. She would just have to keep busy.

She put on a pot of coffee hoping the extra caffeine would help her to stay up as late as possible. The more time she could spend with Aerik the more she could learn about him, about what was happening to her. She re-checked her makeup. She wanted to hide the small cut under her eye so she put on extra cover-up. What if he didn't come right away? What if he only came to her in her mind? What if he didn't want to come? Her mind raced around till she thought she

43

would explode.

"Okay Burl, let's go paint." It would distract her. Painting was like therapy. What a counselor could do for some, painting could do for her. Most of the time she would paint something she saw that captured life happening. Other times she painted images that would just come from nowhere or from things she remembered from dreams. They seemed to be some of her best work lately. She sold her paintings locally and had some at galleries throughout the Olympic Peninsula. Sometimes she would get a special request to do a portrait of a loved one. She had just finished an oil painting of a family that was done from a snap shot Mrs. Snyder had brought her. It was going to be a gift to her husband on his birthday. She had never copied from a photograph before, but she thought it turned out quite well. Mrs. Snyder certainly seemed pleased. Selling her paintings made it possible for her to live comfortably without holding down a nine-to-five job. She also had her inheritance from her parents and her brother. It was really their life insurance money, but her brother used to joke with her about their "puny" inheritance their parents left, and how they were going to build a castle with it, a sand castle. Her brother's life insurance was actually quite large and as long as she didn't live frivolously she would never need to worry about money. So far a comfortable portion of that money just sat in a savings account gaining interest. The rest of it she put into CD's. Her goal was to learn more about investing but what she had read had only succeeded in confusing her more. She would have to sit down with someone who could explain things to her in terms she could understand. Her paintings were turning out to be an investment of their own, and she enjoyed using her creativeness to support herself. Painting not only helped to build her self-esteem but also had provided her with a means to become self-sufficient. The positive impact it had made on her life helped to fight the loss and loneliness of losing her family, in turn keeping her going from day to day.

"What do you think, Burl?" she had donned her painting smock so she wouldn't ruin her white outfit. "Should I finish this bridge," she held up the old wooded bridge painting she kept seeing in her mind, "or this cemetery?" She pointed to the mural she started just after Jimmy died. It took up the entire north wall of the room. Burl waged his tail as she spoke to him. Jamie picked the cemetery mural. It was an old cemetery with lots of character. Some of the stones were white with age and unreadable, some leaning, some fallen over and some broken. Even with some of the stones in such disarray the cemetery was incredible. Old trees shaded the stones that sat amongst the lush green grass. It appeared to be the back corner of a forgotten, much larger cemetery, as there was a large stone wall in the background. A small creek only a foot or two in width ran its own course twisting along the forgotten path, and there was an old stone bench for visitors long past. Jamie called it her Garden of Stones. It was her favorite.

"You know, Burl," she spoke as she studied the mural, "I feel like there's supposed to be a willow tree here, one with great weeping branches. What do you think?" Without waiting for his answer she started painting the tree that she saw in her mind.

When the sunlight through the window began to fade Jamie hurriedly cleaned up, and then nuked her coffee in the microwave. Grabbing her sweater she called Burl and went out onto the porch to await his arrival. The night air was crisp and refreshing, along with the caffeine in her coffee she felt totally invigorated. She almost couldn't contain herself, the excitement, the desire…the need to see Aerik was bordering on obsessive.

The sun was setting and she loved to watch the sun set on the horizon. Her mom used to tell her that since the eruption of Mount Saint Helens in 1980 the sunsets were phenomenal. The colors were astounding to say the least. So vibrant with color it nearly took your breath away. Shades of reds, pinks, magenta, orange, and gold, streaked with a brilliant lavender, all splashed against a blue fading sky. Jamie always thought of it as the palette of the heavens.

As she watched the brilliant colors fade over the ocean she remembered when she was a small child. Her dad each night would whisper into her ear, asking if she could hear the sun hiss as it dropped into the water. She used to stand very still holding her breath as to not make a sound, listening with all her heart. "Yes, Daddy, I hear it," she used to say. Those were the most precious memories she carried of her father, it was "their special time" when the sun would go down. Now here she was twenty years later, waiting with all her heart for the sun to go down again.

The distant roar of the waves rolling onto the beach was like listening to a clock tick in a quiet room. Burl whined and his tail started to thump on the floorboards of the old porch. Like the rise and fall of the tides, he came as promised. He looked as if he had been there for some time, casually leaning against the banister, waiting patiently as she watched the sun go down. Yet she knew he could have only been there mere seconds. Dressed casually in a white cotton button up shirt tucked into Levi jeans, and oh how they fit him, she blushed at the images that fluttered across her mind. He was incredibly handsome and she couldn't take her eyes off him. His shiny black hair was on the long side, full with just enough curl, which rustled sexily as the ocean breeze moved through it. How could he look so casual yet so polished? Had she ever seen a man that could make her feel so....

He grinned at her raising one dark brow.

"Oh...you're reading my mind aren't you?" She scolded rather than questioned. "You need to stop that."

"I'll try," he lied. "Now tell me how it is that I make you feel?" He held out his arm taking her hand, pulling her to him. She smelled so fresh, so clean. The fragrance she wore smelled like fresh roses after a rain shower. He leaned into the silkiness of her hair taking a deep breath, fresh raspberries on a summer day. Drawing another breath he committed the perfumed scent to memory, as he basked in the softness of her silken locks sliding across the skin on his face.

"You were all I could think of today," she confessed. "How is it that you can come into my life such a short time ago and cause me to think of nothing else but you? I saw your image in my mind at least a thousand times today. I feel like I have known you forever, yet I don't know you at all. You have made me feel and experience things that I've never felt before. You inspire me. You make me feel happy. I want to know, what you have done to me?" she demanded as she snuggled into his welcoming embrace. He was a stranger, a predator if he was indeed what he claimed to be. The last creature on earth she should allow close contact with, but she felt right in his arms. "You just make me...feel," she added half under her breath.

Aerik understood what she was saying, he could feel the change in her; it was a good change. He knew that finding her was a blessing. He had spent way too much time lately hiding from his own lonely existence, conducting business. A business that by all rights could run itself. When he wasn't glued to the computer dealing with business transactions he was a Tracker for his people. Centuries ago, they called themselves Guardians of the Night. They would hunt and kill those who committed crimes against humanity. Against nature. He would spend long hours tracking those who were depraved, becoming human monsters, killing their own kind for the pure pleasure of it. He committed himself to tracking, using it as an escape to hide from his own loneliness that ate at him from within. As a Tracker he could give in to his hunger, his drive for blood that the dark feral beast within himself raged for. He showed no mercy to these monstrous men. He would hunt them down, one at a time. He was relentless, fierce, and cruel beyond belief. He brought them the promise of extreme suffering before he took their lives. It was getting harder now that man was becoming more modernized. With the changing times more of the guilty had to be set up and handed over to the judicial system. It wasn't in their best interest to kill all those who committed atrocious crimes for bodies would litter the streets. To protect their own kind their lifestyle had to change with those around them. However when the elements were right death was the preferred option. No sense in overloading an already burdened system.

He hugged her tightly, thankful that he pursued her cries. "Would you like to go out?" he asked her.

Jamie looked up at him, not sure what he meant by going out. "And do what?"

"I could take you for a drive," he paused to think. "To get an ice cream cone."

Jamie laughed. The thought of his taking her for an ice cream cone was ridiculous.

"You don't like ice cream?"

"I love ice cream."

"Then why do you laugh, ma cheri?" He watched her expression intently as she smiled up at him sweetly. Every time she blinked those big grass green eyes at him, her long lashes would sweep down to rest briefly on the tops of her cheeks. He had an over whelming desire to kiss them. He was also silently inspecting the damage done her precious skin by the flying gravel of this afternoon's confrontation with Mr. Edgewood. He had felt Jamie's tension, which awoke him from his deep nocturnal slumber. He had watched with vampire eyes, monitoring the events. He would have been incapable to come to her aid in body, but she was in no danger. He could have manipulated the dog to defend her. He felt again her pain when the gravel from the driveway tore at her beautiful creamy skin. He quelled his anger at the sight of the red spot well hidden beneath her make-up. Make-up she did not need. That human young man was playing a dangerous game with the wrong person and would pay dearly for what he had done. Yes, he would deal with young Mr. Edgewood later.

"I guess I just can't picture you holding a cone," she giggled.

"I want to take you out and show you off," he told her. "Anyone as beautiful as you are should be displayed like the fine precious gem that you are." He took her hand and spun her around, examining every exquisite detail she had to offer, and there were many very fine details.

Jamie blushed at the compliment. Her hand came up to the cut below her eye self-consciously, too quickly for her to catch herself. She didn't want Aerik to know what happened earlier with Jeff. She didn't want anything to spoil their evening together.

Aerik took her hand and looked deep into her eyes. "Jamie, do not feel like you ever need to hide anything from me. I am a part of you now. We are inseparable. There is nothing you can't tell me." He held out each hand on either side of himself as a demonstration.

"Picture in your mind a set of weights." The dramatics really weren't needed but he sensed Jamie was a visual learner so it didn't hurt to help her see. "It's very simple really, when you only have one you have no balance. In nature all creatures, no matter the genre, seek out their mate in life, it's the nature of the beast so to speak. Life is about balance, night to day, warmth to cold, good to evil. From the minute we breathe life till the exact moment of death we are continuing a circle of balance." He looked her deep in the eyes. "You are my counter balance, you are the shining light of warmth to my cold eternal darkness. Together we are whole and complete." He took his thumb and ran it across the small cut on her upper cheek. *Jeff Edgewood's childish display of temper will cost him dearly*, he thought. As he touched the very small wound, Aerik pictured Jeff covered in a swarm of bees. Aerik controlled his temper letting it simmer at what he called the torture but don't kill mode. "Do you understand what I'm saying?"

Jamie nodded. "I do but it's all happening so fast and you have to admit it's not every day a vampire comes to your home and tells you that you belong to him." She gave a little nervous laugh.

Aerik's eyes burned into hers, as he ran his hand lovingly down the side of her face cupping her cheek. His thumb ran lightly across her lips, lips he wanted to taste. Jamie belonged to him, and no other. There would be no mercy for the poor soul who ever challenged otherwise. The very thought of some other male touching her made his fangs lengthen inside his mouth. "We have all night to get better acquainted with each other," he told her softly, seductively. He dared to lean down and tenderly brush his lips across hers. The sensation was electric. He backed away again so he could better view her. Yes, she was the one that he would choose to spend all of eternity with. He thought briefly of the things he would share with her, open her mind to, the places he wanted to take her. He pictured her in his home. The image was so clear, so right. His body ached to make her his...now, here. *Patience*, he told himself. Centuries of patience taught him well, he would bide his time.

So it was over the next several days that he showed up faithfully at nightfall. Always she was waiting for him on the old porch, a smile on her lips. They spent their evenings talking as he courted her in his way, the way it was done years before her time. The only thing missing was a guardian to watch over her but he was that and then some. Besides, there wasn't a creature on earth that could save her from him and he knew it. He would sit and hold her hand listening as she talked about her childhood, about her brother Jimmy, her parents and Payton. He wondered how she managed to keep herself together after Jimmy's untimely death. It seemed that he was the only one left in her life who she could count on to be there. He ached with the loneliness she suffered at his loss. Although she didn't voice it, he felt it deep within her. It was so consuming that most wouldn't have been able to survive it without having gone mad, or worse – taken their own life. Instead she had turned her focus to Payton, her golden retriever. She lived for him through him. She forced herself every day to rise and go on for Payton. Perhaps it was through his death that she was able to break the human boundaries of communication allowing herself to reach out to him, to connect with him. He still didn't see how it was possible but he wouldn't rule it out either, but…why him?

Aerik showed up as promised materializing behind Jamie. She stood at her easel painting by the dim light cast from the old light fixture above her head. Just as he was about to wrap his arms around her Burl thumbed his tail in greeting giving his presence away. "And to think that I picked you out," Aerik scolded the giant dog as he gathered Jamie into his arms breathing in her scent… so fresh. Burl whined and continued to thump his tail on the floorboards.

Jamie quickly removed her apron and laid it aside. "I wish you didn't have to leave, you could just stay here with me. I miss you when you're gone." She had come to trust him to keep his word. He told her would come and he did. She looked forward to his arrival each night feeling as if they had been meeting for years, not days. The thought of his not coming set her on edge and she quickly brushed the nasty thought aside refusing to go there. He was so handsome he took her breath away, his smile so charismatic it sent a shiver down her spine. He had the feel of being dangerous, a predator stalking her with his eyes as if she were his prey. Was she his prey? Yes she was, so why did the thought send pools of heat surging through her body in a sexual frenzy? How was it that she felt so safe with him near? How could she feel hunted yet safe at the same time? What would it be like to make love to such a man? She couldn't help but wonder what it would feel like to have him buried inside her, to feel his weight against her. Would it hurt? What would it feel like if he took her blood while they made love? Would it feel as intense as when he gave her his own? Would it be as good as it was in her dream? Would it feel as erotic? *Oh my god, what am I thinking!* she screamed in her mind. *Where did that thought come from?* She looked up at him, her face rosy with the blush that burned there. He was looking at her with those mesmerizing eyes, looking through her, a smoldering look. He was reading her thoughts! Her blush deepened as she quickly turned her head.

Aerik swept Jamie up off her feet in one quick fluid motion, carrying her into the house. "Naughty little Femme Fatale," he whispered in her mind, deep and heavy with need. "You seduce me, I can no longer wait for you as you assault me with such erotic thoughts." He mentally shut the door behind them. She started to struggle but to no avail, he was far too determined to let her go now. "Let me show you how good it can be, Cara Mia," he whispered in her ear, following it with a raspy deep breath that turned her insides to liquid heat. She instantly stilled in his arms. He glided up the stairs following Jamie's flowered scent to her bedroom. He never took his eyes from her as his hands flowed like water over the suppleness of her petite body. She was intoxicating. She teased his dark soul with questions he ached to answer. He wanted, needed, had to have her, he could not, and would not wait any longer.

Jamie felt his large hand at the nape of her neck, supporting her head as he laid her back onto the white down comforter that covered her bed, his long fingers stroking her neck possessively, as his other hand freely explored her body at his will. His touch sent shockwaves of pleasure up and down her heated skin. She was alive with sensitivity. She was terrified of what to expect yet too afraid to stop him for fear the pleasure she was feeling would stop… if she could stop him, but did she want to? No. Never had she felt this way at the touch of another. Aerik was whispering endearments to her in a language she didn't understand yet she clearly understood the feelings the words conveyed. As his hand spanned the width of her slim tiny waist she arched into his touch, which forced his hand upward to the base of her breast. She heard him growl deep in his throat as his hand caressingly came in contact with the round bud his fingers sought. She felt her breasts swell, aching with the desire for him to touch them.

He pulled her up just long enough to slip her shirt off. As he laid her back down his tongue trailed from the throbbing pulse at her throat to the crevice of her breasts, tracking her heartbeat as he went. It called to him, each beat taunting, torturing him. He lapped at her slowly, teasing, tormenting her with delight. As his lips closed around the hard bud of her breast she cried out softly in pleasure.

As she arched her back she felt his fingers tug gently at her elastic waistband, and then with one pull ripped her skirt from her body tossing it to the floor. Never had she wanted someone, ached for someone to touch her as he was touching her. He wasn't just stimulating her body he was in her mind!

He raised his head from her breast, and looked down at her, starting at her eyes working his way down. He watched her blush shyly as his gaze burned a trail along her body absorbing every detail, missing nothing. When he looked upon her white lace undergarments his eyes turned crimson and his muscles rippled, bulging under his skin then instantly his eyes turned black again.

Jamie's heart slammed against her chest wall a mixture of fear and desire. She saw his eyes change from black to red to black again. Did she imagine it? She felt his muscles expand and tighten.

He felt her tension, heard the beat of her heart increase, read her thoughts, smelled her fear; He took her face in his hands gently. "Jamie, do not fear me, I will not harm you. I made an oath and I will keep it. I will find the strength somehow…to not take from you without your permission. Even if you allowed me the pleasure to taste your blood, I will not turn you into what I am." He captured her lips and drowned in a kiss so sweat it moved his soul. He spoke in her mind. "If I cannot control this beast within myself I will leave you before I hurt you."

"Do not leave me again," she said between gasps of pleasure. Jamie grabbed at his shoulders pulling him to her, wanting to feel his smooth skin against hers. She wondered briefly when he had removed his clothes, then she just didn't care, she was glad they were gone. He was kissing her again, she thought she would go mad if he didn't take her soon.

"Do you know what you are doing to me?" he asked huskily, sending her telepathically the feelings that he was experiencing. He then sent her images of what he wanted to do to her, where he wanted to touch her and how. His lips found her breast again sucking, nibbling, kissing one while his fingers rubbed, pulled and manipulated the other till she begged for more. He used his knee to separate her legs, pinning her with a fraction of his weight. He slid a hand down to rest at the juncture between her legs. He felt her wetness and growled a soft moan with the wanting of her as he slipped a finger into her tight sheath. When she started to rock gently against his hand he inserted another knowing that if he didn't she would never be able to accommodate the size of him without experiencing pain. His thumb brushed her teasingly causing her to whimper. She felt like hot velvet gripping him. He could feel his dark wicked self, wanting to take over. The animal inside was raging to be released. As he held her, skin touching skin, he could feel the electricity of their life forces tingling between them. He was losing the battle with his inner demon. His eyes glowed crimson as he heard her beg.

"Please, Aerik. I can't wait. I want you now."

His fangs exploded in his mouth. He smelled the coppery sweetness of her blood; saw her pulse beat in her delicate throat as she threw her head back in ecstasy. He used everything he had to try to control the darkness, the vampire raging within himself. He whispered in her mind "Mia... I can't do this."

Jamie opened her eyes saw him for what he was. His eyes were as black as night but flickered red deep within as if a candle burned there. His fangs extended, his fierce need evident, he was struggling like an animal caught in a painful trap. She could feel his terror at the thought of hurting her, his shame at not being able to fight the beast he was becoming. She could feel his emotions! She was reaching into him on her own; he was not placing the feelings in her mind. She saw into his tortured, lonely soul so like her own. Saw the passion she stirred in him and his struggle to control it. Above all else, she felt that he would never cause her mortal danger, she was a light in his soul, and he would lay down his own life to protect her. He was struggling with the normal desire to take from his mate during an intimate act, an act that if both were vampires wouldn't even be questioned it would simply be...sharing of each other, an act of love. "Don't leave me," she demanded, staring into his haunted black and red eyes. She let his feelings for her wash away the fear of what he was, of what he needed. He felt so right how could it be wrong? "Aerik, take me...take my blood... please I need you, I want you. Now...please." She moved her long silky hair away exposing her neck to him. "I'm offering myself to you," she was on fire and only he could quench the flames of desire she was engulfed in. He had saved her from herself, could she do no less?

Aerik looked down at her through his vampire eyes. "Do you know what you ask?" his eyes glowing crimson as he sent her images of what he wanted to do to her, what he was about to do to her. He heard her reply in his mind before it left her lips. He tossed his head back and growled his pleasure as the animal within took over. Grabbing her wrists he held them together in one massive hand, and raised them above her head pinning them to the bed, leaving her totally exposed to him. She still did not move, leaving her neck turned to him. He again inserted his fingers stretching her, readying her. He let his tongue flick at her nipple, one then the other then back again. He suckled them again only this time harder with urgency. When she pushed up to meet his greedy mouth he couldn't take any more. He removed his hand to replace it with his thick, hard shaft. He pushed at her forcing his way in. She gripped him like white-hot velvet. Her pulse quickened and drummed in his ears. Her blood rushing through her veins was music to his ears. He felt her intense desire. She rocked with him wrapping her legs around his back. The sweet smell of her blood and the seductive pull of her pulse beating in her neck were too much for the animal he had become to ignore. His tongue slid along the soft curve of her delicate throat, his teeth scraped gently at first then he sank his fangs in the side of her neck as he slammed into her, forcing her to take all of him, stretching her to the limit, filling her with his thick burning heat. Her blood tasted so sweet, so intoxicating, so stimulating it stirred his very soul. Was it possible that anything could be this exquisite?

Jamie felt him enter her with reckless abandon forcing her to take all of him. She felt his incisors pierce her skin like a bolt of white-hot lightning. The pain was mixed with elated pleasure; her feelings of euphoria were so intense it was electrifying. He thrust into her again and again. His one hand was holding her down, pining her to the bed, as the other assaulted her breasts blazing with fervid passion, a pleasure that took her to heights of newfound gratification. Did he even realize that he didn't need to hold her down? She was flying, floating, swirling in a sea of erotic ecstasy she never thought possible. She clung to him like a second skin as he took her to the top letting her entire being crash in sexual delight, like a wave hitting the beach in a storm. It washed over her again and again. As she clung to him reveling in the pleasure he gave her, she felt cool air light and wispy brushing at her heated body. She smelled the salty spray of the ocean and felt its mist. As she came slowly back to reality she realized she was in an upright position and he was holding her, his muscular arm encircling her small waist, her feet were not touching the ground. She felt him suckling her neck followed by a tingling heated sensation, which was his sealing the puncture wounds he had created.

He lapped lovingly at the thin trail of blood that had dripped before he sealed her wounds. There was no pain. He nuzzled her neck then whispered in her ear, "I love you more than I'll ever be able to express in mere words. You're my angel."

Jamie gasped and clung to him with all her might. "We're floating," she exclaimed.

Aerik laughed a deep refreshing laugh that filled the brisk night air with their presence. They were floating about ten feet off the ground above the cliff she so loved to rest on. He drifted down till their feet rested safely on the solid rock. "Yes, we're floating. Oh Jamie, it's so refreshing to see things through new eyes. Floating is as natural to me now as breathing when the sun has fallen."

Jamie refused to let go of him even though they were safely on the ground. She was elated it was a truly wonderful experience. "How did we get here?"

"This place must be special, a safe haven for you in some way. I only wished us outside to cool our bodies," he kissed the top of her head, "you brought us here."

"How could I do that?" she asked softly, her voice full of wonder.

"I don't know, Mia, but together we will find out." He felt her snuggle into him, already cooled down she was now seeking warmth. With a wave of his hand they were clothed.

Jamie looked up at him, her mouth hanging open in total amazement.

"What?" he shrugged. "Were you not cold?"

Jamie hit his muscle-bound chest with her tiny fist. "Is there anything you can't do?" she asked him, a hint of playful sarcasm in her voice.

He held her close as they both looked out over the dark expanse of sea listening to the waves break timelessly onto the log-strewn beach below them. "I can't walk in the sun light with you."

When she shivered again he turned her around, hugging her face to his chest in a loving embrace. The next thing she knew they were back in her living room, and Burl was thumping his tail on the floor in greeting.

Aerik gave the dog a healthy tousle and thanked him for doing a great job at guarding the house. "Yes," he cooed to the dog that just very well might out way him. "Yes, that's a good boy…you can bite Jeff. He's a bad boy…you bite him if he comes here again. Yes you will. What a good boy you are." He spoke to the gigantic dog as if he were but a baby making himself look quite ridiculous.

"How did you know what happened with Jeff?" Jamie asked him in an accusing manner, her hands planted firmly on her hips. "I thought you were sleeping?"

Aerik gave her the tsk, tsk, tsk, with his tongue, while waggling his finger at her. "What was it you called him?" he chuckled. "Oh I remember, something to the effect of spoilt rotten momma's boy?" He laughed again, deep and hardy. "You can be a wordy little snip when you get riled, can't you?"

"Aerik!" Jamie stamped her foot proving him right in doing so. She couldn't believe that he knew about their confrontation and hadn't told her.

Aerik crossed the distance between them with two strides. He moved so quickly Jamie backed up. He laughed softly as he heard her heart start to race. "You are so cute." He took her hand pulling her into his strong arms. "Girl, you have no idea how long I have waited to feel like this."

Jamie smiled up at him. "I feel," she paused searching for the right words, "so alive, like I was missing something all along yet…didn't realize it till now." Looking into his dark eyes she asked, "Do you have me under a spell? Are you controlling me?" She wanted so desperately to hear that he was not, that the feelings she was experiencing were truly her own.

Aerik took her chin in his grasp and gently tipped her head back so he could look directly into her beautiful grass green eyes. "These feelings you are having are very much real. Do not doubt them."

"But you're a vampire," she whispered.

"That I am." Aerik ran his fingers through her thick silky hair as he spoke to her. "Jamie, you need only to reach inside yourself. What do you feel? Our instincts are a subconscious guide that will never let us down, remember that."

"It feels right, but it's not natural."

"You're struggling with logic and reason. Let go and feel. Look past what you have learned, don't justify or validate. What do you feel?" he tapped gently on her chest, "In here, what do you feel?"

"I feel what I have always longed to feel. I feel whole and complete. I feel like you have filled an empty void in my soul," she hesitated. "I feel like I would not want to live without you." That last thought scared her, but she knew it was true. "How can that be? I have only known you such a short time. Is that possible? Well it must be," she answered her own question, "because, that's how I feel. I feel like I have waited my whole life for you. Do you feel it? Do you feel as I do?"

"Yes, I also feel it," he said emphatically. Aerik released his hold on her and walked around the living room. With a sweep of his hand he brought her attention to the portrait above the fireplace. "Some things feel right because they are. What were you feeling when you painted this?"

Jamie scrunched her brow and stared at the portrait of her family cemetery. "Well, this one was different," she hesitated long enough to pull in her bottom lip and hold it there with her teeth, as if that action alone would help her to think better. Aerik thought it was an endearing quality about her and he looked forward to the next time she displayed such intense thought. He grinned.

"What?" she asked. Why was he grinning at her? That smile turned her insides to liquid and made her week in the knees. Lord, she was in trouble if she reacted this way to a mere grin. She could tell that he wasn't going to answer her, as he was still waiting for her to finish. She turned her attention back to the portrait. "It's different because I saw this in a dream. I had this image, this picture in my mind, it haunted my thoughts and I had to paint it."

"You had to paint it?" he questioned her. "You had to paint it because deep inside you knew it was the right thing to do. You felt it. There was no logic or reason. It was purely instinct, it had to be done. It was right."

Jamie nodded. "I had to get it out. The feelings were so intense. In my mind I could feel the wind blowing through the trees and I felt like

I could physically touch the moonbeam that came to rest on Grandpa's headstone. It was as if it was trying to tell me something."

"It was, because it was my vision." Aerik watched her for a response. She appeared startled, her eyes questioning him.

"I don't understand."

"The only thing missing from this picture is you. You have painted what I saw the first time I spoke to you." He waited letting her take in what he was saying.

"This is how you saw me in your mind?"

"You were wearing a gray sweatshirt and blue jeans. You were barefoot. Although I could not see your face I knew you were beautiful. Your back was to me, as you were looking out over the water."

Jamie broke out in goose bumps as all the hair on her arms raised. "I couldn't figure out why this image came to me from an angle that I wouldn't have possibly been able to see it from. I would have had to have been sitting in a tree back here," she pointed beyond the portrait, "to have painted it." Jamie was amazed to say the least. The thought of sharing someone else's thoughts was an amazing concept. She found herself growing excited at the thought. It could explain why she would feel the need the need to paint things out of the blue. Things she had never thought would be of interest to others, images that haunted her till she committed them to canvas.

"Jamie, what's wrong?" Aerik watched her go pale. He quickly scanned her thoughts seeing quick images of paintings, so many paintings flashing through her mind to quickly to really see any one in particular.

"I need to show you something," she grabbed his large hand in hers and yanked him towards another room. She threw open the door and hurriedly pulled him into the large room she had made into a studio. She didn't say anything; it was her turn to wait for his reaction.

CHAPTER 4

Aerik looked around in shocked silence then glanced over at Jamie who was biting on her fingernail. He gently removed her finger from her mouth then slowly walked around the room. There were paintings everywhere. They covered the walls and were propped up along them in stacks as well. Several were displayed on easels and some were obviously still work in progress. There were pictures of his past, his present, his home, places he had visited, and places he had battled. There were others he did not recognize but felt that he should. He stopped and picked up her painting of the bed. His bed. The paint was fresh; he could smell it. She had just recently worked on it. He studied it intently then turned and grinned at her. It was a seductive, sexy smile that smoldered with passion. He sent her an image of himself taking her fervently amongst the burgundy spread and fur blankets. He let her know without a doubt that she had painted his bed. His eyes scorched her as they raked her body with lust and wanting. As Aerik looked past Jamie to the wall behind her, he ceased to breathe. He took in every fine detail of her work. With his vampire eyes he missed nothing.

Jamie watched him study her mural. She knew it was familiar to him, and in some way that pleased her. It was as if she painted it not only for herself but for him as well. She found herself hoping that it was accurate. She wanted to ask him if it was correct in detail yet she didn't want to disturb him while he examined it. That was what he was doing. He was intensely focused and seemed to be following every little detail with his eyes. Twice he had looked over at her only to say nothing and return his attention back to the mural. Then suddenly he paced backward several feet so he could take in the entire wall in its enormity.

"It's very accurate," he said wanting to assure her that her work was indeed correct. He added almost as an after thought, "Honey, you need to breathe."

Jamie hadn't realized until that moment that she had been holding her breath. The fact that he recognized her work sent shockwaves of excitement through her. There was so much she wanted to ask him. Hurrying over to a particular headstone she ran her hand over it. "Do you know the name that is here? In my mind I can see it, yet it's not clear enough to read and it's making me crazy."

"Lord Aerik Bearach," he said softly. "The epitaph beneath has faded to the point that it is forever lost to time." Aerik hesitated briefly and then with a touch of sorrow to his voice he continued, "It should read... *Slan leat, a charaid choir,* which means, *farewell kind friend.*"

Jamie felt the conviction of his words and saw the pained expression in his eyes. She reached out, touching his arm wanting to help ease the pain somehow. His muscles rippled beneath her fingers at her touch. He pulled her close and tucked her under his massive arm. She felt his somberness fade as he held her.

"Oh Jamie, you have done a magnificent job at painting my cemetery," he told her. "Just look at what you have done." Putting his feelings in check he stepped back again only this time dragging her with him so they could take it all in together.

"Your cemetery?" Jamie playfully pushed herself away from him. "I'll have you know that this is my cemetery," she said as if stating a fact that he should well be aware of. "I painted it. It's mine," she stated.

Aerik smiled at her playful little childish outburst. "You forgot to stamp your foot." He knew she was trying to make light of the situation, in hopes to lessen the tension within him. He played along.

"Well...I always thought of it as mine. I call it the garden of stones." She removed her hands from her hips and crossed her arms. "Wait a minute. You said Lord Aerik Bearach?" she stumbled over the pronunciation. "Is he a relation of yours?"

"Actually the stone is incorrect, as it is in fact Gavin Kintour, one of my liege that really lies within that grave."

"One of your liege?" Jamie questioned. Dates were swirling through her head. How old was Aerik? She stood staring at the headstone, while listening intently to Aerik tell her about the man who lay beneath the marker that was not his own. "How is it that he ended up there instead of Lord Bearach?"

Aerik was about to ask her if she really wanted to know all this but a quick scan of her thoughts told him she did indeed want to know.

"I am over 500 hundred years old." Without hesitation he continued, "We fought together in a few skirmishes against raiding clans. He had sworn allegiance to me shortly after his village had been eradicated by the English." He paused thinking back to the days of castles, battles and bloodshed. They were still fresh in his mind as if they happened only yesterday. "He fought valiantly and he had a good sword arm. He was true to his word and fought to his death to protect me."

Aerik walked around the room and began picking through portraits that he had just looked at. With care he laid them out to form a type of storyboard. "Here." He pointed to a rolling green field, a valley that was scattered with large shallow boulders that would have made good chairs for a weary traveler. "I had seven men with me and we traveled by horse through here." Pointing at the next portrait of birds taking flight from a tree that marked the entrance to a forest. "We knew we were being watched. When these birds took to the air it announced the thieves before we actually saw them. We turned about back to the open area knowing that entering the woods would surely bring sudden death. Our only chance was to draw them out into the open and see who and how many we were up against. Three of my men were still recovering from wounds they suffered from a previous battle days before while protecting our boarders against William Lochanier and his sorry lot." He pointed to the next, which was a beautiful scenery portrait of a large boulder beside a pine tree that grew up out of the rocky ground. The painting was very detailed right down to the little sprig of green highland grass that was desperately struggling to take a hold amongst the rocks. "Here is where I went down." He looked over at her briefly, just long enough to once again remove her finger from her lips. "My men were sorely outnumbered. They held them off as long as they could before falling to the bloodthirsty boarder warriors. That's what my men had nicknamed those who patrolled and attacked boarders just for the sport of the killing. Usually the wages they earned weren't worth risking their lives for, it was the lust for blood that drove them. They would go from one area to the next offering their services for a price. Killing for the highest bidder. Anyway," Aerik sighed, taking a moment to mentally send a calm, reassuring feeling to Jamie, he could feel her tension rising as his story progressed.

"I carried this image in my mind for days till I could paint it correctly. I thought I was insane from the grief over the loss of Jimmy, which was why I just couldn't seem to get it right. I started it over and over again because I just couldn't seem to get that little twig just right. There was light shining on it, but it faded from dark to light to very light, yet...the light on it..." she paused trying to find the right words to describe how she saw it in her mind.

"Babe, I can see it in your mind as well as my own, it's okay, you don't need to try so hard. Let me explain what I think was happening. The light was moonlight. There was a full moon that night. When the boarder warriors laid siege to us it was near dark-fall. Normally it wouldn't be wise to start a skirmish so late in the evening, but they had such an advantage in their shear numbers and the moon was already shining brightly. I would think that if I were in their leader's boots I would have used that to my advantage as well. So you see the light you saw shimmering off that twig was moonlight. I also believe that the reason you were so focused on that particular twig was that it was what I focused on when I knew that the wound inflicted upon me was a mortal wound. As I felt the very life draining from my body, I couldn't take my eyes from that one simple little piece of this earth. It was also the last thing I focused on after I made the choice to become what I am. The trickery of light you were seeing was that little branch through my eyes, my eyes as a mortal man... and then my eyes as a vampire. Light, fading to darkness as I passed from the life I once knew to a much brighter night, a night seen through my new eyes…the eyes of a vampire." Jamie's reaction to his words was unexpected. She through her arms around his middle and hugged him close. He could feel her love for him and her happiness at his choice to live on. Her intense feelings were literally showering him with warmth and…gratitude? She felt so good holding onto him like this. He held her back.

"I'm so glad you chose to become a vampire. If you hadn't I would have never met you." She was so happy she was now crying.

She was so overwhelmed with emotions Aerik was quickly sorting through them assessing the situation ready to provide "damage control" as he liked to call it. She was feeling intense relief that he chose the path he did. Great joy at the empty void he filled within her, sadness for him over the loss of his mortal body an old life, guilt over being happy that he was vampire when it meant that he could no longer play in the sun. Panic, that she would grow old and he would no longer want to be with her. She actually ached for him. Her internal feelings harbored such love and caring, that the thought of losing him was more than she could bear.

Not wanting her to suffer even one second more he took control of her mind. Tipping her head up gently so he could look into her eyes, he spoke quietly but with a controlling firmness. "Jamie, you will not feel these hurtful emotions with such intensity. I will not remove your feelings but you will help me make those thoughts that are painful to you small. You will let only the good feelings you are experiencing right now rule your head and your heart." He looked deep into her eyes while scanning her mind. Once he was assured that his orders would be followed he relinquished his control over her. Bending down he brushed his lips across her forehead, inhaling the perfumed sent of her honeyed hair. Then he captured her ripe lips in a kiss so sweet that he experienced an overwhelming desire to take her again, right where she stood. He growled lightly, deeply as he broke away. "You taste like honey."

Jamie felt as if she were drowning in a vat of warm, rich cocoa, lost, caught in the grasp of his mesmerizing eyes. They were like pools of creamy melted chocolate that looked so good she couldn't pull herself away. They seemed to swirl and pull her in deeper and deeper absorbing her, smothering her in comfort. And then she was being kissed. Smiling up at him she stood on the tips of her toes and kissed him again.

"Little girl, you're asking for trouble," he warned.

"I like to hear you growl," she teased as she pushed away from his grasp returning to her mural. "Please tell me more."

"I promise you will hear me growl, my little temptress." Aerik gave her a look that told her in no uncertain terms that he was not finished with this.

Damn! But his smile could make her wet just by looking at her. She desperately tried to concentrate on the previous conversation.

"Let's hope that I will always accomplish such a sweet task." Aerik spoke to her in her mind.

"Stop that," she blushed realizing that he was reading her thoughts. "Seriously Aerik, please tell me more. How did you choose to change into a vampire? Didn't someone have to change you? Did it hurt? How does it happen? How did Gavin end up in a grave that was meant for someone else? Was it an accident or was it done on purpose? Where is this cemetery?"

Aerik burst out laughing a deep full-bodied laugh that almost shook the room.

"What?" Jamie asked knowing it was her that caused the laughter but didn't see what was so funny about her questions. She wanted to know.

Still chuckling Aerik told her that it wasn't the questions that were humorous; it was the manner in which they were delivered, with such rapid fire. It was as if someone took the lid off a jar of marbles and let them spill out, to roll off in all directions. Such were Jamie's thoughts in his mind, scattered and numerous. When he saw her wrinkle her brows and bite at her bottom lip he bit back his laughter and tried to look more serious. "Okay." He raised his hands in truce. "You do ask very valid questions. I'll answer them as completely as I can." He couldn't help but grin; she was so beautiful.

Jamie pursed her lips together knowing that he was trying not to laugh at her. "I have a right to know. You have changed my whole concept of life as I know it, you have to tell me."

He raised his eyebrow at her. He was totally unaccustomed to anyone even remotely demanding something of him.

"Please," she added as sweetly as she could muster under the circumstances. If he didn't start answering her questions she was going to get irritated with him. She had the unmistakable feeling that if Aerik were a dog he would have his hackles raised. This was a man who clearly took orders from no one.

He loved to hear her say that word. "Please." It rolled off her tongue like molasses. Her voice was soothing to his dark soul. He could sit and listen to her talk all night, but with a sigh it was in fact he that would be doing most of the talking this evening. "Jamie, you may not like what you hear. The conversation we are about to have is not going to be pleasant. I want you to tell me when you have heard enough."

"I will, I promise," she said knowing full well she would not.

Aerik raised his eyebrow at her before bringing her attention back to the portraits he had laid out. "This one here of the bridge. That's where I first met Alasdair. He was the one who made me what I am." He paused long enough to let that sink in. "A young girl from the village was raped and I was chasing down the ruthless jackal when Alasdair came from out of nowhere. He joined the chase and we worked together as a team to corner the man here at this bridge. We worked well together; neither of us spoke a word but he seemed to know my every move before I made it. I know now how that is possible."

"What did you do to the man who raped the girl?"

"I dispensed swift justice. There was no need to return him to the keep. He sealed his fate when he raped little Nikiana."

"Go on," she urged, inside she shivered at the images conjured of what Aerik's swift justice would consist of.

"He introduced himself as Alasdair from another highland tribe. He was out soul searching after the death of his *bhean*, his wife. A robber had killed his wife while he was away fighting in a battle for his Baron. With nothing left to live for he spent his time tracking down those who stole for profit or brought harm to others. I had no reason to doubt him. We talked for a time, shared a few stories of the battles we had fought in and the like, nothing of great importance. Then he went his way and I went mine. I figured he was the one responsible for the deaths of the outlaws we were finding on my lands. The next time I saw him he again came from out of nowhere in the midst of a bloody battle. We had been fighting through the entire afternoon and it seemed that it was never going to end, that was till Alasdair showed up. He would swing his heavy broadsword with such ease dropping the enemy like discarded bones at a feast. Again we worked together to lay waist to those warring against us. Again when it was over he would go his own way. It became the way of things for a time. He always showed up when I needed the extra sword or someone to watch my back while I slept, but he only came after the sun had set. There was camaraderie between us."

"He couldn't come to your aid when you lay mortally wounded because night had not fallen yet?" Jamie asked, not meaning to interrupt but speaking aloud her realization of his life and death situation.

Aerik nodded. "As I lay there, my blood pooling beside me and unable to stop it, I cursed that he was not there to aid me in this ambush. It was but minutes later that he appeared. He told me what he really was and that he spent his time hunting down the decayed scum of humanity trying to make the world a safer place to live. That is why he took to me. He said that he read my mind and knew we had the same goals of a healthy happiness for our people. I felt he was genuinely sorry that he could not make it to my aid in time but the sun had just completely fallen and he had to slay the enemy before he could safely help me."

"Why didn't he just give you some of his blood like you did for me?"

"He was giving me his blood. He had slashed his wrist and commanded me to drink. I could do nothing else. It repulsed me yet I could not break away; his will, an invisible force, held me there. I looked past what I was physically doing and focused on that twig in your painting." He stopped briefly to look over at Jamie and remove her finger from her mouth, this time he held onto her hand. "I had suffered great wounds, there was extensive damage done. Even one with powers that he possessed would not have been able to repair what was necessary in time before I passed from this world. So he gave me the choice. A choice that I will live with for all eternity."

"I'm glad you chose to live," she said giving his hand a squeeze. "Tell me more."

"You are tenacious, aren't you?"

"Aerik, tell me what happened next."

"He allowed me to drink of his blood, past the limit of merely saving, but the limit of changing. My physical earthly body died and my new vampire body was born. It was then that I saw the world through new eyes. It's difficult to explain but everything was a lot brighter than I expected. It's not dark in the night as it is to mortals. Colors are much more vibrant and everything is so crystal clear. The clarity in which we see is truly amazing. It is beyond description.

"My first night as the undead was spent changing clothes with Gavin and making him appear to be me. It was grizzly and I will not elaborate so don't ask," he warned. "The point is, we passed him off as Lord Aerik Bearach. It was important to me that my subjects thought I was dead. I didn't want them to think I had been kidnapped. Attempts to rescue me would have only resulted in more spilt blood. Enough was enough." Aerik paused turning her attention back to the mural. "That is how Gavin Kintour came to rest in a grave that was meant for me."

Jamie gasped. Of course! She was so caught up in his story that she failed to realize till now that he was Lord Aerik Bearach. How could she not have picked up on that when he first told her whose grave it was? She chastised herself. "You're a Lord?"

"I've been called a lot of things." He flashed her a wolfish grin.

Jamie scowled. "I bet you have."

Aerik studied her wanting to commit all her little "looks" to memory. "I was Lord Aerik Bearach of Castle Bearach in Glen

Bannatyen," he told her.

"Were you married?" she questioned.

Was that a hint of jealousy he sensed? "There was no need to marry, I was Lord of the manner, I could have the wench of my choosing each night if I wished it." He laughed as she shot daggers of fire at him with her beautiful eyes. "Mia, I was only teasing you. I felt your jealousy and wanted to play with you. Please forgive me."

Jamie struck out at his bulging muscled arm with her small fist only to succeed in hurting her own hand. "Now look, you've made me hurt myself," she shook her hand then added, "and... I'm sure there was some truth to your statement, but I don't want to know any more so don't bother to elaborate."

Aerik took her hand kissing it tenderly. "I was not married. I spent most of my time in the fields or on the battlement practicing or warring. Life then was about protecting our boarders thus, securing our freedom. It was a very long time ago. I was not celibate in my life, but there has never been anyone in my existence that makes me feel as you do. I have never truly loved a woman till now." He surrounded her with his feelings leaving no room for doubt.

"I will try to not let your past infidelities eat away at me," she scoffed.

Aerik snatched her arm pulling her into his embrace. "Woman, you may be the death of me yet. I have committed no infidelity, as I did not know you existed. For that matter in all actuality you did not exist, you are still but a babe in years lived."

Jamie loved the way he spoke, it held an old world charm, but then again, so did his chauvinistic attitude.

"Chauvinistic?" Aerik repeated speaking in her mind. Leaning down he whispered in her ear. "I can think of many chauvinistic things to do to you that I'm certain you would love." He sent her mind images of erotic things he would like to do that involved some form of control.

"You're terrible." Her cheeks were burning up with the blush he helped to produce.

"Come let me show you what a chauvinist can do."

"You forgot arrogant," she chided.

"I thought that was just a given." He swept her up into his arms. "Enough history lessons for now, I need to make love to you."

"You already did that," she protested weekly.

"Ah, ah...." He hushed her.

"But the cemetery," she wiggled in his muscular arms. It was a futile effort to get him to release his hold. She tried to point at the mural but to no avail, he was already gliding towards the door.

"The cemetery isn't going anywhere. I wish to make love to you again before the sun rises."

"But," was all Jamie got out before the thoughts he conveyed to her turned her insides to liquid fire. She throbbed with anticipation of promised ecstasy. The next instant she was on her bed unclothed without having any memory of getting there. She didn't care, she was on fire.

"I'm going to make you burn with desire," he whispered as he devoured her with his eyes.

"Please," she whispered back. "I..."

"Shhh.... Cara Mia. Burn for me." He gently rolled her onto her stomach. He pulled her arms up to rest above her head, and then began a slow soothing massage starting at her shoulders. He sent her images of his taking her in several different positions, positions that would bring her great satisfaction. Positions she had only thought about. His fingers worked their magic as he kneaded and rubbed her satin soft skin. He ran one hand down her leg slowly, rubbing, massaging, soothing her flushed skin, then slowly again, back up the inside till he made contact with her moist heated center. His fingers began to massage the bud he sought, slowly, deliberately, she responded with a soft moan, leaning into his fingers her body crying out for more of his touch. He massaged her womanly core with more intensity till she was whimpering for release. He touched her mind as she moaned and he felt the sparks of pleasure shooting through her body. She wanted him and he was going to oblige her mental request. He ran his tongue along the curve of her back, she tasted like sweet berries and cream, he licked and kissed his way to her ear, where he

70

again whisper seductively. "I'm going to take you now, are you ready for me, Mia?"

"Uh huh," she moaned in response, unable to speak. She was so overwhelmed with pleasure. It consumed her. All she wanted at this moment was to feel him inside her. She tried to turn around to face him, to ready herself but he stayed her with his hand firmly but gently holding her down.

Aerik gently brought her up to her knees and positioned himself behind her. He used his right hand to massage her perfectly shaped bottom while his left circled her waist pulling her back to meet his hard ready shaft. He sank into her feeling warmth engulf him in wet velvety tightness. He moved slowly, rocking, stretching her, slowly giving her more, till she had taken all of him. She was so tight and hot gripping him with such a perfect fit. She was made for him. He ran his hand across her breasts finding her swollen, hard with desire. He pulled ever so gently shaking the hard little bud that was pinched between his fingers, then he pulled and shook it from side to side even harder till he found the perfect pressure that made her gasp with delight. He used his other hand and manipulated both nipples at the same time. Jamie moaned her approval rocking back against him wanting more, wanting to be totally satisfied, wanting all he had to offer. He growled his response, taking her hips firmly into his grip and pulled her to him as he plunged himself deeply burying himself in her moist hot core. When she whispered, "yes" on half a moan it was all he could do to keep from exploding inside her. His eyes turned the color of molten lava and his fangs grew to razor sharpness. His senses heightened; he could hear her blood rushing through her veins, he could smell it, it called to him. He controlled the beast within yet he took her harder, faster. He slipped his fingers into her mane of hair and wrapped it around his hand pulling her head back just enough for his lips to brush at her ear, "Yes Mia; feel me deep inside you." He slipped into her mind using her as an anchor. This way he would know the second he went too far. He wanted her to only feel pleasure beyond the bounds she had thought possible. He would not hurt her. As he opened himself to her thoughts and feelings he was assaulted by a burning need, pleasure so intense it racked his body with waves of euphoria. She was climaxing. He didn't even try to fight the urge to follow suit. He slammed into her precious depths spilling his seed deep inside. That last thrust was so powerful it collapsed them both onto the soft white sheets. Together they lay, locked in place breathing hard, neither speaking. The only sound besides their labored breathing was the sexually sated "Mmmmmmm," that escaped Jamie's throat as she attempted to snuggle back further into his embrace. Aerik smiled. Being able to slip into a woman's mind gave him a definite advantage over the average male. He took another deep breath savoring the scent of her hair. He listened to her heartbeat so strong and steady. He watched each pulse beat within her neck, a rhythm to match his own. Using his thumb he lightly stroked the vein that teased him so. There was no doubt that she was satisfied. If she were a cat she would be purring right now.

Aerik lay with Jamie wrapped in his arms till she fell soundly asleep. Trying to keep his hours had been exhausting for her. Slipping from the bed he couldn't help but admire her perfection before he pulled the feather quilt over her satiny skin. He sighed, fighting the urge to crawl back into the bed with her. What was it about her that totally absorbed him? Here was a girl born literally centuries after him, a continent away, with a prospective life span that was but a moment in time compared to his. Yet…they were connected. He wanted to take her with him deep within the earth as he slept the sleep of the undead. The only thing that stayed him was the thought of her awakening beside his cold lifeless body shut down as he slept the rejuvenating sleep of the vampire.

He returned to the downstairs and walked slowly around the studio. He marveled at the quality of her paintings. In his opinion she was too young to paint with such exuberance. She showed expertise beyond her years, no… this was more than just aged expertise; she clearly possessed an innate capability. He pictured displaying her work on the walls of his home. She deserved her own gallery; making a mental note the thought of which, brought a smile to his lips. Returning his thoughts back to the portraits, he puzzled over the physic link between them. There had to be a connection here.

He spent the next hour looking over each portrait, carefully searching for some correlation no matter how slight it might be. He encountered many surprises, some pleasant; others brought back painful memories of lost friends and family. When he came across a portrait that seemed significant in some way he set it to the side for further scrutiny. He found himself chuckling at what appeared to be Jamie's morbid fascination with cemeteries. Nearly a third of the paintings contained some form of graves. What was even more intriguing was that she painted graveyards from his past in countries that she had never visited...or had she? He would ask her on the next eve. He looked over a painting of a river flowing between two rocky cliffs. It seemed familiar. He stared at the portrait trying to remember if he had in fact seen this particular river. He started to return the picture to the stack then it hit him. He held it up again, looking beyond the river to the land that surrounded it. Killiecrankie Pass. It was during a battle here in 1689 that he met Trayvon, a vampire, or guardian of the darkness, as they liked to call themselves.

CHAPTER 5

Trayvon was like a breath of fresh air. He was ostentatious, reckless and impulsive. Aerik liked him immediately. He had watched from high up in a tree in the body of an owl as Tray played with a man that had committed crimes against his own people.

The man Tray had singled out had battled all day with his kinfolk; a battle between the Jacobites and government troops. The highlanders were victorious in battle that day and were celebrating by telling their stories of personal kills around the fires. The man that Tray had singled out had falsely bragged about how he had watched some of the troops corner his dear beloved brother and stuck him down dead. He continued in a boisterous voice to blatantly lie about how he took revenge on them by chasing them with his claymore off the crag right into the river while he screamed after them like a mad man. He had indeed chased the men off the cliff into the river, the distance to the other side some eighteen feet or so and the men in turn fell to their watery deaths unable to make the long leap. But the fact be known that he himself killed his brother while nobody was looking, whispering to his brother as he drew his last breath that he didn't deserve the fine young wife he had just taken and that now she would be his.

The highlander went to relieve himself for the last time as Tray swooped down on him, startling the man as he came from out of nowhere. The man would turn to flee and Tray would appear out of thin air in front of him at every turn. He taunted him in the manner of a bullying child, tripping him, poking him in the belly, boxing his ears. He then chased the man telling him that he was the devil come to take him to hell for killing his brother. The man ran screaming to the edge of the cliff there at Killiecrankie Pass. He was terrified, begging for forgiveness and pleading for his life. Tray just laughed then lifted his hands up in the air like a little boy playing ghost, his eyes as big as saucers and yelled, "Boo!" The man, so worked up from fright screamed a blood-curtailing cry, convinced Tray was the devil himself, and jumped to his death off the same cliff that he himself had just chased the earlier fallen troops off of. Tray walked calmly over to the cliff, looked off then rubbed his hands together as if he were brushing off crumbs, he turned looked up into the tree where Aerik watched and winked at him, hands on hips sporting a cocky grin. When Aerik remained silent Tray yelled up to him, "I know where there be two more thieves in the night. Want to go huntin' with the likes of me?"

Aerik shape shifted as he landed beside Tray. "You're a cocky bastard," Aerik stated.

"Aye...tis true," he grinned, "I do believe I just may be the rogue of the highway in these highlands." He laughed then added, "Trayvon Cahan. And who might you be?"

"Lord Aerik Bearach."

"Lord, you say..." Trayvon looked him over as if he were sizing him up. "Aye, ye do have the look of being a Lord about ye." Tray grinned big flashing his white teeth. "I'm going to be a Lord someday. Perhaps even a Baron, now that would be mighty fine now wouldn't it?" He looked over at Aerik with total seriousness and asked, "Do you think it possible I may just be a King someday?"

Aerik slowly shook his head no.

Tray shrugged as if it wasn't really that big of a deal after all. "Ock," he waved his hand as if he were dismissing the idea, "tis too much responsibility to be a royal."

Aerik sensed only good intentions from the young whippersnapper but he knew he was also here for a reason. He crossed his arms, which made him appear extremely foreboding. He was direct with his question. "Who turned you and why are you here?"

Tray smiled like a child with his hand caught in the honey pot. "Aye, ye have laid your claim to these highlands haven't ye?"

Aerik wasn't going to play games with the young lad, he turned to leave.

"Wait, Milord," Tray exclaimed. "She was but a vision of loveliness she was. Came to me on the wind whispering in my ear of eternal life."

Aerik had turned back to him providing his complete attention.

"She called herself Jenaver and she saved my miserable life from a farmer who thought I had compromised his daughter. I swear to you t'was not me, my Lord. The farmer had left me for the scavengers he did." Tray looked to the sky and smiled with the remembrance. "She came down like an angel of mercy she did. The most beautiful thing I ever laid eyes upon. She told me that I could have life but I could not have her…she was already taken. She told me the sun would destroy me and that I would have to hide well during the day."

Aerik interrupted him. "I know of whom you speak. Who sent you to me?" Jenaver must have been in a big hurry with this one. More likely she changed him out of pity for the young cuss. The rush was most likely do to the fact that her mate Torin would have a fit over her physical closeness to another male. He wondered why they would have been separated on this night; Torin was extremely possessive. Aerik found it unlikely that he would let Jenaver out of his sight for any length of time, let alone allow her to place herself in such an intimate act as the giving of her life force, her blood to another male. Yet…Jenaver was extremely willful, headstrong to say the least.

"Alasdair sent me to you." Trayvon smiled a roguish smile. "It turned out that my Angel Jenaver had an ogre of a husband who could not tolerate my being near his beloved, so…they turned me over to Alasdair who was to teach me the way of things." Tray ran a hand through his dark blond hair. "A serious man Alasdair. He taught me the essentials but said you could refine me." Tray grinned again, then added, "He said we would be good for each other."

"He said that, did he?" Aerik felt his lip twitch as he tried to suppress a grin of his own.

"Aye Milord, that he did." Tray looked up at Aerik and asked with total sincerity, "Could you find the time, Milord, to teach me to be respectable, to be a gentleman? I would be forever in your debt."

Aerik chuckled to himself. Alasdair…was forever looking out for him. He returned from his memories and sat the portrait down. He would have to ask Jamie if he could make that portrait a gift to his best friend Tray. Alasdair knew that sending Trayvon to him was the best thing that could have happened to either of them, that is until Jamie came into his life.

Aerik reached out to Tray on the mental pathway they used to communicate to each other. With the time difference he should have just started his evening. "Tray, are you available?"

"Always."

Aerik smiled when he heard his friend respond immediately. "Remember when you asked me if I could make you a gentleman?"

"Yes...you told me it would most likely take an act of God, but that we had all of eternity to try and accomplish the task. Tell me, have we finally succeeded?" Tray sent him an image of what he was doing. The vision clearly showed Tray mentally manipulating two drug dealers to shoot each other so their demise would look as if it were just another drug related homicide. Before he had them pull the trigger he passed judgment on them. "You have committed grave sins against your community and fellow man. You have poisoned and killed children with the destructive chemicals you peddle. These drugs you profit from leads to an infestation of degradation, and causes the oppression of the very neighborhoods to which you were born. Thus, you will relinquish your pathetic, wretched, disrespectful waste of a life in hopes that you will no longer befoul the streets of this great city."

Aerik shook his head. Tray always had a flair for the dramatics. He sent Tray the little info he had gathered so far. The psychic link that strengthened upon his arrival, the saving of Jamie's life which in turn allowed him to mark her. The connection through the portraits she painted. Lastly the unheeded warning that he claimed her as his mate.

Tray's message was a little slower in coming. It reeked of caution. "Do you need me to come out there?"

"There is no need. I just thought you might have some input on the paintings she has created. I'm open to opinions, even yours."

"She's a real looker ain't she?" Tray teased his friend using the improper language that Aerik spent years correcting and hated with a passion. The immediate image he received from Aerik was of a wolf ripping his throat out. "Hey…down boy. You know I was only making fun. I'm extremely overwhelmed with great joy that you have found someone with whom will truly make you happy, Lord knows I was having a hard time filling the bill myself. Now on a more serious note, I don't see how she could have connected to you like that, even through paintings without you having given her your blood. I'll ask around and see what I can find out. Torin and Jenaver are in town for a play, perhaps they will have some answers."

"You know how Torin hates your being near Jenaver. He is a jealous man. Sensing his wife's essence that marked your eternal soul will only remind him of an intimacy she shared with you," Aerik warned.

"That is why I am specifically going to seek them out for advice. I so love toying with Torin's overbearing emotions. Gotta go huntin' now, more bad guys out there. Over and out."

Aerik sent him one last message. "You are an instigator."

"I like to keep things interesting."

Aerik shook his head. Tray was his closest friend and confidant, as close to having a brother as one could get. He made the passing centuries more bearable with his wit and charm if you could call it that. He knew that he would be able to trust Trayvon with not only his life, but Jamie's as well if the need arose. But…the thought of his friend, or anyone for that matter, touching Jamie made the beast within rage in protest. The feeling was so fierce it was almost frightening, and fear was something that he was unaccustomed to feeling. He didn't intend to send Tray the vision of the wolf making his kill, it was instantaneous. He would have to examine these feelings closer. It was Trayvon who helped keep him going, gave him reason to face another night when the loneliness seemed to consume him. Some vampires never find their mates; they give into the loneliness choosing to walk into the dawn. Others have searched and waited for over a thousand years, like Alasdair.

He could feel morning quickly approaching. His body was beginning to feel the sluggish sleep that came with the rising of the sun. He appeared up stairs to check on Jamie one last time before he went to ground. As he looked over her sleeping form, he gently ran his fingers over the smoothness of her bare thigh. She had kicked the covers clean off the bed. Replacing them he bent down and kissed her forehead tenderly. With a wave of his hand he made a note appear on the nightstand. Before he disappeared he sent her a command to sleep till her body was well rested.

CHAPTER 6

Jamie awoke late. Looking at the clock she was surprised to see that it was well past noon. Her gaze swept the room looking for Aerik even though she knew she wouldn't find him there. Her eyes came to rest on the note he left. She smiled picking it up admiring the beauty of the letters, which were written in what looked to her like calligraphy. The paper was thicker – heavier. It was what she would expect of a note from Aerik. She smiled to herself, loving the letter and she hadn't even read it yet. She decided to save it till after she had showered. She wanted to read it out on the porch with her morning cup of coffee. Though the temptation to devour it now was almost more than she could bear she forced herself to set it aside. That way she would have something of his to look forward to. As she climbed out of bed she felt sore but in a good way. It had been a long time since she had made love, and never had it been like it was with Aerik.

Sitting down on the swing chair, she used her bare foot to rub Burl's back as she rocked. She was dressed in her jean shorts and Seattle Mariners baseball tee shirt; she felt like being comfortable. The aroma of her coffee teased her into taking a sip despite the fact that it was fresh brewed and steaming hot. There was nothing like that first sip of coffee to start your day. It was pleasantly warm out and she wondered how long the good weather would hold out. Rain was typical Washington weather for this time of year. Here it was bright and sunny, the soft ocean breeze caressed her skin with familiar warmth. The lull of the waves rolling onto the beach below was like soft music to her ears. She reveled in the feelings assaulting her body; feelings of such contentedness, a warmth from within, she was just feeling so satisfied, so right. She was happy. It had been a long time since she felt this good. Had she ever felt this good?

She picked up the letter beside her and read.

Jamie,

You are my cagaran, my grian, my Luan, my re'alta. Now that I have found you I could not fathom what life without you would be like. I only know that I would not wish to exist without you. You are my — everything. It will be your image I will hold as I close my eyes, and your image I will awake to when I arise. Enjoy your day and I will come to you when the sun is no longer ruling the sky.

Your guardian of the night,

Aerik

P.S.

I wish to make you a business proposition. There is a portrait I wish to purchase of a river flowing between two cliffs behind the door to your studio. It would have great meaning to a friend of mine. If you are willing to part with that particular piece I would love for you to send it to:

Trayvon Cahan @ Cahan Hall, Garden Drive, Cheshire, UK SK104 SD7.

I will enjoy haggling over a price with you this evening. Jamie, please bill the shipping charges to:

Wolfe Corp Accounts Payable @ 127 Chichester, Suffex, UK SD7 LR43

Be good, Ma Cheri

Jamie read the note three more times before she finally sat it down. "Burl, we have something to do today." She rubbed the massive dog behind his ear with her toes. Burl gave her a quick glance as if to acknowledge the fact that he was listening.

Jamie spent the next hour packaging the picture, preparing it to be shipped. She then decided she wanted to take the Jeep out so she took the back seat out of it to make more room for Burl. There were times she just wanted to have the air flowing freely around her; today felt like one of those days. As she walked by the computer on her way out of the house she paused. Setting the boxed painting down she took a seat and got online. She pulled up her favorite search site then typed in Wolfe Corporation. "Damn," she swore aloud as she looked at all the hits pop up. It appeared to be the base operations for everything from medical research labs, to worldwide women and children wellness clinics. *Times* article: "Animal Rights Activists praise Wolfe Corp for its policies of non-use of animals." She decided to spend some time later reading everything but not now. She typed in "Trayvon Cahan." "Lord Trayvon Cahan was presented with a prestigious award for generous contributions to help preserve the historical district of Locholm." She clicked the computer off. She had a lot of research to do when she came home. She grabbed a bottle of Diet Coke out of the fridge then snatched the keys to the Jeep off the wall beside the kitchen door. She hesitated then went back to the table grabbing her wrap for her hand. She carefully wrapped up her healed hand in case she should run into anyone while she was out. Once her bases were covered out the door she went.

"Come on, Burl. Let's go to town!" Jamie called the big boy over to her. He lumbered down off the wraparound porch wagging his tail at hearing his mistress's voice. He was a little reluctant to jump up into the back, but once he was loaded, he looked like he was born to ride in a Jeep. "See," she cooed to him, "you look good back there." She patted his side then placed the picture in the passenger seat and climbed in herself. She noticed that the Jag was gone and hoped that it was Aerik who drove it off. She watched Burl closely as they went down the bumpy driveway making sure he wasn't thinking of bailing out on her. When she turned out onto Highway 101 and headed north he lay down, resting his big head on the inside tire well so he could comfortably rest as well as see out.

During the drive Jamie pondered all that had transpired this past week. *A vampire! Vampires don't exist. Well they didn't last week anyway.* She snorted, "I suppose there are werewolves too," she mumbled out loud to herself. Then again just maybe there were, she would have to ask Aerik about that. Hell, why stop there? Witches, warlocks and wizards might as well be on the "are they real?" list too. Perhaps she needed to have her head examined. It could be possible that she snapped and this was all some delusion she was living. After all she had been through in the last several years it would stand to reason that she slip a little. That had to be it. She had to be imagining all this vampire crap. She had lost three loved ones to death, so she invented the perfect person, one that wouldn't die. Or at least wouldn't die easily. That had to be it, she was probably suffering from stress-related schizophrenia and Aerik was simply a figment of her overactive imagination. She had conjured him up. Created the perfect specimen of man. Handsome, attentive a world class lover, someone who wouldn't die on her. She thought back to how he made her feel while making love and hell...if he was a figment of her imagination then she would gladly jump on the "I'm losing it" band wagon. Imaginary people just don't leave you feeling sore and satisfied, or could they? She looked at her hand, then pulled back the wrap to make sure she could indeed see the stitches, needing to be sure she still had the injury she had suffered. The stitches were there in all their blue colored glory, running neatly through healed skin. Now if that wasn't proof that Aerik was real then she didn't know what would be. She really needed to sit down and cut the stitches off, they weren't serving any purpose now. That was not her imagination. Aerik was real.

She looked over at the box beside her and wondered what kind of connection Aerik and Mr. Cahan shared. Could it be possible that he was also a vampire? How was it that Aerik could be so successful when he obviously couldn't attend daily functions? Surely he couldn't conduct all business during the evening hours, or could he? Her mind bombarded her with questions, some new some still unanswered. Where does he sleep? Does he use a casket? What made it possible for them to talk mentally to each other? If there has to be a connection what is it? Does there have to be a connection or could it just be a fluke of nature? How many women has he been with? Does he have her under a spell? Would he tire of her then just vanish from her life? There has got to be a connection, but what? Jamie tapped the steering wheel as she contemplated all the possibilities.

Her dad popped into her mind. Could there be a family connection somehow? Her father's hobby had been genealogy and he'd done quiet a bit of research tracing the family lines. She used to listen to him talk about all the old dead relatives he had found. Some people she felt she almost knew personally since he talked so much about information he had found while documenting them. She couldn't recall any Wolfes or Bearachs, but didn't he say he had thousands of names in his database? His work was called cluster genealogy. That was when you not only traced the direct lineage back but gathered information on all the siblings and their families as well. Perhaps there was a connection, just not of direct lineage. If there were it would surely have had to be from way back. Her family on both sides had been in America since the late 1600s. How old did Aerik say he was... almost 600 years? The thought that he could have possibly been living at the same time as her early ancestors was frightening and intriguing all at the same time. That would put him born somewhere between 1400 and 1500 hundred. She couldn't help but smile to herself. Damn, but he was robbing the cradle. Now where did her family come from? Scotland. The McPhersons were from Scotland. Aerik said he was from Scotland. Of course there had to be some kind of genetic connection. She smiled to herself thinking that she had hit upon something positive, as it was possible to research.

She wished now that she had paid more attention in history class. Mr. Dalton was right. When she had asked him how knowing all this old history would make a difference in her life he had told her, "You never know when you might need or want to know about our past." Of course even now it would kill her to admit to Mr. Dalton that he was right. She had been one of the hardheaded kids that always whined and complained about learning history. She could still clearly remember one of their conversations when she told him, "Who cares what years World War Two was fought, at least I know what's important...it's over and we won." She had been attempting to raise the grade of a low exam score to no avail. In all actuality it landed her with extra homework. Due to her "young and dumb" smart mouth, she had to write a paper about what her life would be like if she were taken from her home with only the clothes on her back, separated from her father and brother, and forced to live and work in a prison camp. In the end the paper had a profound influence on her perceptions of people and life in general. Due to the teacher-student relationship; she couldn't possibly have thanked Mr. Dalton for giving her the assignment. It surely would have breached some student vs. teacher punishment by additional homework ethics rule. Perhaps now that she was no longer a student, if she ever ran into Mr. Dalton, she could – without compromising herself – express gratitude over his choice of class discipline. She would have to ask Aerik what it was like during the war. Now why didn't they find each other earlier, what an asset he would have been during history class. When she got home she was going to start looking through her dad's genealogy stuff. She wasn't sure what she would be looking for but – just maybe she might fine something useful. Besides, she had several hours to kill before nightfall.

Jamie mailed the painting then stopped at the local grocery store to pick up a few things. Burl waited in the back of the Jeep patiently watching the people come and go. He whined his happy greeting and thumped his tail when Jamie returned. Besides another fifty pound bag of dog food she bought him a rawhide bone in the largest size they offered. When he growled low and deep in his throat Jamie stopped loading the groceries and looked behind her to find Jeff's father, Connor Edgewood, glaring daggers at her from his work truck.

"It's okay, Burl," she assured the gentle giant. Jamie stared at Mr. Edgewood waiting for him to speak, not knowing what she had done to deserve the looks she was receiving.

"I don't suppose you know anything about what happened to Jeff the other night do you?" he began. His look clearly said that she did.

Jamie was stunned at his harsh tone. "No Mr. Edgewood, I don't know what you're talking about. Did something happen to Jeff? Is he okay?"

"Someone put a beehive in his truck. He was stung over fifty times; damn near killed him." He stared at her hard, like if he held his eyes on her long enough she would break down and confess to the evil deed. "His mother's over at the hospital with him now. Nancy said that Jeff's convinced your new boyfriend did it." He stared at her again. "What do you have to say now?"

Jamie didn't know what to say. Mr. Edgewood was clearly upset, and rightfully so but she didn't know anything about this. "Mr. Edgewood," she began, "I don't know anything about a beehive being put in Jeff's truck and I sincerely hope that he will be okay. As far as Aerik having anything to do with this...well he's just wrong sir. Aerik has been staying with me and he's not the type who would do something like that." *Aerik! Damn it!* Jamie yelled in her mind. *You did this, didn't you?* She could clearly see Aerik doing this as retribution for the way Jeff had treated her the day he showed up at the house taking his anger over Aerik's presence out on her.

Jamie heard Aerik's voice in her mind. "He was a pompous little ass and he reaped what he sowed." His voice was so soothing, so strong, spoken with perfect inflection. There was no hint of remorse. Regardless she felt relief and strength just hearing his voice.

"Where is this boyfriend? Is his name Wolfe?" Mr. Edgewood questioned.

Burl started to growl again.

Jamie put a hand on the dog hoping to calm him. "His name is Aerik Wolfe and he was a friend of Jim's. He's not in town right now. But I assure you Aerik had nothing to do with this."

Mr. Edgewood cut her off. "We'll see about that. I've already contacted the sheriff's office. As far as I'm concerned this was attempted murder," he spit out with vehemence. "I hope you're right for your own sake because I won't let this lie. You mark my words girl, I'll find out who did this and they'll pay." He slammed the truck into gear and took off without allowing her to say any more.

Jamie was left shaking, her heart pounded against her chest from the unexpected confrontation. She looked around nervously. A few people had witnessed the encounter and were watching, but they quickly went back to their own tasks when Jamie looked directly at them. She wiped her perspiring hands on her shorts and finished putting her groceries into the Jeep. All she wanted at that moment was to leave.

Again she heard Aerik's voice, calm and reassuring. "Mia, you must calm down. Relax and breathe; or I will do it for you."

Jamie took a deep breath and counted to ten. When that didn't work she took another deep breath and counted to twenty. She felt the tremor in her hands ease and a calm overcame her. Was it the counting or was it Aerik? Then again did it really matter as long as she felt better?

"You tell anyone who comes to you that you know nothing. If anyone wishes to question me, tell him or her that I am out of town on business, and that I will be available when I return this evening. Will you be okay now?"

"I'm fine. I just let him piss me off is all. I'll get a grip. How did you know?" she asked.

"You called to me. With an expletive I might add."

"I'm sorry. I didn't mean to wake you, you can go back to sleep now." She felt strange having a conversation with him in her mind as she drove out of the parking lot.

"I trust you will stay out of trouble till I arise? 'Get a grip' as you called it?"

"I'll try."

"You will do," he stated it as a command not a request. He then sent her an equivalent of a hug mentally, and then was gone.

CHAPTER 7

Jamie couldn't get home quick enough. But as she drove down the long drive to the house she was let down when she saw a sheriff's car parked beside her truck in the driveway. Clayton Fisher, a friend of Jimmy's, sat on the porch steps awaiting her return. As she pulled up he stood and walked over flashing his familiar friendly smile that she remembered so well. Clayton and Jimmy had been buddies and used to go out bowling once a week together. Seeing him sitting on the steps without her brother brought an ache to her heart.

"Hi Clayton." Jamie smiled as she let Burl out of the Jeep and then grabbed a bag.

"Hey Jamie. How have you been?" Clayton greeted as he grabbed the heavy bag of dog food and followed her and Burl to the house. "I see you got a new dog. Could you have gotten one any bigger?" He wanted to ask where Payton was but his intuition told him to leave it alone, that Payton had finally reached that golden age of no return. He knew how close Jamie and Payton had been over the years; his death must have been extremely painful for her. That dog was truly the last of her family.

"His name's Burl. We needed each other," she said over her shoulder as she entered the house. Clayton was smart; he'd figure out that Payton had died. She didn't want to talk about it because she knew that to think about Payton would bring a flood of tears that she didn't want to shed right now.

While Jamie put the groceries away they exchanged the normal "good to see you" routine that everyone seemed to follow as a rule of thumb. What she really wanted to say was, "I hurt like hell seeing you because your presence reminds me that my brother's never coming home again. I hate to see how healthy you look because it reminds me of how young my brother really was and that he was cut down in his

88

prime and would never experience all that life had to offer. I hate to see you because you make me see how painful and cruel life can be, you make me remember, you make me feel the pain of losing my brother all over again." That's what she wanted to tell him. What she did say was, "I know why you're here, Clay. I saw Jeff's dad in the parking lot at the grocery store."

Clay stared at her like she was losing it. "What are you talking about?"

"Why are you here?" She realized that the question was a little rude since he was a family friend and quickly added, "I mean it must be business, you're in uniform, right?"

"I'm here to talk to you about Jimmy's shooting. What did you think I was here for?" He nodded his head yes when Jamie lifted a pitcher of ice water in offering.

She poured them both a glass then sat down at the kitchen table with him. "I'll tell ya Clay, it's been a bad day. I guess someone put a beehive in Jeff's truck and he got stung pretty bad. At least that's what his dad told me. He thinks I, well, that Aerik, someone I have been seeing did it."

"Well did he?" he asked in a matter-of-fact manner.

Jamie shook her head no. "He was hear with me."

"All night?"

Jamie blushed which was answer enough for Clay she could see it in his eyes. "Yes all night."

"Well where is he? I'd like to meet him." He gave her a lopsided grin. "I think that's great that you found someone you like. I worry about you being out here all alone." He reached out and gave her hand a squeeze but when he touched her he got shocked and pulled his hand away quickly. "Damn, too much static electricity in the body I guess. Sorry about that," he apologized.

Jamie didn't feel a thing but she heard the snap sound of the charged electricity. *Did Aerik make this happen somehow – perhaps as a protective barrier of some kind?* She wanted to laugh but it wasn't funny. Clay was innocent of any wrongful intentions. "I'm okay," she told him. "Aerik's out of town on business right now and won't be back till this evening." She added quickly, "But I'm sure he would like to meet you also. Now tell me about Jimmy's case. What's going on?" She changed the subject wanting to get at what brought Clay out here.

"Well you know that Lyle Dugan pled innocent and that he has always been adamant that he never shot Jimmy."

"Yeah." She squeezed her water glass feeling the tension within herself rise.

"Well," Clay paused not sure how to say this, "he has been given three polygraphs over the last year and he's passed every one of them."

"What're you saying, Clay? Are they going to let him get away with this? If Lyle didn't shoot Jimmy then Shelly must have." Jamie couldn't believe what she was hearing.

"Jamie, we're not sure what to think. We never found the gun and Shelly has also passed polygraphs. Believe me we checked her out as well. Actually we're not sure what to make of this." He ran a hand through his curly blond hair and shook his head in disbelief. "We know Jimmy was shot at their place. Lyle and Shelly both said they heard the shot and saw Jimmy fall. They were both trying to give him CPR when backup arrived. Things just aren't adding up. There has been an intense investigation on this." He stopped looking Jamie right in the eye trying to convey to her that he knew this was going to be difficult. "They're starting to think that there was a third party. Someone who was hiding in the woods possibly off to the side of the house."

"Clay, that just doesn't make sense. You're saying that it was a setup and someone wanted Jimmy dead?" She wasn't buying this. "But it was a domestic violence call, right? Weren't they fighting when he showed up?"

Clay was nodding his head yes. "Yeah they were, but everyone knows Lyle and Shelly fight when ever Lyle spends all day at the Tavern. Half the town could have predicted the fight they had that day."

Jamie thought back to all she had heard about the couple and Clay was right, Jimmy had talked about the numerous drunken arguments between Lyle and Shelly Dugan. They were called out there just about every other Saturday after Lyle received his paycheck and tied one on.

He continued, "The Dugans are like clock work. Lyle got paid on Friday evening. Saturday he stayed at the Tavern all day. He goes home and within three hours we get a call that they're fighting. Shelly always calls when he starts to raise his voice. We come out and take him in to sleep it off and she picks him up in the morning. It's been that way for years. Lyle never puts up a fight and as far as we can tell he's never owned a gun." He paused. "Jamie, neither of them had powder marks on their hands; they were both tested."

"Clay, who would want to hurt Jimmy?"

"I don't know, Jamie. You said he mentioned being onto something but wouldn't elaborate. Try and think, did he ever talk about anyone being angry with him, maybe someone pissed off over a ticket he gave, anything?"

"Everyone liked Jimmy." She couldn't think of anyone that would want to shoot her brother, it just didn't make sense. "I told you all before, he had said that he was onto something big but he wouldn't tell me, he said what he had was circumstantial and he needed more. The detectives went through all his papers and they found nothing that he was working on."

"So he told you he was onto something and this was in the morning?"

"Yeah," Jamie looked out the window to the porch. That was where they had their last conversation over a morning cup of coffee. "I asked him what was bothering him. I could tell he had something on his mind." She felt hot tears stinging her eyes she tried to blink them back. "He said: 'I might be onto something big, but it's nothing for you to worry about now. I'm going to talk to Clay about it at work today.'" She sniffled. She could still hear his voice so clearly in her mind. "Then I asked him if he could tell me, and he said he didn't want to hurt my feelings but he felt it best if he ran it by you first."

"What did he say next?"

"He changed the subject and we started talking about the stereo speakers in the Jeep. He said the one mounted on the row bar was cutting out." Jamie cleared her throat she felt like she was getting a grip on her emotions.

"Was that it?"

"That was it. He finished his coffee, sat the cup down and asked if I minded taking it in with me when I went in and then he said that he was thinking about stopping by Jeff's work on the way in to talk to him."

"What did he want to talk to Jeff about?"

"Well, fixing the wiring to the stereo speaker. Remember he's 'Mr. Stereo.'"

Clay leaned back in his chair and thought a moment before speaking. "Did he say that's why he was going to talk to Jeff?"

Jamie shrugged. "No I don't think so, but we were talking about the stereo and Jeff would have been the logical one to have fix it. He installed it."

Clay shook his head yet again. When they had interviewed Jeff he told them Jim never came by. There were so many "what ifs." He found himself wishing his friend had confided in him before work. There was never going to be another "after work" for Jim. "Well, I just wanted you to know what was going on. I thought it would be easier hearing it from me. I'm not sure where the investigation is going to go from here but I want you to think about what I've told you. If anything – no matter how insignificant comes to mind, you call me."

"I will," she promised.

Clay stood to leave. "You can call me anytime at work or at home."

Jamie walked him out to his patrol car. "Thanks Clay. I'm glad you told me."

"Lyle's moving back to town, Jamie. This has always been his home and that old house, the piece of crap that it is, well...besides Shelly, it's all he's got." He looked at Jamie watching for her response. She looked apprehensive, but that was to be expected. She didn't look like running into the Dugans was going to create a problem that he would need to be concerned about. That was a relief to him and he felt like a burden had been lifted from his shoulders. "I just didn't want you to run into him in town not knowing what's going on. I believe he's innocent and you know that Jimmy was my best friend and if there was any doubt...."

"Clay, it's okay," Jamie cut him off. "I know. I'm going to trust you on this. The Dugans won't have any trouble from me." That was so hard for her say; she desperately wanted Lyle to be guilty. At least that way she could put it all to rest. "If what you say is true and they are innocent then I owe them an apology and a thank you for trying to give Jimmy CPR. Please find the person who shot my brother."

Clay started to pull out then stopped. Leaning out the window he said, "I'll check on Jeff and see what's happening with the beehive thing. I'll let you know." He waved as he drove off.

"Thanks, Clay." Jamie went back into the house.

Everything Clay said made sense but it wasn't what she wanted to hear. The thought of her brother's killer walking around free made her skin crawl. She sat down at the computer and stared at the black screen. She was trying to decide if she should do more research on Aerik and this friend of his or if she should go directly to her father's family tree stuff, needing to take her mind off Jimmy because if she didn't she was going to start crying and she didn't want to cry right now. With that in mind her choice was easy. The tree was the right choice so she grabbed her diet soda and headed upstairs. "Come on, Burl. I don't want to do this alone."

CHAPTER 8

It had been months since she entered her parents' bedroom. She dusted and vacuumed on occasion but other than that she found it too painful to be in their room. The room was the same as the day her parents died. Neither Jim nor she had any reason to change it. The room just wasn't needed for anything else. Jamie thought of it as her "crying room." If she needed to cry this is where she would come and it wouldn't take long for the tears to follow.

Jamie took a deep breath and opened the door. She walked right in with determination, her head held high. She went straight to her father's computer, removed the dust cover and sat down. "Okay Burl, we can do this. We have a mission." Burl sat down next to her like an old friend ready to lend a hand. Jamie smiled giving Burl a pat on the head.

She switched on the computer and went to work. It took a while to figure out how to work the family tree program he used, but once she got the hang of it she realized it was quite simple. She searched his index of names and didn't find any Bearachs. She did find three Wolfes but they were so far removed and too recent in time. A fourth cousin married to a Bryan Wolfe in 1998 and they had two children thus the three Wolfes that were in the index. There were no parents listed for this Bryan Wolfe. The blood connection if you could call it that was through his wife Shirley Norland. This Wolfe connection was clearly a dead end.

Taking a break she ran downstairs and put on a pot of coffee. She fixed Burl and herself a veggie burger with lots of cheese. She wasn't feeling hungry but when her hands started shaking she knew she needed to eat. When they went back upstairs she had a new plan of searching locations. Her father had lots of books on different families that had been researched by others as well as books and histories on locations that the many family lines originated from. She scanned the bookcase where he kept all his genealogy stuff. She found books on Scotland, Ireland, Early America, several on different ships' passenger lists, ship ports to early America, England and so on. She was surprised at the diversity of all the books he had collected. How to read old handwriting, names of everyday things in the sixteenth and seventeenth centuries, medical terms and their meanings for the genealogist. *Old English Cemeteries Transcribed*, now that one she wouldn't mind looking through. She pulled it forward on the shelf for easier location later. She wanted to stick to her original goal. She decided to start at the top of the shelf and any book with an index she would search first for the names Bearach, Wolfe and she would even look for his buddy Mr. Trayvon Cahan.

For the next three hours Jamie searched, took notes and downed not just her soda but almost half a pot of coffee. Now she wasn't shaking from hunger but from a heavy dose of caffeine. She found herself clock watching again, counting down the hours till nightfall. She had close to three more hours till the sun ceased to dominate the sky.

Taking a break from the genealogy/history research she walked across the hall and wandered around Jimmy's room. Today just seemed to be the day for her to invade on others' space. In all actuality it was now her space but she still felt very much like she were trespassing. She ran her finger over the dresser top, making a line in the dust that had settled there. His desk had papers strewn about from when the detectives had made their sweep of his belongings looking for answers. She had been meaning to go through them and toss what was trash but had put it off. It was all trash now, wasn't it? Nobody was ever going to need or use these things. Jamie pushed a few of them around with her finger scanning the hodgepodge of miscellaneous slips of paper. Little reminder notes Jimmy had written to himself, receipts, old football schedules. She didn't need to keep any of it; he wasn't coming back. As the finality of Jimmy's passing hit her fresh tears stung her eyes.

Crying out in frustration she took her hand, and with one big sweep she knocked the papers off the desk onto the floor. She dropped herself to the floor along with the mess she just created. Burying her head in her hands she sat there and cried. Burl whined and pawed the floor beside her. She looked up at the huge dog as he looked at her with his big brown eyes as if to ask, "Are you okay?" Jamie reached out hugging the dog to her then started to laugh through her tears. "You are a life saver. I'm losing it again aren't I?" Burl thumped his tail on the floor as if in answer.

"Jamie, you are in emotional distress," it was Aerik's voice, soothing, calming, enshrouding her pain in a sea of warmth.

"Really?" she retorted.

Silence.

She ignored him, thinking what a great astute observation he had made, the equivalent of "no brainer," yet she allowed him to comfort her mentally. She could not block his spiritual embrace. Try as she like, it felt too good to deny.

"You're ironic, bitter humor wounds me." His voice flowed over her, through her, touching her. It wrapped around her insides like a down comforter on a cold winter's day. Yet, his voice as pleasurable as it was, dripped with a hinted threat of retaliation to her sarcasm.

She could see him in her mind, his eyes flashing a wolfish smile. Teasing her for choosing to battle with him. A battle she would never stand to win. At least that's what he would have her believe.

"I was just having…a moment," she sputtered out loud. "I'm fine. You can go back to sleep." She swiped at her left over tears and reached out grabbing a tissue from the box she had just knocked to the floor for her runny nose.

"A moment?" he questioned.

"Get out of my head," she ordered. She would smack him if he were within striking distance, not that he would feel it as massive as he is.

"You would strike me? I dare say that the correct response for my mood alteration services should be an emphatic thank you."

"Don't you mean I owe you for the attitude adjustment?" she shot back at him rapid fire.

Her only response was his soft laughter filling her mind till it slowly faded away. She wiped at her eyes one last time then surveyed the mess around her. Sparring with him actually made her feel a little better. She started putting the papers into the trash one at a time, looking them over before tossing them into the waist basket. Half way through she dropped one in the basket them retrieved it. It was a note that simply said call mechanic in P. A. make appointment. That was odd for two reasons. First he always used Big All's auto shop in town when any of the vehicles had a problem. Second, neither the Jeep nor the truck had anything wrong with them. Why would Jimmy want to drive all the way into Port Angeles to see a mechanic? Maybe Big All was too busy or it was something he couldn't do himself.

The phone ringing startled her and she about jumped out of her skin. It was Clay calling to say that he would be stopping by later and wanted to make sure she was going to be home. Hanging up the phone she swore under her breath. Jeff and his parents weren't going to let this beehive incident rest. She was going to give Aerik a piece of her mind when she saw him. He stirred up a bee's nest all right. She went back upstairs to finish the cleaning she should have began a long time ago.

Jamie was kicked back on the porch swing with a fresh cup of coffee. As she watched the sun slowly fade on the horizon, she used her bare foot against Burl's massive body to rock the swing. He seemed to be enjoying this new evening ritual. She wondered who was going to show up first, Aerik or Clayton? It wasn't but a few minutes later that Burl suddenly scrambled to his feet his hackles raised. Jamie listened then heard the distant rumble of a vehicle coming down the dirt drive. Clayton pulled up in his personal vehicle, a little red beat-up pickup truck. The engine knocked terribly before coughing one last sputter and died into silence. Jamie smiled knowing how much Clayton loved that beat-up piece of shit truck. She reached out to calm Burl as Clay exited the truck and came up the porch.

"Hey Jamie," he said in greeting. "I hope you don't mind that I show up on official business out of uniform but my shift ended hours ago and I hate wearing the thing."

"You know I don't care what you're wearing." She took the bottle of beer that Clay handed her from the paper sack he was carrying. "Thought you might like to share a cold one." He sat the bag down on the porch and took a seat on the banister where he always perched himself when Jimmy and he would sit out here and drink beer.

Jamie thought about how nice it was that Clay felt so at home here even after Jimmy died. It was kind of nice, the feeling that things hadn't changed. But they have changed. Jimmy wasn't here. The three of them would often sit out on the porch and talk for hours. Actually Jimmy and Clay did most of the talking, which tended to get louder and boisterous after they had a few beers. She missed the company, the sound of other voices around her.

Clay nodded to the bottle in his hand. "I'm supposed to be conducting official business even if it is after hours, but I figured you wouldn't mind it's been a long day."

Jamie smiled. "Come on Clay, you know I could care less." She didn't want to but she had to ask, "So how's Jeff?"

"I think the bee venom twisted his mind a little is what I think." Clay grinned then added, "He was stung pretty bad and he looks it." He shrugged. "If his parents weren't throwing such a fit I wouldn't even be here asking about it."

Jamie wanted to laugh and almost choked on the beer at his comment. "So you need to question Aerik?" She kept looking out at the blackness of the ocean. The sun had been down for almost fifteen minutes, where was he? She pulled her sweatshirt jacket together feeling the chill of the night. If it weren't for the thick fur on Burl she would have had to put her shoes on to keep her feet warm.

"Yeah, I'm gonna need to ask him a few questions," he drawled. His voice clearly stating that he didn't want to. "This is going to sound crazy but Jeff's convinced that while he was trying to get out of the truck and away from the bees he was seeing your boyfriend in his mind and hearing his voice." Clay snorted a quick laugh. "He said he kept hearing your boyfriend telling him to stay away from you. The kicker of it all is that when Jeff finally yelled that he would stay away from you the bees just disappeared." Clay took a drink of his beer then eyed Jamie for any kind of reaction. "Come on, Jamie, be honest with me. Is Jeff strung out on something? Is that why you broke it off with him?"

It was Jamie's turn to laugh. "Not that I'm aware of but it certainly sounds like he was on something doesn't it?" She agreed with him. "They just disappeared?"

"That's what he says."

"Did Jeff tell you that he was here earlier that day? He had found out that I was dating Aerik and he was a little angry about it. I think this is all just a way to get back at me for breaking it off with him."

They were interrupted by the sound of a car coming down the drive. Jamie could feel Aerik's presence before she could physically see the Jaguar pull up. He parked beside Clayton's truck. The new and sleek beside the old and ugly the site of which caused both Clayton and Jamie to grin.

Clay gave Jamie a questioning look and a half lopsided grin when he saw what kind of car her new boyfriend was driving. "Nice car." He stood up waiting to be introduced as the Aerik came up the steps like he owned them. His charismatic personality clung to him like a second skin. Clay stepped back, not out of fear; it was as if Aerik's mere presence demanded space. He was huge. If it weren't for his charming smile his sheer size would be intimidating. Hell, he *was* intimidating. Who was he trying to kid? Quick calculations put his height at about six foot five. Weight two-forty, two-fifty depending on muscle mass, and there was most definitely muscle mass, they rippled whenever he moved. He couldn't put an age to him though, odd, he was usually very good at age approximation. *Damn...* was the only word that came to his mind.

"I see you have company," Aerik said as he swept Jamie up in a loving embrace and gently kissed her cheek. "I hope I'm not intruding." He released her and turned a warm friendly smile towards Clayton. Holding out his hand he shook Clay's firmly. "I'm Aerik

Wolfe."

"Clay Fisher. Nice to meet you."

"Like wise." Aerik quickly scanned Clay's mind for any harmful intent towards Jamie and found none. He was not a threat, quite the opposite actually. Clay emitted a true brotherly love towards Jamie. What was totally unexpected was the threat he sensed towards himself. Clay was questioning what his own intentions were. He wanted to know why Jamie told Jeff that he was an old friend of Jimmy's at the hospital. He knew it was a lie but wanted to believe that Jamie had good reason to lie to the little snot. Aerik felt that this young man would do everything in his power to protect Jamie as a brother would; he also wanted to trust her judgment, which said a lot in itself. Aerik liked him immediately.

Despite the warm smiles and handshakes, Jamie watched the two size each other up like two roosters in the barnyard. She wanted to laugh. "Aerik," she said softly touching his arm as he sat down on the swing beside her, "Clay and my brother were best friends. Clay's a deputy sheriff, he and Jimmy used to work together."

Aerik spoke to Jamie in her mind. "He knows that you lied to Jeff in the hospital when you told him that I was an old friend of your brother's. When the time is right I will address that issue. You will not need to say anything, he will believe what I tell him."

Jamie responded in her mind knowing he would hear her. "You won't hurt him," she said it as a mixture of a statement as well as a questioned.

She heard his soft chuckle in her mind tickling her sensually. "You need not fear. I know he has only your best interest at heart. I find myself liking him despite the fact that he currently thinks I'm up to no good." Aloud he spoke to Clay, "Jamie has spoken fondly of you. Did you know her family well?"

"I did," he began, then held out a beer for Aerik, which he took with a nod of acceptance. Clay wondered how the porch swing could bear the weight of Aerik let alone the two of them. Jamie looked so comfortable curled up next to him. Clay was not one to be envious of another's advantages but he found that next to Aerik he was puny by comparison. There was no amount of time spent at the gym that would even bring him close to the muscle tone of this man sitting before him. He reeked of physical power. He actually felt as if Aerik were intimidating his manhood just by being present. *How pathetic*, he thought to himself. He had never felt this way before and hoped he never felt this way again. But above all, he hoped he would never have to take on this man in a physical confrontation. He pictured himself being body slammed to the ground with the slightest of effort on Aerik's part. He couldn't help but grin. His skin broke out in goose bumps when Aerik grinned back at him as if he had read his thoughts. "I ah…" he stumbled through his words having trouble getting his thoughts together. "I grew up down the road. I've known Jim and Jamie all my life." He ran a shaky hand over his spiked crew cut. "How did you meet Jamie?" he asked.

Aerik looked down at Jamie his one arm draped around her protectively. His other splayed her fingers entwining them with his own. Her skin was so soft carrying the pleasant scent of vanilla. A nice scent on her, he would have to remember to comment on it at a later time. He inhaled deeply. "I had the pleasure of meeting Jamie at a gallery in Port Angeles. I have been touring the Pacific Northwest purchasing art for my own gallery. There are a lot of fine artists and master craftsman in this region."

"So you have a gallery?" Clay asked.

"I am affiliated with several but my personal gallery is located in London. The London House Museum and Fine Arts. We have some of the finest collections in the world. We premier world renown artists, illustrating major achievements in painting, graphic arts that cover all ages, sculpture, as well as individual artistic creations. Of course I also display art that is suited to my own personal taste at my estate in Suffex."

Jamie tried to not look shocked. She had read about the museum he spoke of. "You didn't tell me," she spoke in her mind.

"There are many wonderful things I have yet to share with you, Mia," Aerik answered privately.

Clay was impressed. Mr. Wolfe seemed to know what he was

talking about, and the gallery should be easy enough to check on. "I always thought Jamie was a great painter."

"Yes, her work is quite extraordinary to say the least. She carries a very special aptitude for creating outstanding works of art. I believe it truly is an innate capability that only a few are gifted with," Aerik complimented. "I'm hoping to give her more of the exposure she rightly deserves. I have nothing against the beauty of this area but it can be stifling to an artist with no means to reach the people of a mass majority. I hope to rectify that."

"I'm not that good," Jamie said shyly her blush was evident even in the dim light that surrounded them.

Aerik ran his chin over the top of her head intimately, letting the silk of her hair tease his flesh. "You are too modest," he told her while patting her hand as if she were but three years old. He continued, "So Clay, tell me what was Jamie like as a child? Was she as tenacious then as she is now?"

Clay smiled. "I guess you could call it that." He paused thinking about what he should say. He didn't want to say anything that might embarrass her like when she was sixteen and she and her girlfriend Sarah snuck a few beers, got drunk and she threw up on her brother's birthday cake. "Jamie had her moments," he decided to play it safe. "She was a typical tomboy, always running around with no shoes on. Climbing trees, riding bikes, playing war, digging in the sand at the beach." He looked her right in the eye. "Always spying on her brother. Tagging along the rest of the time."

"I couldn't fathom this beautiful little girl playing war in the dirt." Aerik chuckled softly. "So you were a tomboy?" he teased.

"I had my moments," she said.

"I bet you have had a lot of moments," Aerik teased her. In her mind he spoke, "I would like to play war with you."

Changing the subject Jamie simply stated. "Aerik, Clay is also here on business. Someone put a beehive in Jeff Edgewood's truck yesterday and he has this ridiculous idea that it was you. I told Clay that Jeff was out here several days back having a fit because I'm not going to get back together with him but he needs to question you anyway. Jeff and his parents are bullheaded." She just had to add that last comment out of spite for the way Mr. Edgewood treated her at the store.

"You need to question me?" Aerik asked.

Clay looked sheepish. He felt like an idiot having to do this now. Obviously Mr. Wolfe was above something so childish. "Yes sir, I have to follow up on the request and Jamie's right, his parents are bullheaded. Jeff's their baby and he can do no wrong in their eyes."

"Well this should prove to be interesting." Aerik grinned. "Question away."

"Have you met Jeff Edgewood?"

"Yes. I met him briefly at the hospital when I picked Jamie up after she injured her hand. I'm afraid that's the extent of my contact with Mr. Edgewood."

Jamie looked down at her hand, she had removed the annoying wrap earlier, glad that she hadn't taken the time to remove the stitches yet. In the dim light of the porch lamp you couldn't see how well it had healed in so short a time. "Now do you see why this is so ridiculous? Aerik introduced himself, shook his hand then we left. I mean come on, he's seeing Aerik in his mind and hearing his voice in his head...let's be real."

"You told Jeff that Aerik was an old friend of Jimmy's." Clay needed to know if she did indeed lie to Jeff and if she did why.

"I told Jamie to tell Mr. Edgewood I was an old family friend." Aerik took control of the conversation. "Jamie told me that the doctor had called him with out consulting her first. As you can see it was not necessary or preferred that she ride with him. Jamie did express her concern to me that Mr. Edgewood would not look favorably upon a relationship between us. So...to avoid an unpleasant confrontation I took it upon myself to suggest the small white lie." Aerik gave Jamie a light squeeze. "I thought that if Mr. Edgewood had the impression that I were a family friend thus not a threat to himself we could all leave peacefully with out incident." Aerik sighed. "I should have known that my feelings for Jamie would be so evident that any fool would see right through the family friend ploy." He leaned down and gently kissed the top of her head. Aerik looked Clay directly in the eyes. His vampire gaze held him, mesmerizing, entrancing him, commanding his undivided attention. "You understand how we were only avoiding an unpleasant situation. Mr. Edgewood and his family have made a mistake accusing Jamie or myself of any wrongdoing. You also understand we had nothing to do with this unfortunate incident. Surely it was a friend's joke gone awry, or the retribution of a jealous boyfriend, which could be one of many. Mr. Edgewood has dated numerous different women since his and Jamie's break up. To further pursue this issue would be a great waist of the department's time. Don't you agree, Mr. Fisher?"

"Oh, certainly, I agree one hundred percent, and please call me Clay," he said while nodding his head in agreement. Yes, of course Mr. Wolfe was right. He wasn't even sure why he bothered them about the silly accusations in the first place. As he looked into Aerik's eyes, they appeared to be pools of swirling black smoke, liquid puddles of charcoal. Totally fascinating the way the porch light created such an illusion. It was the porch light? He questioned himself. He leaned back and rubbed his eyes. Everything normal, damn next thing you know he'd be telling people that he saw Aerik in his mind. He smiled to himself at the ludicrous thought.

"He strikes me as a very immature individual. It's the hearing voices that I would be concerned about. I hope his doctor recommends some kind of evaluation for any future therapy he may need," Aerik commented.

Aerik was effortlessly gracious and tactful in social manner. It was clear to Clay why Jeff would show such resentment towards him. It's one thing to be dumped by your long time love, but to be replaced by one such as Mr. Wolfe who was clearly more of man than he would ever be, not only his social standing but his physical standing as well, must surely have been nothing short of a big slap in the face. There was nothing Jeff could ever do to be of equal caliber to Mr. Wolfe. "I always thought of him as a little spoiled. Maybe this is all a result of years of conditioning on his parents' part. The only child syndrome or something to that effect," Clay said.

Jamie added her two cents, for what it was worth. "I read somewhere that only children were more likely to need professional guidance for things like social inadequacies and character flaws, such as being close minded and egotistical in their adult relationships." She pushed herself up from Aerik's side and asked him directly. "Are you an only child?"

Aerik laughed pulling her back against him but not answering her question. Instead he turned it on Clay. "What about you, Clay? Are you in need of professional guidance do to an egotistical personality?"

"Well actually," he laughed. "I *am* an only child."

The three of them talked and joked around for the next hour and a half till Clay headed home leaving Aerik and Jamie alone. Jamie had no sooner removed her jacket then Aerik swept her into his embrace. He snuggled her to him breathing in her scent, listening to her heartbeat faster at his touch. He kissed the soft curve of her neck, following the line of her pulse with his lips up to her ear where he whispered, "You smell of vanilla and ale, you make me ache for you, Ma Cheri."

He was too damned sexy, a charmer with an innate ability to seduce. He always knew just what to say and how to say it, and she didn't care, as long as he was saying and doing it to her. She didn't know if she could resist him if she tried. She didn't even want to try to resist him, he was every girl's dream man. He was her hero, bringing her back to the real world that she had spent almost a year hiding from. She knew that he had powers, that he was capable of controlling how and what others thought, yet she felt in her heart that he was gifted with this charisma, the very kind that women found so attracting in a man. Of course centuries of practice....

"I assure you it does not take centuries to learn what a woman wants." He cupped the back of her head and brought his lips to hers tasting her sweetness. He wanted more.

His voice was deep, sexy, her body responded immediately. His kiss was demanding yet gentle, filled with the promise of passion still to come. When he released her she was breathless. She pushed against his chest as hard as she could. "You are an overbearing, presumptuous, arrogant man." How did he do that! It was just a kiss yet she felt the heat of desire spreading out to run down her legs. Heat pooled in her womanhood where she throbbed with each beat of her heart. He backed away from her laughing that sexy laugh that made her go weak in the knees.

"You want me." He smiled down at her as he leaned lazily against the door jam.

"You are overly convinced of your sensual power over women."

"You want me."

"That's beside the point," she scolded. "We have only been alone for a few minutes and here you're already pawing me like an animal."

Aerik growled deep in his throat as his eyes burned into hers smoldering with suppressed need. "You do bring out the beast in me."

Jamie wagged her finger at him. "I'll have you know that I had a difficult day while you were off sleeping."

Aerik raised his eyebrow. "You mean trying to sleep," he corrected.

Jamie waved her hand briskly in the air dismissing his counter. "Just where do you sleep anyway?"

"Would you like to see?"

"Really?" she fidgeted at the images that came to mind.

"It's not as bad as you imagine," he stated reading her thought. "It's naturally pleasing to the eyes as well as other senses."

"I watched a movie once," she began, hesitating long enough to bite at her nail. "Do you just lie in the dirt with all the bugs and crawly things and then burst out when the sun goes down?"

Aerik smiled at her imagination, which was quite vivid. He wouldn't tell her that he was very capable of just that minus the crawly things. He abhorred insects and rodents. He made sure that nothing moved in his sanctuary while he slept. "Mia," he mentally hushed her, "your imagination is overwhelming you. Close your eyes and see with your mind," he commanded softly.

Jamie gasped at the beauty of the image he shared with her. It was a cavern of some sort. A cave so beautiful she couldn't possibly believe it existed.

"It's very real I assure you. Your Olympic Mountain range is a geological wonder."

In her mind Jamie saw a cavern that sparkled of color. Carved out of ancient limestone the ceiling and walls dripped with an array of formations. She couldn't tell if some were growing from the ceiling down of from the floor up, it was truly spectacular, from the stalactites, stalagmites, soda straws, and flowstones to a splattering of crystals and mountain gems. There were pools of water so smooth and reflective it was like looking into a mirror. An underground waterfall cascaded into one of the pools causing steam to rise as the cool water hit water heated by the volcanic activity of the mountain. There was a flowstone type shelf in the middle of the room made into a bed covered with white linen and piles of fur blankets. It looked soft, inviting. There were lit candles placed strategically around the room, the light from which twinkled off the gems that grew from the ceiling and walls. Rivers of quarts and gold sparkled everywhere she looked. With a gasp of disbelief it was gone. She was positively speechless. Never had she imagined that her mountains held such inner beauty.

"Being vampire does have its advantages. It is beautiful is it not?" he asked even though he already knew her answer.

"Yes." She looked at him in wonder then asked, "You could take me there and I wouldn't get hurt? I wouldn't have to be like – you?"

Aerik watched her twitch in nervousness before answering. "I can take you just about anywhere on earth," he answered slowly. He was overcome by feelings of reluctance. Had he actually been entertaining the idea that she would someday consider joining him to live out eternity in the shadow of nightfall? His heart ached at the thought of not having her at his side. He should have known better, this was a girl afraid of death. Death had touched her too many times in her young life; it was ingrained upon her soul as an act of pain, extreme sorrow – torture. He also felt her intense resistance to leaving this place she called home. Her roots ran deep here, to this bit of land by the sea. He quickly searched her mind for memories of other places. She had never traveled outside her state. Her exploration of the world came via the Internet, where the world was virtually speaking, at her fingertips. She was frightened of leaving her comfort zone. When she didn't speak he asked, "Jamie, why are you afraid to travel?" He saw it flash quickly through her mind riding a wave of fear, which stabbed at his heart. Her mind screamed that it might rain which made no sense till he felt her pain from her parents' death. When her parents were killed in the car accident it had been raining heavily. She was told it was weather related.

"The roads aren't safe when it rains." It came out as a whisper. Jamie cleared her throat then said it again louder, "Ah...I don't like to drive in the rain."

Aerik watched her a moment letting her collect herself. She was remarkable. She could get control of her feelings quite quickly. "But honey, you live in Washington," he stated.

Jamie laughed a nervous little laugh, her smile brightening her already beautiful features. "I know. Crazy isn't it?"

Her grass-colored eyes sparkled with the tears she was able to keep from spilling, her long lashes holding them back. They made the most beautiful dam, he thought. Yes she was remarkable. He could see it now. How she harbored herself in this big house only going out when she was sure that it wasn't going to rain. He caught a memory of her driving home and getting caught in a downpour. She had pulled off the road in a state of panic and cried for hours till it passed.

She went on, "I'm afraid of driving in the rain. And I'm not just afraid actually – it's more like terrified."

As she spoke Aerik went to her taking her gently into his arms. He felt her need to explain so he refrained from telling her that he knew. He stayed out of her mind and listed to her as she explained about her parents' death and how it had affected her emotionally as well as physically at times, like when the rains came. He enjoyed listening to her talk. He liked the sound of her voice, the feel of it vibrating through her skin touching his soul. Each syllable she spoke was like the sound of an angel's harp. She voiced her feelings freely about the irrational fear she developed after their death. She was unintimidated by any interpretations he may make such as labeling her as weak or emotionally challenged. He made none. When she was finished she looked up at him with her brow wrinkled like she was scrutinizing him. He couldn't help but look bewildered in an amused sort of way.

Jamie asked, "Do you have a problem with that?"

Aerik laughed so hard and so loud he shook.

"It's not funny." She walked away from him with hands on hips.

"You're really quite precious when you get an attitude," he told her.

"I'm not precious," she said for lack of anything else to say.

"Oh you are, trust me," he said then added, "I would never think that anything you said from the heart was funny. Humorous perhaps, but never funny." He crooked his finger at her calling her to him without speaking.

Jamie shook her head no.

Aerik crooked his finger again, this time sporting the wolfish grin that he found to be an effective trigger in eliciting a response from Jamie.

Again Jamie shook her head no, only much slower this time. The look in her eyes betrayed the movement of her head. She jumped in fright when suddenly without seeing him move Aerik was only mere inches from her like an impenetrable wall. She stepped back. "Don't do that, you scared me," she scolded him for the second time in only minutes.

Aerik ran his thumb under the cleft of her chin gently tipping her head back allowing him to look into her eyes. "You are my *grian*," he drawled. "I would never make fun at your expense." He let his thumb run down the expanse of her neck, her pulse beating steady under his touch. His fingers circled around to rest at her back where he proceeded to caress her in a massaging motion.

Jamie relaxed at his touch. She closed her eyes and savored the pleasure his fingers brought to her tense neck muscles. "What does gree-on mean?" she asked.

"Sun. You are my sun."

"That's pretty. Thank you." Jamie thought of the words in the note he had left her. That word grian was in the note as well. She wanted him to tell her the meaning of the other words as well. "Your note," she exclaimed as she dashed off up stairs to her parents' room where she had left it. Once it was in hand she started to head back but as she turned there was Aerik. "You really need to stop that," she said then added, "I wanted to know what these words meant also, here." Jamie pulled up a chair for Aerik then took her seat at the computer desk where she had spent most of her afternoon.

Aerik took the note he had left her and folded it closed. He didn't need to see the written words to translate their meaning he was well aware of what he had written. He sat down on the chair she had offered then handed her back the note. "It says you are my darling, my sun, my moon, my stars. I'm sorry I should have used your words instead of the words of my youth."

"Oh no, I loved the note. It was sweet." She took the folded paper from his hands. "I'll cherish it forever." She smiled up at him clearly happy about the translation.

"You are too easy to please." Aerik reached out taking a lock of her silken hair and let it sift between his fingers.

"Oh I wanted to show you what I did today," Jamie said excitedly as she turned to the desk and looked over her notes.

"You mean besides having a bad day?" he teased.

"I know it could have been better," she conceded. "It started out good though." Jamie's smile turned into a blush. "I woke up feeling great."

"I would love to make that a habit." Aerik grinned at her. His eyes kept being drawn to her delicate throat where her pulse beat strong, steady, calling to his animal need. He hadn't fed before he came knowing upon waking that another male was with Jamie. He was feeling the need growing within, a thirst he must quench. As Jamie showed him her notes on the family genealogy and what she had weeded out he forced himself to concentrate on her words. Her pulse was thrumming in his mind his own heartbeat regulating itself to match hers beat for beat. He felt his fangs begin to grow as the smell of her blood assailed his senses; its sweetness beckoning to him. "Jamie, I must leave for a little while." Aerik stood. "I will return within the hour so that we can finish going over your work."

"Where are you going? Why do you need to leave?" she questioned.

He reached out again running his fingers through her silky tresses. "I must feed now. I will return soon."

She asked hesitantly, "You don't want to feed from me?" The look on his face told her that he would like nothing more but his words said otherwise.

"I will not use you to satisfy my hunger, Mia. I only take from you out of desire; it is not the same as to fulfill myself for nourishment. I will return soon," he promised. Then, in the blink of an eye, he dissolved into a fine mist and disappeared.

CHAPTER 9

She was disappointed that he left yet she was thankful as well. *At least he behaved like a gentleman*, she told herself. After all what was she going to do argue with him? "Oh please baby, stay and sink those razor sharp fangs into my neck, let me be your entree this evening." She smiled at her own humorous remark.

"I'm saving you for dessert."

Jamie whirled around before she realized his voice was in her head. She shivered at his words despite the sexually charged way he conveyed them. It was the unexpectedness of their delivery that threw her. She could hear him chuckling softly, his voice like a feather tickling her from the inside. "Shame on you for eavesdropping on my thoughts."

"Trust me, when you speak like that I will be listening."

"Typical male," she chided.

"Some things will never change."

Jamie set her notes aside and took this time to refill her coffee. When she returned to her parents' room she found that Burl was still asleep on the braided rug at the side of the bed. He did open his eyes as she took her seat. Once he acknowledged it was her, it was lights out again. Her heart thudded when she thought of what his fate would have been had it not been for Aerik. She leaned back in the chair resting her foot on the edge of the desk. She sipped her coffee. Too hot, she sat it down to cool. "Can you hear me?" she tested.

"I will always hear you when you wish to communicate with me."

"Can I talk to you while you're – having dinner?" she asked smiling to herself.

"Mia, I could listen to you through all of eternity and never tire of hearing your voice."

"If my voice sounds as good to you as yours does to me, then

112

we're both in trouble."

"Why would you say that? I would think that enjoying the sound of each other's voices would be a good thing."

"Well yours – turns me on," she admitted.

"You know I'm going to do more than turn you on when I return. You should rid yourself of those cumbersome clothes and save me the time."

It was Jamie's turn to laugh. "I will wait and let you do that," she teased. "I was looking through my dad's papers. He was into genealogy and I thought maybe there was a family connection somewhere. When you return I thought you might want to look over his trees index and see if any names looked familiar. I also thought that perhaps your family and mine were in the same area at the same time."

"Look at the list and I will see it through your eyes," he told her.

"Now why didn't I think of that?" Jamie asked with playful sarcasm. She scrolled down the list slowly till he told her to stop. "Did you see something?"

"The names aren't going to be enough. I'll need dates and locations as well. I have just realized that I have, shall I say…known many people, we also share a common heritage. I grew up in Scotland, as did your Craig, McPherson, and Stuart lines."

Jamie felt the letdown of failure. The spark of hope he ignited when he told her to stop was quickly extinguished. The problem wasn't that he had recognized a name; it was the fact that he recognized many names. Letting out a big sigh, she realized that this could prove to be a very tedious undertaking.

"Mia, do not fret. I will be there momentarily and we will search together." His voice was reassuring. "I spent many years living near Iverness. This particular area of the highlands was literally over run with the Clan McPherson." He didn't tell her that sharing a common ancestor was probably not the reason for their connection, but he would not rule the possibility out. Heredity had nothing to do with the turning from human to a guardian of the night. Everything he had learned and read about being vampire was due to a blood exchange;

not just the taking of blood when a feeding took place, but a sharing of blood. He had not fed during this century in this area until he followed Jamie's spiritual cry to these beautiful Olympic Mountains. He had never turned anyone in this region. For that fact he had never changed anyone in the United States. Yet in the name of science he wouldn't rule out any possible theory. If Jamie wanted to research a common ancestral background as a possible answer then he would encourage and support her. He also wanted to find the connection that brought them together but the bottom line was that no matter what the connection was it wouldn't change the choices that they were going to face together. He was going to have to sit down with Jamie soon and talk to her about their options. First he wanted to make love to her.

"A moment's up. Where are you?" Jamie asked still playing with him.

"I'm right behind you," he answered.

Jamie let out a small scream at hearing his voice behind her. As she jumped up she yelled at him. "You scared me!" She patted her chest trying to still her racing heart.

"Take a deep breath." Aerik helped to calm her without her knowledge by regulating her breathing and heart rate. "Jamie," he said calmly. "I didn't mean to startle you. Next time I will let you know before I appear," he promised.

Jamie smacked him lightly in the arm then reluctantly allowed him to embrace her in those same massive arms. She could feel his corded muscles swell and undulate beneath his skin at the slightest of movement. *He must have been something to see dressed in armor on the battlefield*, she thought.

Aerik smiled at her mental compliment. He steeled himself when he felt her run her hands along his biceps in exploration. She didn't stop there, continuing to run her hand across his chest and down his stomach. Aerik drew his breath in sharply in response. He felt himself grow hard with need as her fingers lightly caressed his flesh through the thin fabric that separated his flesh from hers. When she stopped and looked up with those big green eyes he could think of nothing else but the fire she had stirred within him. "You're playing with fire, little girl," he warned.

Jamie looked up at him grinning like a child who was caught being naughty. She could feel his need. She couldn't explain it but she felt it. And his need was spilling over and running through her like erotic liquid fire. The feeling reminded her of the warmed shot of apricot brandy her brother gave her on Christmas Eve years before. It spread through her like a warm inviting burst of sunshine on a cold winter day. She continued to let her hands explore and he didn't stop her. She slipped her hand inside his shirt feeling him lightly jerk as her fingertips touched his heated skin. She pushed his shirt up exposing his abdomen. He was the most muscular man she had ever seen. He was as hard as a rock. She traced her fingers along the ridges of each well-defined muscle. Leaning forward she replaced her fingers with her tongue. She smiled to herself when she heard him suck in yet another breath then she felt his hands sink into the thickness of her hair at the back of her head. She fumbled with the button to his jeans. As they dropped to the floor she looked up into his dark smoldering eyes and said simply, "I want to make you feel good."

Aerik felt his insides tighten in response. Her hands slid over his heated skin like silk leaving a trail of passion in their wake. He bit back a moan as her hand glided up over his chest and the other up the inside of his thigh. When she wrapped her tongue around his swollen shaft he shivered in delight at her intimate touch.

Jamie encased his hardness with her hot moist lips. She let her hands explore wandering seductively, touching, rubbing, massaging everything within reach. She felt his desire, the burning need, the wanting, the passion. She didn't know if she was experiencing it on her own or if he was openly sharing what he was feeling with her it was beyond the bounds of what she thought possible. She didn't care she only wanted more. It was all consuming and it was consuming her.

Aerik threw back his head in reflex as a carnal moan escaped his lips. His fingers flexed, his hands fisted in her bountiful hair, a lifeline grounding her to him. She pleasured him unmercifully; his feelings of extreme gratification were so intense, so fierce, that it bordered on the verge of sexual torture. "Cara Mia," it barely escaped him as she rocked his very world. He firmly took hold of her wrist and pulled her up to stare into her eyes, only to find them glazed over with passion. "Enough," he said hoarsely. His eyes held hers, spellbound, mesmerizing, keeping her from moving. He took control just long enough to simmer the beast that raged within himself. He continued to shower her mind and body with the sensations she herself had ignited in himself. If she were a vampire he wouldn't have to be so careful. His fear of hurting her mortal body kept him in check. If he were to unleash his feral appetite on one not of his own race, the results could be construed as nothing short of rape. He killed men for less. Sweeping Jamie up into his arms he kissed her deeply. He floated them to the bed never once breaking their kiss. It was his turn and he was going to show her what sexual torture was all about. As he cupped her cheek he trailed feather light kisses down the long column of her delicate throat, only to reverse and go up again to her ear. He licked, suckled and breathed deep whispering of the pleasure to come. His breath was hot against her ear his voice racked her body with tremors of ecstasy.

Jamie screamed out in her mind. His voice was so pure so magical it created a sexual symphony singing through her very being. She would never tire of hearing his voice. When he whispered for her to open herself to him, she obeyed with out hesitation. She cast all her inhibitions aside, lost in the passion of the moment. Her body was burning with desire, a fire blazing out of control, a fire that only he could put out. "Aerik, please I want to feel you inside me." She didn't know how it was possible to feel this good and survive it. He ignored her plea; his tongue continued to tease, tantalize, torment her ear as his fingers sought out and manipulated her breasts. Just when she thought she couldn't possibly stand any more he slid down taking first one breast then the other. Back and forth he suckled, nibbled, pulled then sucked again till she squirmed and shook with tremors of fury and rapture. Again she asked him to fill her, again he denied her only to move his head lower his mouth kissing, sucking laving at the upper inside of her thigh. One hand massaged and pulled gently on her nipples as his other sank into her wet hot core. She moaned out loud and rocked against his hand that filled her. When she felt his tongue glide over her wet heat, his lips following, manipulating, she burst like a damn that had reached its limit. A waterfall of extreme sexual hunger surged through her veins reaching every inch of her body, followed by rippling spasms of sated euphoria. "Aerik," it was but a whisper on her lips.

He slid his head over, teasing her womanly bud with his tongue as his fingers worked their own magic. He felt her experienced the pleasure that he still denied himself, yet he built her up again. He could feel the tightness of her muscles squeezing, clenching his fingers as he stoked her over and over. If it weren't for his strength holding her to the bed she would have fallen off for all the squirming she had done. He looked up at the window and raised it with a thought, allowing the cool misty air of the ocean to wash over their heated bodies. The coolness of the breeze had its own aphrodisiac effect. It brushed across their skin like invisible satin stroking them in places that their skin didn't touch. He grabbed both her ankles gently lifting and spreading her to accept him. She not only allowed him to manipulate her legs, but she arched her back upwards to meet him. He groaned his approval of her eagerness and obliged her unspoken request as he sank into her, stretching, filling, pushing till he filled her completely, he did not stop till he was buried deep inside able to go no further. She was so hot, so tight he felt like he had squeezed into a well of hot moist lava. He growled low, deep. With their bodies meshed together he began a slow circular rocking. She writhed beneath him begging for the sexual release she knew only he could provide. He smiled as he read it in her thoughts "only he" yes, he liked that, "only he." Changing the grip of his hands on her ankles he flipped her over onto her belly effortlessly without missing a stroke. Her long luscious honey colored hair cascaded down over the smoothness of her back. He released her ankles so he could stroke her long legs and small rounded bottom. Nobody was put together so perfectly, she was flawless. When she started to moan while bucking back against him in wanting, he threw all caution to the wind and entered her with all the fervor he had. Matching her stroke for stroke he sent them both sailing off the edge of elated bliss. Two shooting stars, brilliant golden fiery arks racing across the night sky in all their glory. As was their mutual climax, their entwined passion.

His eyes took in everything about the beautiful angel that lay beneath him. They fit together perfectly, she had been made for him and him alone. Everything about her was appealing to him, even her tenaciousness struck an adoring chord within him. She was beautiful and strong spiritually. She was a glowing light surrounding his darkness. Together they glowed the colors of the rainbow. He did not want to ever lose her. The thought that he may someday not have her, that these wonderful feelings she produced within him may be gone forever scared him. Fear...twice now since finding her he had experienced fear. It was a feeling he hadn't experienced in centuries. It was...he didn't like it.

"What's wrong?" Jamie asked as she ran her fingers down the side of his masculine jaw line. She felt his mood change suddenly and she wondered what she had done wrong.

"I allowed myself to think of what life would be like without you," he admitted. He played absently with her hair letting it sift through his fingers as he spoke.

"Is making love always like this for your kind?" she asked shyly. "I mean I never thought it could feel so good. Is it just our chemistry or would it be like that if I was with any other of your race?"

Aerik sat up quickly his eyes blazing crimson flames. A growl so sinister escaped his throat that Jamie scrambled to retreat but he held her fast. As fast as the change came on it disappeared. He stood quickly moving away from the bed – away from her. He didn't speak, but with a wave of his hand he was cleansed and dressed, as was a stunned Jamie. He ran his hand through his dark thick hair then paced the distance back to the bed. Again Jamie tried to shy away from him. He stayed her with a mere pointing of his finger. "Do not," he ordered.

Jamie sat motionless, scared of the almost instantaneous change that came over Aerik. She was terrified, her heart pounded against her chest, almost painfully when she realized that she couldn't physically move. He held her prisoner in an invisible grasp. Her eyes grew wide as she watched him pace like a lion caged at the zoo.

"You will never sleep with another, especially another vampire. Do you understand?" His male animalistic jealousy burned at his mind. The mere thought of her with another man, let alone another vampire! The very image consumed him with blind rage. Aerik forced himself to stand still taking a few deep breaths. When he looked back up at Jamie his own fear nearly suffocated him. "Oh…Mia, I'm so sorry," he said as he released his hold on her. "I don't know what came over me. Well I do." He hesitated then went on, "It's just that my reaction – my jealousy, it shocked me. I have never experienced jealousy as a vampire before. I am extremely self disciplined." He confided, "To lose my self-control was something I haven't experienced in quite some time, centuries to be exact. The last time I had no control was when I lost the mortal life I was born with. The death of my natural body I could not control." He reached out to touch her but she moved back. It was a subtle move, yet a flinch was enough to stop him dead in his tracks. "I'm sorry to have frightened you. But I must reiterate to you, that I would never hurt you, you must remember that above all else." He scanned her thoughts and eased her calm gently so she wouldn't notice it was he who controlled her fear. He needed her to feel in control of herself. He spoke softly aloud and inside her mind. "No matter how bad you may think the situation, no matter how angry I become I would never harm one hair on your head." He said it with such conviction that when she nodded he knew she understood it to be the truth. He would not harm her. He grabbed the desk chair pulling it over and sitting down. He felt that his massive bulk looming over her wasn't helping to de-escalate the situation. He sat backwards on the chair, his arms resting on the back of it. As he looked at her his eyes filled with regret for not leashing the beast that he was.

"Aerik, I'm sorry. I didn't mean to imply…" she began.

Aerik cut her off shushing her. He reached out again taking her hand. She didn't pull away as he held it. He felt instant shame. Her voice was so soft, so musical. He knew she meant no harm by her questions. "I love you so much that the thought of you with another was simply unacceptable. We vampires are very jealous, and we do not, will not, share our women. It is not in our nature. Our feelings for each other, for our soul mates are so much more intense than that of humans. It's those feelings that we share while making love. The feelings, the passions of the vampire." He looked her in the eye wanting to be sure he had her complete attention with out commanding it. "Jamie, I have watched over the centuries how sexuality in humans has changed. The commitment that used to be so important in the human relationships isn't the same anymore. I didn't stop long enough to assess that it was you asking an innocent question from the heart about something special we share. All I heard was what a typical jealous male vampire would hear – if I slept with another vampire would it be as good?" He shook his head again in shame. "Please forgive me for my lack of better judgment and my quick jealous temper. I need you to know that it's okay to ask me anything without fear. It will not happen again. I give you my word." He opened himself to her and shared with her his feelings. He didn't want any confusion on her part. She must understand that he meant what he said and that he would be true to his word.

Jamie felt so bad for him. She could feel his remorse…it tugged at her heart. Tears welled, stinging her eyes as she tried to hold them back. Failing miserably they spilled down her cheeks in a silent cry.

Aerik produced a cotton cloth from nowhere and gently wiped her face. "Mia, I know I frightened you." He tipped her head back. Her eyes were rimmed with redness from the sting of her tears, tears that he caused. "I must have looked pretty scary to you."

Jamie couldn't help but smile. It was a small smile, but a smile nonetheless.

"Can I tell you something?" she asked timidly.

Aerik smiled back the mood lightening. She was so damn beautiful. "You can tell me anything."

"I almost wet my pants," she admitted.

Aerik burst out laughing at her sincere honesty.

"I thought you were going to bite me," she added.

Aerik rubbed his chin as he chuckled. "I've bitten you before – was it so terrible?" he asked, his eyebrow cocked in question.

"Well, I was certain that from the look on your face it would surely hurt this time."

"Come here, little girl." He stood up slowly drawing her into the great strength of his corded arms. "I believe that the only punishment I could be capable of where you are concerned is possibly a sound spanking, you do flash an attitude of your own on occasion." He gave her a squeeze.

Jamie laughed at his attempt to be humorous. "Aerik, that was really funny," she teased.

He swatted her behind then released her. "Okay now that we have addressed love and war this evening let's see what you have been working on this afternoon while I wasted the day away sleeping." He teased her back.

Jamie plopped down in the computer chair and took a sip of her soda. "Are you thirsty? Do you drink anything?"

"What I drink you don't keep on hand." He grinned that sly wolfish grin then added, "Unless you're offering me dessert?"

Her eyes grew big. "Well I was wondering if you wanted some water or soda, something along that venue." She cleared her throat. He was such a rogue.

He burst out laughing again. He hadn't laughed like he laughed with her in years. Usually only Tray could get him going. More seriously he said, "We can create an illusion of drinking and eating so that we fit in while socializing. The only substance that is not painful or dangerous for us to ingest is blood."

"So you really didn't drink those beers that Clay offered you?"

Aerik shook his head no.

"So if we went out to dinner for instance you would only appear to be eating?"

"Correct." He walked slowly around the large country style

bedroom. He looked over the large bookcase. "Your parents have collected many books," he observed out loud.

"My dad's hobby was genealogy. He was always working on the family tree. He used to say that his greatest joy besides us kids was digging up dead people," Jamie told him. "Okay I have the name index up, come see if you recognize anything." She turned the chair over to Aerik. "You must have seen a lot of history happen."

"More than I care to remember," he told her as he scrolled through the tree.

"This afternoon I was thinking about how I wished I had paid more attention in history class."

"What would you like to know?" he asked, dividing his attention to both Jamie and her family history. "Perhaps I can answer your questions."

"Well, I don't really have any particular question in mind. I did wonder why Hitler was allowed to kill so many people."

Aerik turned to face her, his look more serious. "There have been times when we have gathered to discuss such events. We are guardians yet we must also let fate, history take its course. World War Two wasn't only the actions of just one man. Hitler, he had a great following. If it were solely due to the workings of one man, then we would have taken him out long before we did."

"What do you mean taken him out long before you did?"

Aerik grinned. "Let's just say that Hitler didn't shoot himself nor did anyone in that bunker take cyanide capsules of their own free will."

"Who killed them?" She was stunned at the implications of what he was claiming.

"It wasn't me, though I would have gladly accepted the job had it been offered to me."

"Anyone else that I would know from history?"

"Curiosity killed the cat," he teased.

"It's just so amazing. I find it hard to believe."

"How about King Henry the VIII? Now Jenaver didn't actually kill him but she scared him to death." Aerik chuckled at the remembrance. "You would have to know Jenaver," he explained. "She answers to no one but Torin."

"Torin?" Jamie questioned.

"Her husband," he answered. "I remember I had come to visit Torin and while we sat in the great hall Jenaver came storming in as only she could, spouting off about what a horrid, tyrant Henry was. That he was a mean ogre that didn't deserve to have a woman for company let alone as a wife. It took me a minute to figure out whom she was referring to. Jenaver was fond of Henry's sixth wife Katherine Parr. King Henry didn't have a great reputation for treating his women well and Jenaver not wanting to take any chances paid him a visit. According to her she appeared to him in all her vampire glory, with eyes glowing and teeth bared and threatened his life. She told him that if he so much as touched one hair on another woman's head, that she would torture him with methods he couldn't possibly conceive even in his own depraved mind. And when she was done torturing his hateful self then she would drain him dry and leave his retched carcass for the rats to fight over."

"Well, what happened?" Jamie asked, totally enthralled by his tale.

"She scared him so bad he had a heart attack and after that he went down hill rather quickly. Bottom line is that he never recovered, nor did any more women lose their heads at his hand. It was said that he had been mellowed by Katherine's gentle nature. I have always wondered if he wasn't mellowed by a very pissed off female vampire." He grinned. "Wow, look here. I know this person." He looked over one of the family pages on the computer screen. "Imagine that." He leaned back letting Jamie look at the family page of the person he recognized.

"Othiel McPherson born 1654 near Iverness Scotland," Jamie read out loud.

"Here honey, you sit here." Aerik gave up his seat.

"How do you know him?" she asked her excitement building.

"I bit him a few times." Aerik waited for her response then laughed when she spun around looking at him with her mouth hanging open. "I'm just kidding," he joked. "He tended my sheep and worked the plot of land that bordered my own," he explained then added, "and I bit him a few times, though I made sure that he never remembered it."

"Aerik!" Jamie exclaimed.

He casually shrugged. "A man's gotta eat." He grinned while using one of this generation's expressions. He briefly pictured Trayvon smiling at his use of the word "gotta."

"Well could that be our connection?" Jamie asked.

Aerik more seriously now thought about Othiel. He had fed from him and on more than one occasion, but never had he given him blood. "I don't think so. Why don't you read down through his children and I'll try to remember them. Maybe something will jump out at me." He paced around the room as Jamie read what little information her father had collected on Othiel's children and their descendants.

CHAPTER 10

"Anything?" she asked stopping to sip her soda.

Aerik shook his head no. "By this year I was no longer living in Scotland and I rarely visited. When others around you age, yet you do not, timing and visits must be carefully planned. When I returned to the estate there I was supposed to be an heir of myself, a nephew coming to claim his great granduncle's possessions." He returned to the bookcase and ran his fingers absently over the book spines deep in thought. There was something nagging at him but he just couldn't put his finger on it. "Jamie, have you ever traveled outside the country?"

"Nope," she answered quickly, easily. "Why?"

"I'm standing by the blood exchange. I can connect...*if I choose to*," he stressed the "if I choose to" part, "to those whom I have given my blood. The more blood exchanged the stronger the connection."

"I've not really been many places," she told him. "My parents weren't crazy about traveling after their disastrous honeymoon." She laughed thinking about how unlucky they had been. Suddenly Jamie came flying up out of her seat. "Aerik, what about my parents? They went to Scotland for their honeymoon. My dad wanted to go there to see where the family came from, how they lived."

Aerik marveled at how beautiful she looked as her green eyes sparkled with excitement, shining with a light all their own. The way her hair floated around her as she jumped up out of her seat, the way it gently swished up against and around her supple body. Ethereal was the word that came to his mind. He smiled at the wonder of her natural beauty.

"But," Jamie added talking quickly her smile fading, "they were only there a couple days before they were involved in a car accident. They spent some time in the hospital then came home. My dad never traveled much after that. He said that if he was meant to visit faraway lands he would have been born there, and that if he was going to die he wanted to be near his family." Her excitement dissolved as quickly as it came and she sunk back down into the chair.

"They were in an accident?"

"Yeah, they were taking pictures at some cemetery and when they left the brakes failed in their car and they crashed. At least that's how I remember the story. A horrible outcome for a time in your life that's supposed to be so happy."

Aerik's skin prickled as memories overcame him. It couldn't be, the couple he helped wouldn't be that old right now. What year was that? "Jamie, how old are you?"

"Twenty-three. Why?"

Aerik looked around the room in frustration. "Where are the pictures of your parents?"

Jamie jumped up and went to the bedside table. From inside the drawer she removed a photo of her parents that had been taken shortly before they died. "Do you recognize them?" she asked all her excitement back.

"Do you have any pictures of them when they were younger, I need to be sure." He knew. He knew that this was the couple that he had met. Had it been twenty-three years already? They were wandering through the cemetery near his estate just outside Iverness. They said they had been enjoying the sunset when he came upon them. The young man was so refreshing and filled with questions about the area and the families that had lived there. Aerik had put them under his spell after their long pleasant talk. He had fed from him – Jamie's father, James was his name. He didn't take from the girl, Shannon. Yes she was very pretty with long honey colored hair and a splash of freckles across the bridge of her nose. Now he could see the resemblance in her daughter. He didn't take from her because she was carrying a new life. He could barely sense the baby's spirit starting out its new beginning, but it was there safely wrapped inside her womb. When they left the cemetery true to Jamie's tale their brakes failed on the long descent down the winding country road. He had heard the crash and went to investigate. Like Jamie – her mother was going to die if he didn't intercede and give her his healing blood. He almost waited too long, trying to decide if this was their fate, for him to be there. Like Jamie – he made a quick decision, the baby being the deciding factor. He felt in his heart that the baby this young woman carried deserved a chance at life. He gave the injured woman his life-giving blood. He gave Jamie his blood. She was that baby. Through her mother she took his ancient healing blood thus connecting them irrevocably for all of her natural life, and if she chose for all of eternity. She was of a good and pure spirit deserving of the choice he himself had made. He stared at her, the realization of their connection taking his brain by storm. Other questions, questions of an ethical nature came to mind. He asked, "Your brother, was he adopted?"

"Jimmy is my half brother. My mother was my dad's second wife. Jimmy's mom died from complications of childbirth." Jamie looked at him questioningly. "Aerik?" Jamie asked softly. She could see that his mind was preoccupied. What was it that he remembered? Did he know her parents?

Aerik took the picture she was handing him. It wasn't even necessary to view it now. He knew without a doubt, that the young honeymooning couple in that old cemetery was in fact her parents. He looked at the photo anyways.

"Do you know them?"

He looked her right in the eye knowing how important this was to her. "Yes, I know them."

"Yes!" Jamie jumped up and down and clapped her hands together like a child that was just told they could have what they wanted. "Yes!"

Aerik watched her as she did a cute little dance around the room. He grinned and shook his head at her enthusiasm. That girl had spunk, he wondered if her attitude would change when she learned the whole story. Even he was concerned about the implications of what he had done.

She stopped jumping long enough to look more serious. "Did you bite my parents?" She looked him in the eye then pointed her finger accusingly at him. "You did – didn't you? You bit my parents."

Aerik was leaning against the bookcase with his massive arms crossed nonchalantly across his chest watching her intently. He hesitated before answering. "I, as you put it, bit your dad." He slowly walked to her leading her to the bed sitting her down then taking a seat beside her. "I was at the accident, Jamie. I gave your mother my blood. If I hadn't she would have died. You would have died."

"What do you mean I would have died?"

"Your mother was pregnant at the time of the accident. Ma Cheri, that's how we are connected. When I gave her my blood I inadvertently gave it to you as well." He sat there silently giving her time to absorb what he was telling her.

Jamie didn't say anything as she mulled over his words. "You saved my mom's life."

"Yes, she would have died had I not intervened."

"So you have saved me twice now."

"You could say that."

"Do you think that I wasn't supposed to be born? That fate keeps trying to take me out of the game plan?"

"Jamie, no good will come of thoughts like that. You were meant to be here. Fate finds a way. I believe that there is a reason for everything that happens to us, everything we do, every choice we make. I also believe that I was meant to have a connection with you. I believe that you were born to be my soul mate. In turn fate made that a reality."

Jamie was confused, her mind raced with all kinds of possibilities and questions. "You in a sense made me." She nervously rubbed her hands on her shorts. "Would you have been attracted to me if you hadn't given me your blood before I was born?"

Here it comes, he told himself. This is where things were going to get complicated. He could easily control the situation, make her think whatever he wanted her to think, but he wanted, he needed to keep things between them honest, real. "First I must reiterate that I believe that this happened because it was supposed to, that we were meant to be together. I also believe that we may have not ever met each other had we not connected mentally. As for the question of would I have been attracted to you? Yes, I would have been physically attracted to you. Any sane man would. You are truly beautiful in every sense of the word." He took her hand rubbing his lightly over her own as he spoke. "Would the attraction be as strong? I don't know. I would like to believe that it would be; that fate would have seen to that regardless of what preceded our first face-to-face meeting."

"I'm glad that we found out what connected us. You were right you know, about the blood connection." She slid her hand from his and went back to the computer. "My dad wrote about their honeymoon. It's in the notes section of his family page." She clicked a few buttons bringing up what she was looking for. She read silently then aloud. "Shannon and I watched the most incredible sunset at the old McPherson cemetery. It was hard to imagine that my ancestors of so long ago watched the sun set from this very hill. We met a wonderful man who owned the manor nearby. His name was Lord Aaron Von Wulff." Jamie hesitated as she looked over at Aerik. "We will forever be indebted to this kind generous young man, as he not only shared his knowledge about the locals; he saved my beautiful bride's life. After leaving the cemetery the brakes failed in the car we had rented. We suffered a horrendous accident and Shannon was thrown from the vehicle. If it weren't for the heroic and quick actions of Lord Von Wulff my Shannon would have bled to death on that little country road. He was skilled in first aid and kept pressure on her wounds till I could reach the nearest farm house and call for help." Jamie stopped reading and looked over at Aerik. "That was you. You were Aaron Von Wulff."

Aerik nodded. He was moved by her father's kind words of appreciation, and the fact that he immortalized them in his family history by writing them down. Aerik had always had a love for books and took an active part in their preservation. He would on occasion loan some of his personal collections to the museums for viewing. "I am very pleased that your father included me in his family history.

It's truly an honor."

"Would you tell me about my parents? I want to know everything."

"Everything?"

"I want to know what color socks they had on. Yes, I want to know everything from the first hello till you left the accident."

"Well I'm glad you don't want too much." He lay back on the bed, his hands behind his head, staring up at the ceiling. "When I awoke that evening I was famished," he began.

CHAPTER 11

It was nearing dawn and they had talked all night. Aerik stayed out of her mind and enjoyed each surprise she shared about her life. He in turn he shared several stories as well about growing up through the centuries. Aerik had wanted to avoid this moment that was at hand, but knew it was inevitable. He needed to tell Jamie that a time would come when she needed to make a choice as to how they would proceed with their relationship. He had made up his mind that he would explain each choice with her then he would give her time alone to think about the options. He knew in his heart that he would never give her up. She was his soul mate, a shining star to his blackest night, the light to his darkness. If he had to give up their physical relationship, then so be it. If he had to shadow her in secret, be her personal guardian of the night to protect her from harm then he would do it till she breathed her last natural breath. Almost as hard would be to live as a couple as she aged as humans do. He would love her as much now as he would if she were eighty. That type of relationship would be most difficult for when she passed from her natural life he could grieve so intensely that he may choose to walk into the dawn giving up his own existence, not wanting to go on without his love. It has happened before and surely would happen again. If she chose to join him to walk in the *camhanaich*, the twilight, then he would spend all of eternity showering her with love as he showed her the wonders of the world through new eyes, vampire eyes. Leaving this decision, their fate to her, could prove to be the hardest thing he had ever done. He would love nothing more than to take the decision out of her hands. Change her, turn her, make her a guardian, a vampire. But…the sanctity of their relationship required that he used no control, that she make this choice of her own free will. So, as Aerik felt the approaching of the sun, he carefully broached the subject of their relationship. He laid it all out for her. He left nothing out. He made her aware of all their options, and covered all possible scenarios of what could be. She listened intently, neither interrupting nor questioning. When he finally finished she still sat silently.

After several minutes he slipped unknowingly into her mind. He needed to be sure that she was okay. He found her mind so overloaded with questions, thoughts and the playing out of each possible action that he became angry with himself. He shouldn't have waited till such a late hour. She had little sleep and had been awake all night with him. Clearly she was exhausted. He sent a silent command to calm her troubled thoughts. He accomplished this by simply slowing her thought process, hoping to reduce her agitation.

Had he to do it all over again, he would have, everything in him said that the time was at hand. He carefully chose the questions that were important for her to know the outcome to and he answered them. Would it hurt to die? Would she need blood as he did? Would she have to leave her home, her friends? If she died how would she know that she would wake up like him or if she would just be dead? He could validate all her questions but only had time to answer the ones that he felt were most important. He then told her that he would give her time alone to think about her choices. He didn't want his presence to influence her decision. It was Monday and he would come to her Wednesday night to check on her. He let her know that he wouldn't contact her, even mentally, during that time. In return she must also refrain from contacting him. If she found that she needed more time, then she would have it without question.

Aerik pulled Jamie into his arms. He felt her panic, her uncertainty, not only at the decisions that faced her, but also at the thought of his leaving her. Since his arrival she had come to terms with how truly lonely she had been. He had made her face her fear of the loneliness that had all but consumed her.

Nevertheless, he knew this was something he must do. Not only for her sake but his own as well. He wanted her to be free of his influence. Women were attracted to him and he knew it. The vampire species had an animal-like magnetism that drew the opposite sex like bees to a fresh spring flower. This ability was necessary to sustain their very survival. The ability to draw a person to them easily allowed them to be able to feed without great difficulty. Being absent for a few days would give her time to regain some of the normalcy prior to his arrival. Thus, assuring that his presence wasn't controlling her thought process in any way. He wanted her to be confident, sure of her decision, to know that it was hers and hers alone with no outside pressure from him. It would be imperative that she experience no regrets from the choice she makes. Regrets after the fact would be totally devastating, with disastrous results.

Aerik was now assured that he had covered all bases, and that she understood all that was at hand. He cupped her head gently in the grasp of his large hands. He kissed her forehead tenderly trailing angel wing kisses across her brow then down the side of her cheek to the edge of her mouth. He waited for her to turn her lips to his then kissed her fully. In her mind and allowed he spoke, "I know that we have physically known each other only a short time, but I feel that I have waited over five hundred years for you. I will not lie to you, I have known many women in that time, but none have ever filled me with light from within. It is only you and you alone that my darkened soul cries out for. You are my soul mate and I wish to make you my wife. I believe that you were born for me as much as I was for you. I believe this with all that I am. I want you to take these few days to contemplate all that has transpired between us and apply it to all that you have experienced in your life before you make your decision. If you choose to walk away from me I will accept your choice and respect it. It will be the hardest thing I have ever done but I will honor your wishes. I love you beyond the boundaries of time. Just know this," he looked deep into her eyes then pushed aside a stray lock of her silky tresses, "if I can not have you in this life then I will wait for your next, and I will find you again, this I vow." He couldn't help himself, he opened himself just enough for her to feel the conviction of his words, the genuine love he had for her. He captured her lips gently committing her feel, her taste, her tenderness to memory. He then claimed her lips with the passion of a lover who would never have another kiss. It bordered on aggressive, punishing, leaving her lips swollen, red and pouting for more. And that was how he left her. He faded slowly turning into a fine, colorful, shimmering mist. Like a whirlwind of sparkling glitter he swirled up into the air in an awesome display of glistening colors and light, and then with a blink of the eye he was gone.

"Go to sleep now." Those were the words that she heard in her mind as Aerik left her. Those were also the words she remembered first as she awoke. The first thing she heard were raindrops pelting against the glass of the windowpane. She grabbed the blanket and pulled it over her head. She felt the bed jiggle which caused her to sit up quickly, her heart in her throat. Burl looked over at her with his big brown eyes. He was stretched across the bed beside her as if he had slept there all night, and it was she who disrupted his sleep.

"What are you doing up here?" she asked while stretching sleepily, her words being replaced with a yawn.

The big dog just looked at her and whined snuggling closer to her.

"Ah, don't you try and kiss up to me." She dropped her arm over her new companion and hugged him to her. "You're a good boy aren't ya?" Jamie lay there a few minutes longer then forced herself to climb out of bed. Burl needed to go out and she needed a cup of coffee and an aspirin.

Dressed in jeans and a sweatshirt she pulled her hair up into an alligator clip and slipped on her jacket. Taking her notebook and pen she grabbed her coffee and went out onto the porch. The sky was gray and the wind blew the rain in the form of sheets from off the ocean. The porch along the front of the house would be exposed to the elements blowing in. No doubt drenched, with not only the rain, but the salty spray of the ocean. On days like this when the wind blows hard the rain will always taste of salt.

When she was only six years old she came out onto the porch pouting and stomping her feet, she was mad because her father told her she couldn't go down to the beach and play while it was raining so hard. An old Indian friend of her father's named Nushiu was visiting at the time and he told her:

"Did you know that you can taste the sea salt in the rain? This is because the Maiden of the Ocean is mad. In her anger she stamps her foot onto the ocean's surface. When she does this, the salt water of the ocean flies up to mix with the rain. In her fury she blows the sea spray onto the shore."

"But why is she mad?" Jamie had asked him.

"That is simple." He had paused waiting to be sure he had attention. "Her father told her that she could not play in the rain. Perhaps you should try to blow the rain away too."

Jamie sat down in the plastic patio chair that rested outside the back kitchen door. She was safe here from the Maiden of the Ocean's temper. This side of the house faced the east; there was less wind and very little rain that fell on this area of the covered porch. She looked out at the puddles in the dirt driveway. Her parents had many discussions on the paving of the driveway. Her mother wanted it paved and her father liked the natural look. Her mom disliked the fact that her car was always dirty. Her dad was convinced that if they paved it tourists would always be driving down it looking for an entrance to the beach. They finally decided on paving it and putting up a gate. They had been saving for it when they died. Her brother never saw a need to pave it and she really never cared. Driving a truck it just didn't seem to matter if it was dirty. Her brother used some of the money to help cover funeral expenses that insurance didn't cover. The remainder he put into a CD in Jamie's name.

She sat and thought about what was as she sipped at her coffee. What she was really doing was avoiding what was to be. She felt mentally tired, sluggish, drained, or was she coming down with something? A rush of wind whipped around the edge of the porch and rustled the notebook lying on her lap. It was as if the Maiden of the Ocean were urging her on to the task at hand. She thumped the ink pen absently on the paper then made four columns. At the top of each she wrote a heading. Go on with life as before/no contact. Friends only. Relationship without changing who I am. Relationship as a vamp. She started scribbling down the pros and cons then peppered both with questions to ponder. It only took about a half an hour and she had totally eliminated the idea of ever being "just friends." She took her pen and drew a large X through that section. The phone ringing saved her from having to think further on the subject for now. She had the cordless out on the porch with her, but had to retreat to the kitchen in the house to hear over the wind and rain. She was cold anyways and it was past time to go back inside but she had gotten caught up in the mapping out of her future.

"Hello." She held the phone to her ear with her shoulder as she refilled her coffee.

"Miss Jamie McPherson please."

Great a sales man, she thought, he had that kind of voice, one that could sell dirt to a farmer. "Speaking."

"Miss McPherson, this is Trayvon Cahan. I just received your painting. It's magnificent."

Jamie started to shake, nervous, cold, a combination of both probably. She looked at the clock; she did send it over night express. "I'm glad you like it, sir," she answered. She didn't really know what to say. This was Aerik's friend. Her heart began to race as her mind assaulted her with an array of questions. This could be another vampire. She looked at the clock wondering what time it was in London.

"I take it that Aerik had you send it?"

"Yeah, ah – I mean yes, he did." She tried to calm herself down but when she went to take a seat at the table she tripped and almost spilt her coffee down the front of her. Instead it just sloshed over the cup splattering on the floor at her feet. "He said that it was of a place that held special meaning to you," she said while scrambling for the paper towels. She heard him laugh deep and boisterous...like Aerik did.

"It most certainly does. I wanted to thank you for sending it to me."

"You're welcome," she said as she threw some paper towels onto the floor and used her foot to wipe up the mess.

"It couldn't be more perfect. Leave it to Aerik to find the gift of a lifetime."

Jamie was glad that he enjoyed the painting but she wanted to know what meaning it held for him but she was afraid to ask. Instead she said, "Aerik's not here right now but I'll tell him that you called."

"That's not necessary I will speak directly to him myself, I'm flying out that way on business. I just wanted to thank you personally for being so kind as to send me the painting. It truly is spectacular. It is absolutely amazing how you captured the image of Killiecrankie Pass so perfectly; it is as I remembered it, and in vivid detail I might add. Well done."

"I'm glad that you're happy with it."

"While I'm in your country I hope to schedule a visit with Aerik. Perhaps then I will be able to view more of your work."

Sensing that he was going to hang up she wanted to keep him on the line but she didn't know why. Was it that he was a connection to Aerik, or was it her overwhelming curiosity as to his genetic makeup? "I'd like that, Mr. Cahan. To meet you that is." He talked like Aerik. They both spoke with a gentlemanly old world charm, as if they were from another time.

He was silent a moment too long. Jamie nervously continued. "Meeting a friend of Aerik's should prove to be interesting. I'll be looking forward to seeing you soon." Why did she say that! She scolded herself for her poor choice of words. There was that dead silence again. Why did she feel like she just overstepped her boundaries? Why did she not want him to hang up? She didn't really want to talk to this man, did she? He was silent. The hair on her arms stood on end as her skin prickled with uneasiness.

"Interesting…I do like that expression. Yes, I also believe that it should prove to be quite interesting." His voice was cool, washing over her like a wave of ice water, despite the pleasant harmonious sound of his voice. He paused then finished his conversation by simply saying, "Until we meet then." The line went dead.

CHAPTER 12

"Damn!" Jamie exclaimed. She rubbed her arms in an attempt to remove the goose bumps. He gave her the creeps, or as her brother would have said when they were children, "the willies." It wasn't that she felt threatened by him, or did she? He called to thank her. He didn't say anything threatening; it was only a harmless little conversation with a friend of Aerik's. She was just overreacting to a chill from being outside in the weather. If she didn't have all this vampire crap on her mind right now she wouldn't be justifying her feelings like this, she rationalized. Who the hell was she kidding, it was night time in Europe and he probably had fangs long enough to scare Dracula.

Jamie turned to hang the phone up on the wall mount and screamed as she saw a man standing at the door staring at her through the window. Her heart slammed into her chest with fear, and then again as Burl came racing from the living room barking. As the giant dog hit the linoleum at a gallop, his feet went out from beneath him on the slick surface. Burl slid right into the side of Jamie's legs knocking her down and sending her sprawling onto the kitchen floor, the two of them ending in one jumbled heap. When she looked up at the door the man was still standing there, only now he looked worried. Burl scrambled to his feet, his toenails clicking loudly against the smooth surface of the kitchen floor, as he continued to bark at the stranger. Jamie picked herself up and tried to push past Burl to the door. Through the glass windowpane she asked the man what he wanted.

"I'm Detective Neely. He held his picture ID up to the glass. Jamie read the information on the ID not that it would do her a lot of good since she wouldn't know the difference between a fake detective ID and a real one. The picture did match the face if that was any consolation. She stamped her foot on the floor to get Burl's attention. Her scream had sent him into watchdog frenzy.

"Burl!" she raised her voice. "Down." She pointed to the floor between herself and the kitchen table. Burl lowered his hackles and sat down beside his mistress. She gave Burl a stay signal with her hand, hoping not only that he knew what it meant but that he would mind the command as well. She hesitantly opened the door watching Burl through the corner of her eye.

The detective also eyeing the humongous dog entered the house slowly. He removed his hat that was dripping onto the floor. "Miss McPherson, I'm detective Benjamin Neely. I'm sorry I startled you," he apologized. He wiped the hat across his pant legs in an attempt to absorb some of the excess rainwater. "I was hoping to talk with you about your brother's murder investigation." He started to hold out his hand in offer of a handshake but when Burl growled he retracted it, putting his hand inside his jacket pocket instead. "That's a big dog you have there," he said.

Jamie composed herself and smiled. "It's nice to meet you. I'm sorry but I don't remember you as working on his case." He looked to her to be in his thirties; a lot younger looking than her preconceived idea of a detective, no doubt do to her choice of television programming.

"I'm new to the case. I was transferred out here about a month ago. I'm working under the supervision of Detective Lewis Northcutt. I believe you've met him?" He removed his jacket revealing a casual but neat dress of a button up short-sleeved green shirt tucked neatly into khaki Dockers.

"Mr. Northcutt's the one I remember talking to." Jamie offered him a chair at the table and a cup of coffee, both of which he accepted. She noticed that he looked over at her notebook that she had sat on the table when Mr. Cahan had called. How in the hell was she going to explain that! With a big smile she flipped it over so he couldn't further read her pros and cons of becoming a vampire lists. "Notes for a book I'm working on, I have a thing about people seeing my work before it's finished."

"You're writing a novel?"

"Working on it," she lied. Taking a sip of her coffee she smiled at him from over her cup. "So what can I do for you, Detective Neely?"

Jamie sat silently listening to the detective talk about all that had transpired in the case over the last year. He then went on to explain how the Dugans were no longer prime suspects and how they were going to have to look at other possibilities as to the death of her brother. She was happy that they were still working so diligently on the case and was comfortable throughout his conversation till she sensed where he was leading…to her.

"Now there had already been one paying of insurance monies when your parents died, if I'm correct, to both you and your brother. So can you tell me again how much was the insurance settlement that you received from your brother's passing?"

"Two hundred and fifty thousand." Jamie sat her coffee cup down on the table a little harder than she should have. "I'm sure that you are already well aware of how much money my brother left me. Why don't you ask me what you really want to know." She glared at him…at his silent accusation.

"And what would that be, Miss McPherson?" He eyed her back meeting her glare head on with his own iron demeanor.

"If you think I killed my brother you couldn't be more wrong. If you think I killed my brother for his insurance policy then you haven't done your homework. Either way you're wasting your time on me. You," she pointed her finger at him for emphasis, "should be out there looking for the asshole that took my brother away from me." She realized that she was almost yelling, she lowered her voice and said, "You need to leave now." She slid her chair back almost knocking it over in her anger. She opened the door in a silent "get out," while Mr. Neely put his jacket on.

Burl came to his feet a low growl rumbling in his throat. Jamie again stayed him with her hand.

"I'm only covering all bases, Miss McPherson." He smiled a cocky smile at her. Pleased that he had riled her.

"Like I said, do your homework before you waste my time. I'll do anything I can to help put away my brother's murderer, but you're barking up the wrong tree." She was so mad it was all she could do to refrain from slapping the smirk off his face. It was the desire to toss her coffee in his face that was almost her undoing.

"I don't suppose you wouldn't care to elaborate on the missed homework?" he asked standing in the doorway inches from her face. He slid his gaze sideways as Burl inched closer his lips pulled back twitching in a silent snarl. Fear clutched at his insides when he thought of what kind of damage the massive canine could do. He backed away from Jamie and went out the door without taking his eyes from the menacing dog.

"You're a detective, you figure it out." She slammed the door shut behind him.

Detective Neely felt instant relief the minute the door slammed shut behind him, putting a barrier between Cujo and himself. The old saying "don't let the door hit you in the ass on the way out" would have been appropriate for his exit. He looked out into the rain and smiled. He was aware of the fact that Miss McPherson didn't need her brother's insurance policy. He had done his homework. The problem was, they had about exhausted all their options, and the case was going nowhere fast. Being new to the case he was looking for anything, and found himself resorting to lessons learned from textbooks in his days of training for the bureau. One of which was to stir up a potential suspect in hopes that they would in turn do something to compromise themselves. Well he managed to stir her up all right, but would it produce any results? Time will tell, he'd just sit back, watch and wait. Smiling to himself at a mission accomplished he stepped off the porch into the driving rain.

"Jerk." Jamie watched through the window on the kitchen door as the young detective got into his car and drove off. Turning to Burl she lavished praise on her dog for being so well behaved.

Jamie spent most of the next hour on the phone, but did manage to accomplish a few things. She called Big Al to ask about why Jimmy might have taken one of the vehicles into Port Angeles and if he knew what the problem might have been. Big Al was happy to hear from her but he didn't think he was going to be much help. The last conversation he and Jimmy had was about shortages in a cars electrical system. Jimmy was asking what the warning signs of an electrical problem would be. Big Al assured her that the electrical problem wasn't for either of their vehicles because he had told Jimmy to just bring it in and he would look at it. Jimmy told him he wasn't asking about the truck or the Jeep that he was doing research for a case he was working on. Jamie wasn't sure what all that meant because the only case Jimmy was working on that she knew of was monitoring possible drug traffic of some local dealer they suspected of growing marijuana in his barn. Clay had assured Jamie that all they were doing at the point of Jimmy's death was writing down license plate numbers and the make of cars seen coming and going from the residence. They weren't actually staking out the home they only took note of the goings on when they actually passed the house on their normal daily business. The narcotics division out of Hoquiam had been notified and had officially taken over. There was no need for the local guys to take a chance of tipping off the grower by appearing too nosy. It was to appear as "business as usual" with the local deputies.

Next she called Clay just to verify what Big Al had told her. Clay wasn't much help suggesting that the electrical questions and the wiring issue were more than likely connected but he would stop by Big Al's at his lunch break and pick his brain if it would make her feel better.

Jamie was frustrated. Jimmy told her he was going to stop by Jeff's work and speak to him that fateful morning. Jeff said he never saw him. What was it that kept him from stopping at Jeff's work? This minor little detail nagged at her then, as it was nagging at her now. Jimmy wouldn't lie to her about something so trivial. She thumbed through the yellow pages and dialed the phone.

"Vic's Custom Sound Waves. This is Kyle, can I help you?"

"Kyle Lassaro?" Jamie asked.

"Speaking."

"Kyle, this is Jamie McPherson."

"Hi Jamie. I haven't seen you in a while. How have you been?"

Jamie was relieved that Kyle answered the phone. They had all attended school together and Kyle and Jeff were pretty good friends. "I was wondering how Jeff was doing? I heard about the bees."

Kyle was silent a moment. "Jamie, he says that it was your new boyfriend that put the bees nest in his truck. Is that true?"

"Kyle, if you knew my boyfriend you would know that that's crap. I just wanted to see if he was doing okay and ask him about Jimmy coming in to have wiring done on the Jeep the day he died."

"I didn't mean to upset you, Jamie. Just spreading the word is all." Kyle chuckled at the way Jamie took offense to the idea of her boyfriend being responsible. Actually Kyle didn't believe that Jamie would date someone who would stoop to such antics. "Hell, I didn't buy it when he told me anyway," Kyle admitted. "My first thought was he probably ran into a tree limb with the darn thing attached to it knocking it into the truck. It'd be just like Jeff to make up a big story to hide his own stupidity."

"It's okay. I'm sorry I've just had a rough morning." She apologized then added, "You know you may be right, Jeff does like to stump jump in that truck of his."

"I talked to Jimmy that morning. Is there something I can tell you?"

Jamie was suddenly stunned silent. She grasped the edge of the table till her knuckles turned white then asked. "You spoke to Jimmy?"

"I saw Jeff and Jim talking out in the parking lot and it looked like their conversation was getting a little heated, so I went over to see what was up. Ya know, cool things down a little. It doesn't look good to the customers to see confrontations at the work site."

"They were arguing? Do you know what about?" Jamie's voice was almost a whisper. She cleared her throat.

"When I walked up they quit talking. I think they were talking about a wiring job that Jeff had done on the side. I heard your name mentioned too." Kyle paused. "I believe Jim told Jeff to stay away from you. Then he noticed I had come up from behind and quit talking. I asked Jim what was up and he just shook his head and walked away. Ya know, Jeff went one way and your brother another. Jim got half way across the parking lot then walked back and asked me about fixing the speakers on the row bar of the Jeep."

"You heard him tell Jeff to stay away from me?" she asked, totally lost as to why Jimmy would do such a thing.

"I'm pretty sure. It's been a while but yeah I'm sure. That's why it didn't surprise me that you two broke up. I figured there was a problem."

"Was that it? Did he say more?" Jamie asked. Her mind was spinning. What was going on between Jimmy and Jeff?

"That was it. I know that it upset Jeff. The next day, after the shooting and all, he was telling me that he wished their last conversation had been on better terms. He didn't like the idea of Jim being upset with him when he died."

"Did Jeff tell you what they were arguing about?"

"He wouldn't tell me, and since he was so upset about it I just left him alone."

"Did Jeff say when he was coming back to work?"

"He doesn't work here anymore. About four months ago he quit and started working for his old man. I guess dad told him it was time to quit playing around and start working like a real man." Kyle chuckled under his breath, adding, "You know Mr. Edgewood."

"Yes I do," Jamie said. "Kyle, thanks for talking with me. I really appreciate it."

"Anytime, Jamie. Hey, if you're still having problems with the speaker bring it in and I'll fix it for ya, no charge."

When Jamie finally hung up the phone she sat there staring at it. She picked up the ink pen and thumped it methodically onto her notebook never taking her eyes from the phone. She snatched the hand set up and punched in Jeff's home phone number. She could tolerate just about anything but she didn't like being lied to.

Once Jamie managed to get through Nancy Edgewood, Jeff's mother, alias Jeff's watchdog, she was almost shaking with anger. She didn't feel like playing Nancy's game of twenty questions, but she knew that if she refused then she would never get to talk to Jeff. The woman had a way of manipulating a conversation to meet her own needs; others' personal knowledge slash business was her need. She was a pro at pumping you for information then finding a way to use it against you for her own gain. Never had Jamie ever met a person who could use gossip as a way to control a situation or a person like Mrs. Edgewood could.

Jeff's voice filled the receiver pressed to Jamie's ear. "Jamie, I'm glad you called we really need to talk."

"You got that right," Jamie snapped.

Jeff was silent a moment. "If you're mad about what I told the police there's nothing I can do about it. I just told them who I thought might hold a grudge against me."

"Why would Aerik hold a grudge against you?"

"Well because I'm a threat. You're my girl, and I know you better than anyone," he said using a matter a fact tone.

Jamie wanted to throw the phone across the room. What did she ever see in this guy? "Look, that's not what I'm calling about. I want to know why you lied to me about Jimmy. I know you talked to him the day he died. Why would you lie to me about something like that?"

Jeff didn't answer her; the phone was just silent.

"Well?" Jamie demanded. "I want to know why you lied to me, and I want to know what you two argued about."

Again there was only silence.

Throwing caution to the wind and losing all merit, she yelled into the phone. "Damn it, Jeff! Are you going to answer me?"

"Look I can't talk right now. How about I come over tomorrow and we'll talk about it." His voice sounded strained.

"I don't want to wait till tomorrow, Jeff. I want to know now. Please..." she added out of shear desperation to know the truth.

"I can't do this now. I'll stop by tomorrow and we can discuss it then."

Jamie wanted to scream when the phone went dead. She hit redial then hung up knowing that she wouldn't get anywhere. Jeff would use this opportunity to control the situation. After all he learned from the best, like mother like son. She punched in Clay's number next, then again, hung up before completing her call. She wanted to wait and talk to Jeff before calling Clay.

Picking up her notebook she went to the living room and lay down on the sofa. She grabbed the remote from the coffee table and clicked on the Weather Channel. She wanted to see how long she was going to be house bound. Besides that the Weather Channel was fairly mindless and at the given moment mindless was exactly what she needed to regroup. Ironically she couldn't even concentrate on the Weather Channel, missing her local forecast as her thoughts strayed. She mulled over all that had transpired in the last twenty-four hours. It was no wonder she was experiencing a complete lack of forethought and good sense.

Try as she might she just couldn't seem to get a grip on her scattered thoughts and turbulent emotions. Her mind was being tugged in to many different directions. Jeff and Jimmy, Aerik, and let's not forget the new Kojack and his accusations. What she needed was to do some serious dumping. Hitting number five on her speed dial she resorted to making a call that was a long time in coming. She waited hoping to catch her long time friend Sarah at home. Sarah had made it out of the "sticks"; which was their personal reference to their hometown of Klahaya. Sarah had to join the military to accomplish this small feat, but as long as she was happy it didn't matter to Jamie how she got out. After all it was Sarah's dream of great escapes, not her own. Jamie was quite happy living in Klahaya. She felt at home nestled between the majestic Olympics which hovered over her on one side and the rolling endless waves of the Pacific Ocean on the other. Regardless of Sarah's moving every three years, as was the fate of Navy families, she always stayed in touch with Jamie. Currently she was all the way across the United States in Virginia. Jamie looked at the clock aware of the three hour time difference. It wasn't too early to call, she should be home from work by now. The bottom line was it really wouldn't matter what time it was. She needed her friend and Sarah wouldn't care if it was seven at night or three in the morning. If she wasn't home from work yet she would just talk to her answering machine.

When Sarah answered the phone Jamie burst into tears. When she hung up three hours later she knew without a doubt that calling Sarah was the right thing to do. She felt in control again. Forget seeing a shrink, she just needed her friend. She smiled to herself at the image in her mind of sending Sarah a check for mental health services rendered. Jamie had confided all the drama taking place in her normally non-eventful life. Sarah was so happy that Jamie had found a real man. The key word being "real," which had brought a smile to her lips. Jamie did omit the fact that Aerik was a vampire, figuring she would spare her friend the trauma of that one little detail. After all she didn't need Sarah showing up at her door in complete hysterics.

CHAPTER 13

Jamie made frozen pizza for dinner, which she shared with a very appreciative Burl. Also on the menu was an extra thick homemade chocolate milkshake, which she savored, as its taste by far exceeded all her expectations. Some would argue that it wasn't the healthiest of meals, but for now she was indulging the "it's all about me" attitude.

Despite the calmer demeanor she still felt herself wanting to reach out mentally to Aerik. His image simply would not leave her mind. She was experiencing a strong desire to just assure herself that he was there. As the sun faded on the horizon she wandered restlessly around the house cleaning for lack of anything better to do. Cleaning, like watching the Weather Channel, was a mindless task she used to fight the ever-growing urge to connect with him. When the sun was no longer visible she found it almost impossible to think of anything other than Aerik.

"Burl, I'm obsessed." She sighed. "Or possessed," she added as an after thought. She put away the orange oil she was using to clean the wood furniture with. As she headed up the stairs she stamped the steps allowing her growing frustration to vent itself. Half way up she did an about face and went back for her notebook. Glaring at it, disliking the unnatural yearning to keep it close at hand. She felt as if the darn thing were a lifeline to the devil himself, then again maybe it was. The problem was simple. She was copping an attitude towards Aerik because she couldn't control her own emotions where he was concerned. If she couldn't talk to him then she would be mad at him. It was much easier to be angry with him. This was the first night and she had two more to go. If the next two nights proved to be as much of a struggle as this one was turning out to be, then she would more than likely be furious with him by the time he resurfaced.

Jamie drew herself a hot bubble bath complete with candles and soft music. She had been staying up most of the night with Aerik and hoped that a long soak would relax her enough to get to sleep at a fairly decent hour. Not that it really mattered what time she went to bed, it wasn't like she had pressing engagements to attend. She was fortunate enough to be in a small class of people, mostly artists of some kind, that didn't have to conform to society's classic work hours. She thought about that fact for a while in relationship to her list of pros and cons. If she chose to accept Aerik's gift of immortality then she would never be able to paint in the sun again. Now that was a major fact to consider. Granted she could paint under false light but she rather enjoyed painting outside. Didn't Aerik say that it was bright out to him, that the night sky was different through vampire eyes? She reached for her notebook and quickly wrote down her thoughts.

While unwinding in the tub she examined the most significant ideas that were plaguing her troubled mind. Aerik kept saying that he felt that she was born for him, that they were meant to be together. He may be more correct about that than she cared to admit. If he hadn't given her mother his blood she would have died, taking her unborn child with her. Jamie was alive solely due to Aerik's interference with the natural course of her mother's, thus her own life. Again he intervened when she had cut her hand, again giving her life, when reality as she knew it, would have denied her a future. Her relationship with Aerik was anything but natural. What she felt and experienced with him couldn't possibly be the norm of others. Her relationship with Jeff, despite his immaturity, was fairly normal by majority's standards. Yet, she knew from the bottom of her heart that he wasn't the one. Never had she felt so complete as she did when Aerik was with her. Even now, through his absence, she felt like a part of herself was missing. Her rational side wanted to say that what she was feeling was his fault. He genetically altered her, by the giving to her of his blood in utero. This action predisposed her to him, sealing her fate. She would be forever connected to his soul — it was predestined. It was very well possible that she had more of his blood coursing through her veins than her own mother's during her critical development. That thought intrigued her. No doubt she existed because of him. So did that make him her creator? And if he had created her, shouldn't he be able to claim her? Or was that in fact what he was doing? Was it her fate to be his soul mate? Fate was a strange thing. Fate had taken her entire family. Was it fate or was it fate's way of helping her make the correct choice? By all rights there was nobody to hold her back from joining him to walk in the darkness, to become a vampire.

She had no family ties to keep her confined to a human time frame. For that matter she could drop off the face of the earth and the only person who would take notice would be Sarah. Jamie hadn't seen Sarah in over six years. It would be very easy to continue their friendship without actually having to see each other face to face. Sarah would never move back to Klahaya. She picked up her notebook and added a new column. What's keeping me here? Under this heading she wrote: memories, house, cemetery.

When the water finally grew tepid she reluctantly climbed out of the tub. Looking at her list again those three items stood out like a sore thumb, as they were still the only three items on her new list. As she dressed for bed she thought about how important those things were to her. She could take her memories with her. She had painted her cemetery, would her painting suffice? Yes, she knew that it would. There was nothing she could do about her house. When it really came down to it, the house was the base of all her memories. Leaving her house would be emotionally traumatic. It was also her safe haven when it rained. It wasn't the rain she feared it was driving in it…yet she had become accustom to being in her home when the rain fell. Just thinking about being in a strange place while it was raining gave her a twinge of panic. *People move all the time*, she told herself. Perhaps a change of scenery would in fact be beneficial to her well-being. She could rent out her house and visit on occasion. Then again why would she have to leave? Aerik could move in with her. Different scenarios scrambled around her head playing each other out.

"Oh great," she said out loud. Burl, who was lounging on her bed as if he owned it, looked over at her and whined. "I'm setting myself up for having a panic attack." She picked up her remote and crawled onto the bed. She pushed against Burl who was taking up far more than his fair share of available space. When he looked at her like moving would be way too much work she gave up. Using his body as a pillow she propped herself up, then clicked on the television to the news hoping to catch the weather. She moaned in disgust when the five-day planner showed rain showers for the next four days. Of course things changed day to day in this area, bottom line is you couldn't trust the weatherman as far as you could throw him. Up to this point it had been exceptionally warm and dry, for which she was very thankful. She really needed to get a grip on the whole rain issue. It was insane to live Washington State and have a phobia of the rain. It was after all, the evergreen state, and those evergreens didn't stay that color from lack of water. The Olympic Mountains located just outside her back door, was home to Washington's Hoh rain forest. Realistically, Jamie's problem with the rain would be in equal comparison to a dieter living next door to a pastry shop.

Jamie channel surfed, not really watching anything. Her mind was focused on Aerik and when she finally fell asleep it was Aerik she dreamed of.

CHAPTER 14

The following morning Jamie found herself literally pacing the floor, always to return to the kitchen table where she had placed her pros and cons notebook. In frustration she moaned. In reality what she really wanted to do was have a full-blown temper tantrum. She knew she had serious choices that needed her full attention yet she found it hard to concentrate. She wanted...no needed to reach out to Aerik. It was like an itch she couldn't quite reach. She thought that having distance and time away from Aerik's overwhelming presence would allow her to see that she was just latching onto him because of her loneliness. Instead of getting a grip about herself, she was missing him fiercely. His image dominated her thoughts. The need to touch him, to hear his voice, was almost more than she could bear. She felt as if she were losing her flipping mind. Her thoughts kept returning to why Jeff lied to her about talking to Jimmy. Why would Jimmy tell Jeff to stay away from her? Jimmy didn't say anything negative about Jeff to her that morning. There wasn't anything said to lead her to believe that there was issues between Jeff and Jimmy. It was already noon and as the day wore on Jamie found it increasingly difficult to think of anything else. Where was Jeff? He said he would be over and you would think that by the way he had been acting he would have been pounding on the door at the crack of dawn. Walking over to the phone she called his house. When the answering machine came on she hung up.

Jamie paced the floor a while longer then let Burl outside after realizing that he had been standing at the door for a while now. She wanted nothing more than to hear Jeff's truck pull down the driveway. She may just give him an earful for taking his sweet time in showing up. Reaching for the phone again she dialed Clayton's number. The phone rang twice and she slammed the receiver down.

"What am I doing?" she mumbled to herself. She knew she needed to calm down and get a handle on her emotions. She wasn't being rational and needed to think about what she was doing. What she wanted to do was tell Clay to come over and confront Jeff and make him tell the truth. In all actuality things just didn't work like that. There may be perks for being a deputy sheriff, but physically forcing someone to talk was clearly dramatics reserved for television.

She poured herself another cup of coffee and looked out the window for Burl. Not seeing him yet she sat down with her cup and took a few deep breaths and gathered her thoughts. *Yeah, more caffeine that ought to help,* she chastised herself. Jimmy wanted Jeff to stay away from her. They were arguing over a wiring job? Jimmy wanted to talk to someone in Port Angeles. What job did Jeff do for Jimmy? He didn't work on the Jeep's speakers because the row-bar speaker was still blown. He did some wiring in the garage – it seemed fine. He wired the vapor light outside the house but there were no problems with it either. She kept thinking back to all the little jobs that Jeff had done around the house. It had been so long. Jeff had been doing electrical type work back in high school. He was in an apprenticeship program throughout school that was supposed to have led him into a career after graduation. The only problem with that golden opportunity was that Jeff was offered a job with the Aberdeen Power and Light Company. He would have had to move about fifty miles south. His mother being the control freak that she was made him turn the job down. It was a shame since the job would have made him a great career with plenty of advancement opportunities. Jamie drummed the tabletop with her fingernails. He rewired a lamp for her mom and he installed a ceiling fan in the living room. He installed a stereo in her dad's car.

Jamie got up and went to the door and called for Burl. He was going to be absolutely drenched when he came in. The rain was really coming down. She called him twice wondering if he would hear her through all the noise, the wind was literally howling around the sides of the house. The sky was a dark gray as the rain fell in torrents pelting at the already saturated ground. It looked like evening time instead of the middle of the afternoon. Jamie liked the rain in one sense; she liked the smell of the damp earth that only a good rainfall could produce. Yes, she liked the smell of rain and the smells rain created. She even liked the sound of rain as it drummed the roof and tapped at the windows. If only she could bring herself to drive in it.

As she stood there at the door with that thought in mind her body went cold. A shiver ran down her spine as all the little hairs on her arms stood on end. She broke out in goose bumps that not only covered her arms but her legs as well. Could Jeff have done something to her parents' car that could have caused their accident? *No…that's crazy, it was just the stereo he worked on wasn't it?* She was only succeeding in getting herself all worked up. She called for Burl again this time with more urgency. Jamie just couldn't shake the deep cold that flooded her insides with dread. She went to the drawer and pulled out the phone book. With shaking fingers she dialed.

"Hi Big Al, this is Jamie McPherson again. I'm sorry to bother you but do remember what kind of car Jimmy was asking you about before he died? Was it a Ford Taurus by any chance?"

"1991, darling."

"1991?"

"That's right he asked about a 1991 Ford Taurus. I remember the year because I bought my daughter one that same year."

"Thank you."

"That's it?" he asked.

"Yeah that's it. Thank you." Jamie hung up. Her insides were aching and she felt like she was going to be sick. That was when she felt an impact at the back of her head followed directly by blinding pain. Blackness claimed her as she sunk to the kitchen floor.

Detective Neely grinned as he watched Jeff Edgewood turn down the McPherson driveway. "Finally," he mumbled aloud. He had been going stir crazy staking out her residence. He shrugged into his camouflage rain jacket and slipped out of his car into the heavy downpour. He started to jog down the long driveway towards the house till he realized that Mr. Edgewood only went half way down the drive then parked. "What the hell?" He swore as he quickly made his way into the tree line. He watched as Jeff exited his truck and disappeared into the trees on the opposite side of the road from where he himself was hold up. He slowly backtracked then crossed the drive. He contemplated calling for back up. He had a bad feeling about this yet there still wasn't any evidence of foul play. The mere thought of blowing his first real investigation didn't sit well with him. He really didn't want to believe that Jamie had anything to do with her brother's murder since all of his psychological training pointed to the fact that she was innocent, however she did have a stake in his insurance monies and the sole control of the family property. He was just out here stirring things up. They were out of leads and about to put the case in the dead file. It was time to grasp at all straws. Now things were looking a little more than "just interesting." He hit the ground when he heard the distinct sound of a gun with a silencer attached. "Damn it." He swore again as he spat muddy water and wiped at is face. He reached for his radio, back up would be a good thing but he wondered how long it would take them to get all the way out here.

CHAPTER 15

"Well at least you were smart enough to hit her in the back of the head." Were the first words clear enough for Jamie to hear as she tried to fight her way out of the debts of darkness. She felt like she was swimming underwater and couldn't quite reach the surface. As physical feelings returned she was assaulted by pain not only shooting down her spine but radiating out from the back of her skull, it wrapped around her head in a throbbing ache unlike any she had ever experienced. She struggled to no avail; she couldn't move her arms or legs. Whose voice was that? She recognized the voice, but couldn't think clear enough to put a name to it. Was it a female voice? She struggled to see but it was too dark. Trying to see or speak was all but useless as she realized she had been blindfolded as well as gagged. At this point all she could do was squirm, which only increased the pain her body was racked with. The voices around her lowered to whispers she couldn't discern them. Panic…shear stark terror gripped her in its icy clutch as she realized her vulnerability. Her heart nearly jumped from her chest pounding unmercifully as she broke out in a cold sweat. She could taste metal in her mouth as if she had bit down on a copper penny. At that moment Jamie felt that if her assailants didn't kill her, she would surely die from the rigors her body was subjecting her to, for she was clearly suffering from a horrific panic attack. Her heart began to race so quickly she felt as if it had stopped beating all together. Fear sucked at her sanity and she wiggled around trying desperately to free her hands. Her gasps through the gag were choking her; she couldn't seem to get enough air – she couldn't breathe. She tried to cry out for Aerik but it only came out as a strangled whine. Suddenly as if by magic a calm flooded through her. She could feel the warmth as it permeated, filled, surrounded her very being. Her heart was slowing from the frantic flutter to a rapid pounding but at least she could feel it beating, which meant she was still alive. She could breathe easier. The immediate calming of her body made her realize just how close she had come to losing her mind. Then she heard his harmonious voice, drawing her out of the debts of hell, cascading over her in a waterfall of tranquility and peace.

"Jamie, can you hear me?"

"Help me," Jamie pleaded to him with her mind.

"Shhhh," he shushed her as a mother would a crying child. "You're going to be alright. I'll take care of you. I have slowed your respiration and taken away your thoughts of death. You will not think about dying. Do you understand?" He commanded her to obey him.

"Yes. I will not think about dying," she replied to him in her mind.

Her thoughts were in such disarray he was having a difficult time ascertaining them. He was now in control of her body as well as most of her thought process. As quickly as he could he sifted through her recent memories watching, experiencing her events of the day. He was disappointed when he realized that she did not see her attacker nor did she know where she was. He felt the prick of a foreign object entering her delicate skin quickly followed by a drug. He scanned the properties finding them to be a non-lethal dose of pain medication combined with a sedative. He stayed in control of her body till he was satisfied that the medication was working and she truly was asleep. He was in trouble. He had at least six hours till the sun safely left the sky and he could arise. He had no idea where she was or who had her. In his weakened state while the sun ruled the sky he was all but helpless to aid her. He reached out to Burl hoping to see through his eyes. He found Burl near the north edge of Jamie's house. He was bleeding from a bullet wound. Aerik eased the dog's pain and assessed the damage. It was a clean shot and if he could slow down the bleeding then he would make it. Aerik mentally helped Burl to roll onto his other side, which in turn put the pressure he needed on the wound to slow the flow of blood. He flooded the dog with warmth, reassurance and praise.

"Aerik, I sense that you are in distress."

"Tray, I may be in need of your assistance." Aerik was relieved when he heard his friend's voice in his mind. "Where are you?"

"Why I'm in Seattle. I was going to surprise you with a visit. Where are you?" Tray asked.

"You're down." It was their term for sleeping.

"Well I was..." he gave a mental image of a sigh, "but I was awoken by an overwhelming feeling that you needed my assistance."

Aerik began to fill Tray in on the details.

Hours later Jamie slowly regained consciousness. She was no longer gagged or blind folded, but she was tied at the wrists and ankles to the chair she was sitting in. Feeling extremely disoriented, her vision came in and out of focus; everything was so hazy. Her head felt like a balloon that was about to pop, swollen and full of pressure as it throbbed keeping time with her pulse. Her mouth was so dry she could barely swallow. Her vision was fuzzy but there appeared to be two people sitting at a little table across the room from her. She blinked several times trying to clear the fogginess to her sight. Trying not to move she checked out her surroundings. They appeared to be in a cabin.

"Good girl, keep looking around." It was Aerik's voice – strong, powerful, comforting. "Who is sitting at the table?"

Jamie tried to focus on her two kidnappers. The sting of reality, confusion then anger overwhelmed her when she realized that it was Jeff and his mother sitting at the table. They looked like they were playing cards. "Jeff and his mother Nancy Edgewood," she answered in her thoughts. "Why? Why would they do this to me?"

"Shhh...Cara Mia, it does not matter. Mark my words, Jamie, they will pay dearly for what they have done to you." Aerik's voice wrapped around her like a warm blanket, so gentle and reassuring. "Do you know where you are?"

"No."

"Do you know why they did this?"

"No." She thought a moment realizing that Jeff had to be angry over their breakup but did it warrant such drastic actions as this? No that couldn't be what it was about, could it?

"Jamie, listen carefully to what I'm telling you. They have given you drugs to dull the pain and sedate you, to make you more compliant. If you fall asleep again I will not be able to see through your eyes. It is imperative that you stay awake."

"I'll try."

"I want you to do whatever they want. If you are accommodating they may not drug you again. Do you understand?"

"Uh huh." Jamie found that each time she blinked it was harder to open her eyes. All she wanted to do was listen to the sound of Aerik's voice and give into the beckoning call of a drug-induced sleep. "I'm so tired."

"I know you are, honey."

Jamie shook her head slightly trying to dislodge a hair that lay across her field of vision. Her movement drew the attention of the Edgewoods.

"Look, the princess is awake," Jeff exclaimed.

"Great." Mrs. Edgewood jumped up in delight. "Let's take some pictures." She grabbed a throwaway type camera off the table and headed directly towards Jamie. "Did you have a nice nap, dear?"

Jamie didn't say anything, she didn't know if she could. Whatever it was they had given her was playing havoc with her senses.

Mrs. Edgewood paced the floor in front of Jamie's chair. "Well I guess that you have made some poor choices in your life lately, what a shame. I don't think that you realize how some decisions a person makes can destroy another's dreams. It really is a shame how you have chosen to throw your life away like you have. But," she smiled brightly as she clapped her hands together, "we're going to fix all that, aren't we, Jeff?"

"Yeah, whatever Mom." He glared at Jamie as he lit a smoke tossing the match to the floor.

"Oh come now, it's all going to work out just fine. Let's tell Jamie of our plans shall we?" Mrs. Edgewood took a brush from her bag and started to comb through Jamie's hair without so much as a hint of gentleness. The brush caught pulling the hair causing Jamie to cry out in pain.

"What are you doing?" Jamie asked as a tear slid down her cheek. It came out as half cry half horse whisper but she was heard.

"Well we're going to take some wedding pictures of course," she said as she finished brushing her hair then sprayed Jamie's head generously with hair spray. She pulled up a chair directly in front of her and proceeded to inspect Jamie's face. "I think we need a little make-up." Opening her bag she removed her cosmetics.

"Wedding pictures? Why are you doing this?" Jamie asked. She didn't understand what was going on. It all seemed like a bad dream and she would wake up at any moment. Nothing was making any sense.

Mrs. Edgewood took Jamie's chin her hand firmly and started to apply some foundation. "Well it's quite simple, dear." She smiled giving Jamie one of those… you should know this, but I'll explain it to you anyway looks. "You should have married Jeff. We had such grand plans for the two of you. We were going to turn your place into a bed and breakfast then add a string of rental cabins lining the bluff. We would have made a fortune on tourism. Not to mention the fact that we would be starting our own chain of oceanfront resorts. We would have had a monopoly on the northwestern coastline. With your talent as an artist we would have had show quality galleries that catered to the rich. While the husbands were enjoying their beautiful quiet get away their wives could have shopped in our galleries and gift shops. With your work it would have been nearly a 100% profit, not to mention the items we could have sold under the table to those willing to pay a little more and forfeit their bill of sale."

Jamie jerked her head from Mrs. Edgewood's grasp. A sharp stinging slap to the side of her face quickly followed her movement. "But…" she went on as if it never happened, "you had to go and throw it all away." She started to apply the mascara and Jamie moved her head back again. Mrs. Edgewood used the hairbrush she held and smacked her on the side of her head only harder this time.

"Jamie, hold still or I will do it for you," Aerik commanded. "Do not provoke her further she is dangerous."

Mrs. Edgewood smacked her painfully one more time when she saw a tear slide down the side of Jamie's face. "Stop that crying, you're going to mess up the make-up, and I won't have it."

Jamie gasped and tried to hold still. She heard Aerik growl inside her mind. She felt the pain leaving her body as he pulled it into himself, shielding her from this crazed woman. Aerik was now giving her strength, his strength. She felt as if a current of electricity were running through her veins filling her with feelings, feelings of courage, vigor, and power. She sat up straighter in her chair and looked Mrs. Edgewood dead on.

Aerik silenced Jamie before she could spout off which was exactly what she was about to do. He obviously gave her just a little too much confidence. She was feeling fearless at the moment. He wanted her to feel empowered but not to this extent. "Jamie, you must do as she says. I can not come to you till the sun is down."

"I want to rip her head off, Aerik," Jamie cried out in her mind.

"No Babe, those are my feelings not yours. You must as you say, 'Get a grip'."

"Well can't you make the sun go down any faster?"

"There are some things that even I can not do." He sent her the feeling of his sigh. Fact be known he was experiencing feelings of his own that were new him. He was feeling helpless and scared. This was truly the first time that he felt trapped by the earth. He was being held within, a prison of dirt of rocks unable to break free from its crushing grip till the sun no longer ruled the sky. He thought about Jamie's assailants. Their fate was sealed as he was beyond anger. There would be no contemplation of retaliation for their actions ruled their fate. Vengeance was no longer an issue it was fact. These people who threatened the life of his beloved would pay with their lives.

He felt her close her eyes then struggle to reopen them. He had to keep her awake. "Ask her what their plans are."

"What are you going to do?" Jamie asked.

Mrs. Edgewood went back to applying Jamie's make-up with the expertise of an aged glamour girl. She made a pursing of her own lips to let Jamie know that it was what she wanted her to do. Jamie pursed her lips allowing the lipstick to be applied. "You're going to sign a forged marriage license. That way it will look like you and Jeff were married this weekend. "Then we're going to take some wedding photos. I bet you didn't even notice that you had on a wedding gown now did you?"

Jamie looked down at her clothes and realized that they weren't her own. They had dressed her in a white lacy summer dress, one that could easily double for a casual style wedding. How did she not notice?

"The drugs," Aerik told her.

"Then what?" Jamie asked.

"Then you're going to have a little accident." She finished with the blush and carefully put all the make-up back in her bag except for the cover-up. "All finished. Jeff, how does she look?"

"Like the tramp that she is." He walked over to stand behind his mother, inspecting the make-up. His face clearly showed his unseen encounter with Aerik. He had several red dots from the bee stings that resembled a bad case of acne. He glared at Jamie with an intense hatred then walked back to the table.

"Honey," Mrs. Edgewood exclaimed, "some people just have character flaws and there isn't anything you can do about it. It's simply bad genetics. Come here and let Mother cover up those nasty marks on your face. We need these pictures to look good. We'll have to display them long enough for you to have suffered through a proper mourning period before you marry again."

Jamie was overcome with intense anger at the implications that they were making. "How long have you been making all these plans?" she asked.

"For years now. It's amazing really," she said while working on Jeff's face. She continued talking as casually as if she were attending one of her luncheons. "Everything was going along so well just like clock work. Then," she wagged her finger at Jamie as if she had been naughty, "you had to go and break up with my sunshine."

"Mom," Jeff whined. He hated it whenever she called him "sunshine."

"Be quiet and hold still," Nancy reprimanded her son.

"Were you responsible for my parents' death?" Jamie blurted out.

"You know we made them very solid offers on their land several times, but they were stubborn, your parents."

Jamie tried desperately to hold back the tears that welled up in her eyes. She stared out the window and noticed that it was getting darker. If she could have willed the sun to fall from the heavens she would have done so. Never had she felt so angry, and confused as she did right now. "You shot Jimmy too."

"That was to easy," Mrs. Edgewood laughed softly. "That drunk will never know what happened. At least his wife won't have to make weekly phone calls to the police station anymore. Quite frankly they were a disgrace to our community. I do believe we killed two birds with one stone that time." She seemed very pleased with herself and it showed in her giddiness. She actually thought she had done society a good deed by framing Lyle Dugan for Jimmy's murder.

"Mrs. Edgewood, I'm really thirsty. Can I please have a drink of water?"

Nancy nodded to her son to get it.

Jeff brought Jamie a glass and held it to her lips so she could drink.

"Time to sign the license and take some pictures." Mrs. Edgewood picked up the camera and instructed Jeff to slip on the dress jacket that was hanging over the back of his chair and to sit beside Jamie. She handed Jamie a pen and instructed her where to sign. "Oh that won't do," she exclaimed. "You're going to have to look happy dear. You need to smile."

Jamie looked at her like she was insane. There was no way she could smile; this sick bitch killed her family.

Mrs. Edgewood snatched up a piece of kindling from beside the fireplace and thumped Jamie on top of the head with it. "You will sign that paper. And you will sign it with a smile," she said firmly as she stood ready with the camera. "I want a good picture of the signing."

Jamie felt the initial pain, which was quickly absorbed by Aerik.

"Do not fight her." His command was nothing less than that, a firm command; she was compelled to obey him. It was with a shaky hand that she signed the marriage license. She couldn't help but think that she had just signed her own death certificate, sealing her fate. Jamie allowed the two tormentors to pose her for several shots, "wedding photos."

"Jamie, it's almost time. You need to stall them." Aerik sent her an image of the sun setting on the ocean.

"What makes you think you'll get away with this?" she asked out of the blue.

"Well that's a given since you and Jeff have dated all these years nobody will question the fact that you decided to marry," Mrs. Edgewood declared. "Of course your habit of staying cooped up in that big house painting all the time certainly didn't hurt matters," she said while flashing Jamie a big smile. "You never were one to swarm in the social circles, always keeping to yourself. Quite honestly there just aren't that many people who will question your marriage or your whereabouts. I really doubt there will be anyone who will even care that you're gone."

The truth of Mrs. Edgewood's words stung. Her lifestyle had indeed created the ease in which their plan could flow. "They know that Lyle didn't kill my brother," Jamie blurted out desperate to keep Nancy talking.

Mrs. Edgewood shot Jeff a sidelong glance.

"She's lying, Mom," Jeff said as he blew out a stream of cigarette smoke. He then proceeded to flip the butt onto the floor of the cabin squashing it with the toe of his shoe as he pulled out his pack to light another.

"I'm not lying," Jamie said adamantly. "Clay Fisher was by the house to tell me that they were releasing Lyle. You can call and check it out."

"She's lying," Jeff repeated as he shifted nervously from one foot to the other.

Jamie heard the doubt clinging to his words as he spoke. "Jeff, please don't do this. It's wrong. Don't you care about me at all?" she pleaded.

Jeff glared at her. "Don't you get it?" he spat out. "I never cared about you. It was always about the land." His agitation was definitely showing through and he began to pace the floor as if he were a caged animal.

"Honey, calm down," Mrs. Edgewood cooed to her grown son. "I think you just need to go outside and get a little fresh air. Don't let her rile you so. You can calm down then we'll finish this." She smiled sweetly at her son then added, "Go on, go on outside for a while."

Jeff glowered as he stalked over to the table and snatched up the handgun that lay there. He shrugged out of the dress jacket tossing it into the corner. He slapped his ball cap onto his head then grabbed a flannel shirt off the back of the chair and headed for the door.

Aerik's voice filled Jamie's mind. "Jamie, I didn't know they had a gun on the table."

"I didn't either. Oh God they're going to shoot me, Aerik!" she cried out in her mind.

"Jamie, listen to me. When Jeff goes outside you need to get his mother to look you in the eyes. Do you hear me?"

"Why? Then what?"

Jamie was giving up hope and he felt it slowly encompassing her spirit. He was extremely weak, having forced his body to refuse the sleep that it demanded while the sun was up, but he refused... he would not allow her to give up. "I'm going to try and control her through you. Jamie, you must get her to look you in the eyes. If this works you will go to the window opposite of the door and climb out. Do you understand?" Aerik knew that they were ready to finish her off. They had accomplished all that they needed her alive for. The sun was fading fast but not fast enough. The fear that he might actually lose her enraged him. His emotions at the mere thought of losing her were a crushing weight on his dark soul. It was fate that created their bond; let it be fate that they survive this ordeal together. For if she were to be taken from him, from this world, then he would not want to exist any longer. The anguish that he would suffer at her loss would in itself extinguish any innate will to live that he might harbor. With grief as his guide he would choose to walk into the sun in the hopes of following her into the next world. This had to work. As Jamie called Mrs. Edgewood over to her, Aerik directed all his attention and focused on her through Jamie's eyes. He commanded Jamie to speak his words. "You will listen to me."

Nancy Edgewood looked at her questioningly then shook her head slightly. She neither spoke nor moved.

"You will to listen to me."

"I'm listening," she mumbled, staring at Jamie with a vacant look in her eyes.

"It's working, Aerik!" Jamie cried out from within. "You will untie me so I can climb out the window. Do you understand?"

Nancy was clearly struggling to break free from his vampire hold as she reluctantly untied the ropes that bound her hostage.

"I said you will let me go out the window. You will obey me."

"I will obey you," she answered despite the fact that she appeared to be internally fighting against whatever controlled her body and mind.

"Jamie, go to the window. Be quick. I do not know how long she will stay under my power when you are no longer looking at her. Go now. Go fast," he commanded.

Jamie flew to the window only to find that it was nailed shut. She tried pulling on it to no avail. She struggled with it in shear desperation. "Look at what's stopping the window," Aerik commanded through her. Jamie did as she was told and watched in amazement as the nails came out of the wood as if by an invisible hammer.

CHAPTER 16

Detective Neely found himself again lying in the mud, only this time he was at the base of an ancient cedar tree with his service revolver aimed directly at Jeff Edgewood's chest. He had been watching the cabin for quite sometime now. It was only till he reached this new spot that he could visually see Jamie McPherson through the window. He was mad as hell that he was still waiting on back up. His last communication with them was over twenty minutes ago. He clearly stated that if he had a free shot he was going to take it. The McPherson girl was suffering head blows from her assailants. Neely knew that due to the circumstances surrounding the suspects' involvement it was pretty clear to him that they were going to kill her. The radio sure came alive when he announced what was going down. Seems that Deputy McPherson and his artist sister had many friends in this community and in some pretty high places to boot. He turned his radio down when Jeff Edgewood walked out of the cabin to have a smoke. He wondered again where his backup was. The only close contact he had was from a Deputy Sheriff Fisher who said that he was making his way through the underbrush to his left but he had yet to see him. He left his car on the side of the road about half a mile back but then again the weather was bad and they were in the woods on logging roads, it couldn't get any worse than that. His vehicle not being four wheel drive just couldn't make the climb. He was thankful that the road ended only this far in. He had no idea how much further the logging road went. The longer the road the further away Edgewood was to him. His only fear now was the possibility that he provided his back up with incorrect directions. He had been in a hurry trying to keep a tail on them, but he doubted it. Detail should have been his middle name. His friends in the bureau were always joking around referring to him as "Mr. Detail" in their quest at badgering him for why he took so long on essay questions. He looked over to his left hearing the cracking of a small twig. He caught a glimpse of the deputy who waved an acknowledgement that they had a visual on each other. Neely returned his attention back to Jeff Edgewood. He was a little nervous about the prospect of having to use his weapon. This was the first time that he actually had his gun trained on a suspect. He quickly evaluated his choices then asked himself if he could in fact pull the trigger. It took all of about two seconds to realize that he would under the circumstances have no problem pulling the trigger. Yet…he had heard stories of the so called "trigger test," where good men in the bureau had done exemplary work in their fields, only to throw it all away when they realized that they couldn't follow through with discharging their weapon when called upon. He glanced at the deputy who flashed him the sign "for take him out." He looked back at Jeff who was rocking nervously from one foot to the other. Neely knew that Jeff was working himself up to commit an act he knew was wrong. He had learned a lot about reading body language. This kid was about to blow. Jeff Edgewood flicked his cigarette into the mud puddle in front of him then turned to go back inside the cabin. Neely's gut instinct told him it was now or never, he pulled his trigger. As Jeff Edgewood fell Neely felt a rush of adrenaline unlike any he had ever felt. He smiled to himself as he darted towards the cabin thrilled that he had passed the trigger test.

Jamie was stopped dead in her tracks by a loud report of gunfire. She waited for the impact but none came. She whirled around to find Mrs. Edgewood looking at her with a dazed and confused look on her face. It was at that same moment the cabin door slammed open as the weight of Jeff's body collided against it. He landed with a loud thud on the floor of the cabin. His dark red blood began to slowly pool around him spreading out onto the cedar floorboards from a hole in his upper chest. Nancy Edgewood looked at her son with shocked horror in her eyes. She dropped to her knees and let out a blood-curtailing scream of anguish that filled the evening air.

Jeff blinked once then locked eyes with Jamie as a thin trail of blood began to seep out the corner of his mouth. With a ragged gasp he raised the gun still in his grasp. The last thing he did before he died was to pull the trigger.

Jamie caught the bullet in her left shoulder. The impact lifted her up off her feet pitching her into the wall behind. Pain burned through her in an intensity that took her breath away. As she slid down the wall to the floor she saw Detective Neely come through the door kicking the gun from Jeff's dead hand and slamming a screaming Nancy Edgewood to the dusty floor.

Aerik felt his world shatter. He cried out as Jamie's pain racked his body. He fought to rise from the ground that kept him safe from the sun's rays but found that he was being held fast. He tried to fight the barrier that surrounded him but could not break through it. "Do not die. You will not die!" He commanded her to breathe. When he realized that he could not rise to go to her he concentrated solely on assessing the damage that was done to her body and regulating her heart and lungs. She was bleeding to death. He could see that the man she recognized as the detective that pissed her off was handcuffing Mrs. Edgewood. He knew that he would aid Jamie as soon as it was safe. "No!" Aerik cried out, as Jamie's eyes closed and he could no longer see what was happening around her. With all the strength he could muster he tried again to break free of the invisible web that held him.

"You can not rise yet."

It was Trayvon's voice that entered his mind. Aerik was surprised and shocked that his friend was holding him back. "If you do not release me I will kill you," Aerik responded.

"If you rise now you will die before you reach her."

"I must try." Aerik cursed at the loss of his strength. He cursed his friend.

"You must keep her alive mentally for only three more minutes. You will be of no use to her if you are dead. She can survive this. She has a strong will if she loves the likes of you," Trayvon stated. "I will not let you go till the sun is down. Then together we will aid your love and take vengeance upon those who have harmed her."

Jamie heard Aerik's healing voice. He was but a whisper in the recesses of her mind urging her to hold on, to hold on for him, for them.

As the last ray of sunlight gave up the sky for nightfall Aerik burst from the earth in an explosion worthy of the rage that consumed him. In all his vampire glory he tracked Jamie's essence, something he could not do till he had risen, to the cabin nestled in the lower Olympic Mountains. As he swooped down on the cabin from the darkened sky he felt Jamie slipping from him. Aerik zeroed in on the scent of her blood as he entered the cabin in a blaze of blind fury. The door literally exploded. Anything in his way flew from his path as if pushed by an unseen wind. He was solely focused on Jamie, who lay so lifeless against the wall, soaked in her own precious blood. Aerik looked wild, clearly not human. His eyes flamed as if lit from within the unholy red of burning torches, they carried the promise of retribution. As he seethed with anger he wanted nothing more than to kill those who dared to do harm to his woman. He snapped his head in the direction of the detective causing his gun to fly from his hands rendering him helpless. He had been bent over Jamie trying to stop her flow of blood. Now he looked up at Aerik with terror in his eyes as his gun was ripped from his fingers by an invisible force. A second later he was slammed roughly across the floor, his body slamming into the opposite wall by a wind that came from out of nowhere. Aerik commanded him to not move with a single thought as he went straight to Jamie. As Aerik kneeled down before her, he was hit with gunfire. It jerked his body three times in rapid-fire succession. Standing quickly he snapped his body around fangs bared hissing at what assailed him. A loud deep animal growl erupted from his throat as his eyes blazed red with pain and raging fury.

Mr. Edgewood was standing in the doorway of the cabin in shock at what stood before him. Smoke curled up from the barrel of his rifle. He backed up in stunned disbelief; the man he shot did not fall. As his eyes settled on Aerik he saw him for what he was; stark terror consumed him as he stared at the unholy beast that was before him. He felt something wet run down the inside of his leg to scared to realize that he was wetting himself. His eyes grew wide as Aerik took two steps then shape-shifted into the form of a giant black wolf that sprang at him with it teeth bared. His last words just prior to Aerik ripping his throat out were, "Holy shit."

As Aerik shape shifted back he went to Jamie's side. She was barely alive. He let out an unholy cry that would have woke the dead when he realized how far gone she was. He cradled her to himself trying to reach her on the mental path they shared.

"Aerik." Trayvon appeared at his side. "You must make a decision, my friend, before it's too late."

"I can not lose her." Aerik lengthened his nail preparing to slash his wrist so he could give Jamie his blood.

Trayvon grabbed Aerik's wrist and stayed him. "You are too weak, it will kill you. You're bleeding freely yourself; you need blood as badly as she does."

"I don't care." Aerik glared at his friend, not having time to debate the issue.

"You will die," he stated anger, tinged his words. "Then where will she be? I am not babysitting her for the rest of eternity, that will be your job." Tray slashed his own wrist. "Give her to me."

Aerik shook his head. He wouldn't let her go.

"If you want her to live give her to me, it's the only way and you know it. You are weak and you must feed to heal yourself or you will die. Take from him while I give to her." Tray nodded towards the detective. "Now is not a time to have a battle of wills. Do not make me force you because I will win, you are too weak to fight me in your condition. As you will not give her up I will not give you up."

Aerik released his hold on Jamie and turned her over to his friend.

Tray sat on the floor and pulled Jamie into his lap so his front was to her back. He cradled her to his chest then opened a wound at his wrist; he held it to her mouth commanding her to drink. He never once dropped eye contact with Aerik. He knew what he was doing and he knew how dangerous Aerik was at this moment in time. He felt his friend's emotions raging inside his own mind as they were also connected. He watched as Aerik made his way to the detective and started to feed. He did not break eye contact.

Aerik was overcome with an intense weakness from lack of sleep and loss of blood. He knew his friend was right but it was all he could do to turn over his love, his life to the care of another. His animalistic instincts wanted to lash out and attack Tray in a fit of jealous rage as he shared an intimacy with his woman, the giving of his blood. He also realized that with their sharing Tray would always know where Jamie was and would be able to communicate with her if he chose to. Watching Jamie take nourishment from Tray, her lips locked to Tray's wrist, taking his ancient blood made Aerik see red. He felt as if he would lose his mind. He tried to control the rage burning inside him to kill his own friend. To kill him for an act that was necessary to her very survival. He just kept repeating to himself that he was saving her life.

"You need this," Tray told him knowing that to let Jamie go, especially into another male's arms, was a difficult thing for a vampire to do. They were extremely protective of their mates. Tray could feel that although he was saving Jamie's life and they both knew it, Aerik was fighting the urge to attack him as he held his mate in his arms and let her feed from him.

"Aerik, she suffers a mortal wound," Tray spoke out loud and inside his friend's mind simultaneously.

Aerik shook his head no, despite the fact that he had his fangs sunk deeply in the neck of the detective and his eyes locked to Trayvon.

"Aerik."

"No." Aerik gave an emphatic mental negative response.

"I turn her now or she dies. She is at her limit." Tray studied the pain on his friend's face as he waited for his answer. He read Aerik's thoughts of wanting her to be able to make the decision on her own. He couldn't live with himself if she hated being a vampire and held it against him, changing her without her consent. Then he saw that his friend was thinking about letting her go only to follow her to the next world if that was his fate. There were no rules where they were concerned and like mortals, what happened to them when they died was unknown. Bottom line was Tray was not ready to lose his best friend. He would turn this girl and if she decided she didn't like being a vampire then she could just blame him. He continued to let her drink. When he knew he had given more than her limit and there was no going back he spoke. "You need her."

Aerik stopped feeding. To take any more would put the detective at risk. He had consumed enough to make the necessary repairs to his body. He knew that Tray had turned her, taking the choice out of his hands. He watched as his friend removed his wrist and seal the slash in his arm closed as he continued to cradle Jamie to him. They watched together as her body reacted to the overdose of Tray's ancient vampire blood. He held her firmly as Jamie's body jerked as it tried to reject the genetic altering changes that were causing her mortal body to die and her new body to live. They looked at each other again as Jamie gasped her last mortal breath, her green eyes opened falling to rest on Aerik as her heart ceased to beat. At the last pulse her eyes closed as if saying goodnight to the world she knew. A minute passed, two minutes – they waited. Both had been here before and they were somber. Her last heartbeats as a mortal were intensely loud to their vampire ears. Literally pounding inside their heads like the beat of a bass drum. Not just a sound, but a moment, they would carrying with them through all of eternity. Jamie's hair a golden honey brown changed instantly to a brighter more vibrant golden shade of her natural color. Her skin took on the glow of eternal beauty as her lips darkened to a deeper red as if she had applied a coating of lipstick. Her wound mended itself before their eyes. Her body took on an ethereal quality. And as if on cue Jamie's eyes opened. Aerik sucked in his breath as she looked at him with the most beautiful sea green eyes he had ever seen. They sparkled with colors so intense, so profoundly beautiful he ached to look at them. He never thought that it was possible for her to become more beautiful than she already was; yet here she was the most beautiful creature he had ever laid eyes upon.

"Damn," Trayvon whispered as he watched Jamie's transformation. He looked up at Aerik who was looking at him with death in his eyes. Tray looked down at Jamie who was still cradled in his arms. He heard Aerik growl deep, menacing inside his head. He slowly, carefully removed his arms from around Jamie and mentally lifted her into the arms of Aerik. "I know she's your mate. I'm your friend, remember? I did this for you," Tray said as he raised his hands in the age-old motion of surrender as he backed up a few paces.

Aerik took Jamie protectively into his arms and held her close. Looking into her eyes he compelled her to sleep. She complied instantly. He then looked up at Tray, the fire gone from his eyes. "Thank you."

Tray knew that those two little words spoke more than just that. He grinned. "You're welcome." Tray surveyed the cabin. Two dead two living. Mrs. Edgewood lay on the floor with her hands cuffed behind her back watching them her eyes as large as saucers she reeked of fear and urine from where she had wet herself. The detective looked just as fearful but was clearly more dazed due to lack of blood. "What about them?"

"This man tried to save Jamie's life. He had been staking out Jamie's house when that one over there," Aerik eyed Jeff's body, "kidnapped her. The detective followed them most of the way in then hiked in the rest of the way on foot. We don't have much time left. He called for backup when he found the cabin." Aerik had read his mind while he had fed from him.

"So…" Tray said, "what I hear you saying is that I don't kill this one."

"Correct."

"And her?" Tray nodded towards Mrs. Edgewood.

"Justice," was all Aerik had to say. Tray knew that she was to die.

Mrs. Edgewood started to scream in protest knowing that they were deciding her fate. With a wave of his hand Tray silenced her. "Take Jamie and go. I'll do the clean up work here." He paused then held up his hand in the gesture of silence. "Someone is outside."

Aerik listened with his vampire ears. Now that he had fed he was stronger. He could feel his body mending itself inside. "The detective was not alone, there was a deputy out in the woods with him." They waited. He heard footsteps nearing the cabin. Suddenly standing there with his gun aimed right at him was Deputy Fisher. He looked stunned to find Aerik Wolfe in his sites. Aerik did not have time for this. "Put that gun down," he commanded.

Clay was visibly shaking, trying to fight whatever was taking control of him. He did not want to let go of his gun. Why couldn't he look away from this man!

"Everything is fine here and you will put down your gun. Now," Aerik said, only this time he used a more calming yet firm tone.

Clay slowly laid his weapon on the floor of the cabin being careful to not sit it in the puddle of blood that ran freely from Mr. Edgewood's body. He also hesitated making sure to not sit it too closely to Jeff's deceased body either. He wrinkled his brow as he assessed the ripped neck of Mr. Edgewood then looked back at Aerik.

"How did you know to come here?" Aerik asked him.

Clay felt as if he was being drawn right into Aerik's eyes. Swirling black smoke, that's what they reminded him of. "I saw Jamie's number on my caller ID and went to check on her. I found Burl shot and then I heard the chatter on the radio."

"What did you do then?"

"I called it in and requested they also send a vet. The dog was still alive. When I heard Edgewood's name as a suspect I figured if he was running he would come here. He uses this cabin every hunting season."

"What did you see happen here?" Aerik asked.

"I saw some real weird shit," Clay began but Aerik cut him off.

"You will stand still and close your eyes now. You will not feel anything till I tell you. Do you understand?" Aerik directed.

"Yes," Clay said as he closed his eyes.

He now turned to his friend and without saying a word he reluctantly handed Jamie's sleeping body to Tray.

Aerik was instantly at his neck, fangs bared. The extra blood was exactly what he needed to completely heal himself. He had only taken enough from Detective Neely to allow him to function at a safe level, to heal critical damage. Clay's blood would restore him back to full strength. He drank quickly then sealed the wound commanding the deputy to sit beside the detective. He then, with great care, took his mate from his trusted friend's arms.

Aerik ran down a quick scenario for Tray so he could plant false memories in their minds of the events that took place. "Detective Neely got here just in the nick of time with Deputy Fisher as back-up. They exchanged gunfire with the Edgewoods and were victorious." He looked over at Mr. Edgewood who was missing most of his throat. "This one needs to be placed in the woods near Jamie's home. They'll assume that her dog made the kill. Jamie escaped out that window," Aerik pointed to the window where he had released the nails earlier, "during the shootout and they assumed that she is on her way to a safe place."

"I'll handle it but you had better get going. I have work to do and we don't have much time. I'll catch up to you later." Tray reassured him that he had everything under control.

When Aerik was satisfied he tucked Jamie safely against his chest and they dissolved into mist then disappeared.

Trayvon looked down at Mrs. Edgewood and smiled flashing her his long sharp fangs. "Damn but I'm famished."

CHAPTER 17

Aerik took Jamie to his cavern deep inside her beloved mountains. He placed her on his bed admiring her as she slept so soundly. He was almost afraid to awaken her. There was always a chance that she would not accept the changes her body experienced. If this were to happen she would go insane and Aerik would be left with no choice but to destroy her. He blocked the thought from his mind and said a silent prayer that she would handle this life-changing burden he forced upon her without her consent. She was so beautiful he could sit here like this and be content to just watch her sleep. She was sleeping the sleep of an immortal for the first time. He committed every detail to memory…her hair, her clothes, this cavern lit with a thousand candles; the fact that her chest didn't rise with breath as she did in the sleep of a mortal. By nature they only drew breath when they were awake. It was a safety mechanism really as they did not need to breathe. It did however allow them to mingle with humans without detection. Aerik leaned down and gently kissed the edge of her lips. "Jamie, it's time to wake up. Come and see what the night has to offer you."

Jamie's eyelids fluttered. Her heart began to beat as she drew in the breath of being awake. When her eyes opened they rested on Aerik. When she saw his face she felt relief and when she felt him touch her mentally she wanted to weep with joy. "Oh Aerik, I was so afraid I had lost you."

"Never will I let you go." He pulled her into his embrace stroking her hair. He refused to think of how close he came to losing her. He kissed the top of her head as she snuggled into his chest.

"Jamie, do you know what has happened?" he questioned softly.

"You saved me and now we will not ever have to worry about being separated again."

"You realize that you have become one of us?"

Jamie looked up at him with her new vampire eyes. "I am?" She was feeling so may emotions that she had to stop talking just to concentrate on what all she was feeling. She looked down at her arms and hands as if they would somehow be different. They appeared the same as she always remembered them.

"It's okay, you are still the same beautiful girl as before," Aerik hushed her, "everything you felt before you will feel ten fold now. You will adjust. I remember it was quite overwhelming to me when I became a vampire."

"Aerik, you're worried that I will hold this against you." Jamie looked at him questioningly. "I can feel...I can read your thoughts!" she exclaimed.

"I wanted the choice to be yours. It was important for me to know that you chose this way of life of your own free will."

"I had pretty much already made up my mind that I was not willing to lose what we have together. I didn't want to spend my life without you," she said softly reaching out to twine her fingers through his.

"Pretty much made up your mind?" Aerik mimicked her then laughed a deep hearty laugh. "Oh Mia, I have so much to teach you I'm not sure where to begin."

"So this is your chamber." Jamie looked around for the first time. Although she had seen it through his eyes once before, being here was something else all together. The beauty of it was intense. The candles flickering were about the most breathtaking thing she had ever seen. Never had flames held such an appeal. If she wasn't seeing it with her own eyes she would never have believed that they would produce all the colors that glistened within the flickering lights before her. She could sit and watch them dance all night.

"Jamie, let me take you outside so that you can see the night through your new eyes."

In the next instant they were standing on a deserted bluff that looked out over the great Pacific Ocean. It was raining, yet Jamie didn't feel cold.

"The rain, it sparkles like diamonds," she exclaimed as she held her hands out to catch the drops as they fell. "And the water, it's bluer. All the colors are so much more dramatic. Aerik, why didn't you tell me it would be like this?"

He chuckled as he stood back and watched her experience the new night with the delight of a child that was just given a new toy.

"Oh Aerik, can I still paint?" She turned to him, her whole being emitting such amazing exuberance. "Can I still do all the things I used to do?"

"You can still paint and do all the crafts you did before. You may even find that your skills as an artist have been enhanced," he told her. He looked more serious as he pushed a lock of her hair away from her face. "There are things however, that you can not do any longer." He sighed hoping with all his heart that she would be able to handle the truth of her situation and learn to adjust. "You can not ever let the sun come in contact with your skin and you can not eat or drink human nourishments." He ran his thumb across her bottom lip as he looked into her eyes. "You must drink blood to survive." In her mind he whispered, "I will help you adjust, Ma Cheri."

Jamie was quiet as she contemplated all he had said. The thought of drinking another's blood was so repulsive it turned her stomach just to think about it. Yet, she had done it on two separate occasions and survived it. Well not really survived it but she was still walking around in her same body, sort of, with her same memories. Perhaps that could, in an essence, count as surviving it, couldn't it?

Aerik was monitoring her thoughts, which was so much easier now; it was as if he were but a shadow in her mind. Suddenly the thought of her taking sustenance from anyone other than himself made his hackles raise. The image he drew of her feeding from another male made the dark beast within himself rage, his fangs lengthening in his instinctual need to solely possess and protect her from others of his gender. Males were not an option. There would be no exceptions to that rule, unless she had a death wish for the one she chose to take from, for he could not promise that male would live. "Jamie, you took from us because we compelled you to. It will be different on your own but I will be there to help you through it. Trust me it's not as bad as you are envisioning it to be." He kissed her lips softly. She tasted so sweet...so tempting. "When it's time you can feed from me. I will take care of your needs till you are comfortable and learn our ways."

Jamie turned her back into his front and snuggled back against his chest. "Yuck...God Aerik that's so gross. There has got to be another way."

"I don't find it...gross."

"Well I guess you could just put me under one of those spells of yours and feed me. You could probably even take the memory away when you're done," she thought out loud, then added, "yeah, I bet you can do that can't you?"

Aerik laughed then leaned down to gently kiss the top of her precious head. "I believe you will come to enjoy sharing such an intimacy." He could do what she suggested but didn't want her to know it. Not yet anyway.

"Just the thought sounds so nasty." Jamie wrinkled her nose in disgust. She refused to think about it further and changed the subject. "How did we get here?"

"You need only to close your eyes and concentrate on where it is you wish to go." Aerik dropped his arms around her casually looking out over the snow capped mountain peeks. He felt Jamie shift then realized she was fading. His arms went from holding her to falling through a rainbow of mist. "Damn," he mumbled connecting to her with his mind. He quickly dissolved to track her. When he materialized he saw her standing in her studio at home smiling at her accomplishment.

CHAPTER 18

Aerik wagged his finger at her then brought it to his lips to silence her. In her mind he spoke. "Do not do that again. Only with me until I'm sure you have safely mastered the art of moving from one place to another," he scolded her. "For instance did you know that there are police officers in the kitchen and others going over the grounds outside? You must speak to me with your mind," he added tapping his temple in visual cue.

Jamie heard him loud and clear but decided to let the arrogant tyrant think she chose to ignore him. "Did you see me?" she asked grinning from ear to ear with the excitement of her triumph.

Aerik looked at her out the corner of his eye while reading her mind (arrogant tyrant?) then grinned as he watched her basking in her newfound powers. *Why the tenacious little snip,* he thought. Suddenly he felt very old. It had been centuries since he experienced such simple delights in his abilities.

"Where's Burl?" she asked.

"Babe," Aerik began but she was already dissolving into mist again. "Damn it," he swore as he quickly took off after her.

Jamie was standing in front of a veterinarian who was holding up a clipboard ready to defend himself with it if necessary. "No don't be afraid, I just want to know if my dog's okay?" She was trying to calm the doctor down. When she saw Aerik standing beside her she looked at him for help. The poor doctor's eyes were huge with disbelief at the sight of these people materializing out of thin air.

"Jamie, you can't just go around appearing in front of people like that." He scolded her for a second time. He turned to the doctor and asked, "Did she just show up out of the thin air?"

The doctor nodded his head yes looking from one to the other.

"Did she scare you by doing that?"

181

Again he nodded yes, still afraid to speak for fear he would have no voice.

Aerik turned to Jamie and pointed at the veterinarian for emphasis. "You see, you nearly scared him to death."

The doctor was looking at Jamie nodding his head yes in agreement to Aerik's statement.

"I will not tell you again, young lady," he wagged his finger at her again, but this time he clucked his tongue as well. "If you do it again," he stressed the word again, "then you my girl, will be the recipient of a sound spanking."

The doctor looked at Jamie still nodding his head in agreement with Aerik.

"Do I make myself clear?" Aerik asked.

"Yeah, but…" Aerik shushed her.

"I know you were concerned about Burl. But like I said, you almost gave this young man a coronary. Now how can he help make Burl well if he himself drops dead from a heart attack that you gave him?"

"But, I…"

"Tell the doctor you are sorry."

"But, I was…"

"Tell him."

Jamie looked at the man whose eyes were as round as saucers and skin as white as a sheet. "I'm sorry."

The vet nodded his acceptance.

Aerik looked at the vet's nametag then said, "Doctor Sheraton, you will not remember any of the conversation we just had. You will remember only that we just entered and were inquiring about the status of our pet the American Mastiff that was shot in the abduction case at the McPherson home earlier today." Aerik tucked Jamie neatly under his arm kissing her on the top of her head, as he so loved doing. In her mind he scolded, "I'll deal with you later." To the vet he said, "So Doctor Sheraton, how is Burl?"

The doctor looked at his clipboard and wondered briefly why he was holding it in such an awkward manner. "Oh, ah…he is doing quite well. Much better than I expected considering the circumstances. The bullet went in at such an angle that it missed all the internal organs. Very lucky dog, lucky indeed." The doctor looked at Jamie finding it hard to look away as he continued to speak. "It basically passed through tissue and fat and I expect a full recovery within a month or two." He realized he was staring but he couldn't help it, he was compelled to keep looking at this woman. She was the most beautiful woman he had ever seen, a true natural beauty. She seemed to shine from within, and her eyes, they were the most brilliant color of green that he had ever seen. He wondered if she was wearing the color changing contacts that were all the rage now among the younger generation.

Aerik stiffened then stroked Jamie's arm drawing the doctor's attention to himself in doing so. "My fiancée and I were very concerned about Burl's health. He is a very special part of our family. We would like to take him home as soon as possible."

"Oh I would say that he could possibly go home in a couple days, I would like to keep him for at least two days just to make sure that we didn't miss anything and that there are no unseen complications." *My God but that man is massive*, he thought as he looked at Aerik. *Good thing too, with his fiancée's looks; he will need all that brawn just to keep the guys away.* There was no way he would want to tangle with him.

Aerik smiled. "I will provide the receptionist with all the pertinent information you may need and please call us anytime with information regarding Burl's health. We will look forward to bringing him home as soon as possible." Aerik reached out to shaking the doctor's hand. "Of course my fiancée would like to be able to visit with him."

"Oh of course, anytime Miss McPherson." Doctor Sheraton shook Aerik's hand then reached to shake Jamie's.

As Jamie took the doctor's hand she swore she heard Aerik growl like a wolf giving a warning before the attack. She could feel his jealousy as he told her to "let go of that man's hand if you wish him to keep it." Jamie released Doctor Sheraton's hand and smiled up at

Aerik. She spoke to him silently, "Aerik, you're jealous."

He silently answered her, "The man is positively drooling over you."

"Thank you so much, Doctor Sheraton. We'll be in touch." Aerik directed Jamie out of the room and away from the man that was undressing her with his mind. It was all Aerik could do to keep his cool. Obviously Jamie had acquired the vampire's gift to attract like a magnet. He didn't know how he felt about that.

Jamie looked around the old mansion that belonged to Aerik's friend Trayvon Cahan. While Aerik and Trayvon talked she wandered around the great room examining all the works of art he had displayed for just this purpose. It was amazing how she could still hear their conversation regardless of the fact that she was so far away from them. It seemed that if she concentrated or focused on them she could tune their voices in almost in the same manner as tuning in a radio station.

"Another perk," she heard Aerik speak softly in her mind.

"Are you always listening to my thoughts?"

"Mia, you have nothing to keep from me; we are as one." He caressed her without physically touching her.

Jamie looked across the long room and smiled seductively at Aerik. "He can't hear our thoughts can he?"

Aerik knew she meant Trayvon. "Not on the path we are using. However, if you were to mentally call out to Tray you would connect to him, he has marked you as I marked you."

"But can he hear what I'm thinking like you can?"

Aerik was quiet a moment. "Why don't you ask him yourself?"

Jamie looked at the equally imposing vampire who was talking to Aerik. She shook her head no and walked on directing her attention back to the portraits on the wall. She stopped to admire one in particular. The artist had a way with painting roses that Jamie admired.

"They are beautiful are they not?" Trayvon asked.

"Yes they are," Jamie said turning to him. He wasn't there. Aerik and Trayvon were still at the opposite end of the room but instead of talking they were both watching her.

"Very funny," Jamie yelled out across the room to them knowing full well that using her voice wasn't necessary, nor was raising it.

Aerik returned his attention back to Trayvon. "You know, I felt something when I shook that boy's hand at the hospital. I should have paid more attention. I didn't sense life-threatening thoughts towards Jamie. I'm assuming because they were the mother's." Aerik told him. "That woman had a tainted mind. She killed not only Jamie's parents but her brother."

Tray was not surprised by this revelation. "It's truly amazing how greed can so consume a person. It sickens me when they twist the minds of their children to achieve their goals. I saw how she had manipulated her boy through the years, changing his character, shaping as well as warping his perspectives on life." Tray flashed a wicked grin then added, "I gave her a little taste of warped and twisted."

"Tray, you will never cease to amaze me with your dynamic forms of justice." Aerik knew that to have Tray as a tracker would be any criminal's worst nightmare. The only problem was they had no idea Tray was stalking them until it was too late. He may dispense swift justice when the crime warranted it, but it was sure to involve some sort of pre-calculated radical punishment, as was Tray's style.

"Jamie, come and join us." Aerik held out his hand beckoning her to them. He watched as she gracefully walked across the great room. She looked radiant, positively regal, and luscious he thought. He suppressed a strong desire to kiss her ruby red lips. He wanted immediately to be alone with her only manners prevailed and he sighed, *Later*....

"All right. What are you two talking about?"

Tray and Aerik looked at each other and grinned.

Aerik pulled her into his arms in a loose hug, his fingers stoking the back of her neck possessively. "Well, we were talking about you," he said in a matter-of-fact tone. "We were working on how to tie up loose ends here. You will need to be interviewed by the police tomorrow. I'm sure they are already frantically searching for you. I will place a call letting them know that you are well and that they will be able to speak with you tomorrow. There aren't enough hours left tonight to chance meeting with them," he explained. "However since your becoming one of us wasn't planned, I do not want to make things difficult for you. I want your transition to be as smooth as possible. The stress of being interrogated isn't in your best interest at the present time and I will not allow it."

"What are you really saying?" Jamie's insightfulness told her that he was beating around the bush about something more important than being interrogated.

"We haven't discussed where we will live and how we would handle all the legal aspects of your change."

"And what exactly will that entail?" she asked.

"We need to decide how to sever ties to your home. I would suggest a mortal marriage and a simple move. If you choose you could retain your property and rent it out, or perhaps close it down and use it as a summer home where we can come to visit."

"I keep this home for when I feel a desire for a change from the European countryside and wish to come to the great Northwest," Trayvon told her. His voice carried that same magical quality that Aerik's did, more so in person than over the telephone. What was it about their voices that made her feel dreamy when she listened to them?

Aerik ran his fingers seductively, possessively down her neck turning her gently to him so he could kiss her full lips tenderly. In her mind he spoke, "Our voice is one of our most powerful tools, it helps us to control others. You also have this gift."

"But I don't hear it in mine as I hear a difference in both of yours."

"We hear it," Aerik told her releasing her as she slightly pulled away from him.

Jamie paced the floor obviously in deep thought. Tray watched her intently. He recalled his own transition centuries before. His brow knotted in thought. She was willful; she would survive this change. Knowing that he had made the correct decision he turned to

Aerik and grinned. "I remember that not long ago it was you who was wearing holes in the carpet. Perhaps you two do belong together," Tray chided his friend.

Aerik shot him a look that told him in a friendly way to not go there.

"So what you're telling me is that I need to leave my home…" she paused, turned and begun pacing in the opposite direction. She was looking at the floor while she talked directing her conversations to no one in particular. "But, I can come back and visit whenever I want." She glanced over at them then returned to pacing. "Why do I need to leave my home? Can't I just stay with you in the mountain during the day and come home at night?"

"Jamie," Aerik sent her a compulsion to calm down he could feel her heart rate picking up at the decisions she was facing. "We could continue to live in such a manner if you wish."

"But you don't suggest it?" Her agitation was clearly starting to show.

"No." He shook his head. "I don't."

"Why?" She walked over to the window looking out at the night. Only it wasn't the night she was used to. Even in the overcast sky it looked as if it was only twilight. Touching her finger to the windowpane she traced the outline of a raindrop as it slowly slid down the cold translucent glass.

"I know that we haven't discussed it much but I have several businesses that I am directly responsible for and I will need to attend to them. I also fear that your situation here will draw the media, and we are extremely careful of how we draw attention to ourselves. In your case I believe that reporters may wish to dig into your personal life. It is not only their nature, but it will give them the back ground they will need to write about your relationships with the Edgewood family." Aerik watched her as she rubbed her arms as if she were cold. It was apparent to him that she was struggling internally as they did not suffer from things such as temperature changes. Their bodies regulated heat as needed.

"I don't think I would do very well with people I don't know asking me a lot of questions," Jamie told them.

"I would propose that we let anyone with an interest believe that you decided to leave these bad memories behind you. To start a fresh life in Europe, a place better suited to displaying your artwork to a broader audience. When the media frenzy has died down here we can return and settle things however you see fit." Aerik took her chin gently in his large hand tipping her head back till their eyes met. Her sadness pierced his dark soul and he felt her pain at the thought of leaving her home. It wasn't just a house, it was a palette for her soul. He ached to protect her from the conflicting emotions causing her such turmoil.

"You're probably right. I'm just really confused right now. I'll be okay once I have time to think things over." Jamie looked up at him confused at what it was she was feeling inside only knowing that something wasn't right.

"She needs to feed," Tray said more as a statement than an observation. He was well aware that Aerik was witnessing the same signs as himself.

Aerik nodded his agreement. He was worried that she wasn't going to be very receptive to what lay ahead. He spoke to Trayvon silently. "Jamie is not going to like the feeding process."

"Make her feed," Tray silently said in his casual matter-of-fact tone.

Aerik looked sidelong at his centuries old partner. "You should not force a woman to do anything that is not of her choosing. Haven't I taught you anything through all these years?"

"Ha," Tray laughed out loud, slapping Aerik on the back playfully. "You, my friend, apparently have not spent much time with the twenty-first century woman. I do not have the patience nor the desire to deal with stubborn obstinate, inflexible, feministic women, with their 'I want it my way or no way' attitudes." Tray cringed at the mere thought of having to cater to such a person. "Now," he added with a wolfish grin, "submissive, obedient, passive, those are traits of a good woman. The only problem is, they died out two centuries ago. Who would have known?" He sighed.

"Tray, I look forward to the day when you find your soul mate. It should prove quite interesting to see what kind of girl you end up with. I do not think she will be the least bit submissive or obedient." Aerik chuckled at the mental picture he had envisioned of the woman Tray would fall head over heels in love with. He then called Jamie to his side.

"I am content as I am," Tray told him only not so convincingly.

Jamie looked at the two realizing that they had been talking excluding her from their conversation. She frowned at them both and walked away from them in frustration. The feeling of something amiss was growing inside her and she was feeling extremely agitated.

"Are you going to stay here in the area or return to England?" Aerik asked.

"I have an engagement to attend in Switzerland. There's an arms dealer that I wish to make acquaintance with. He has been very unconcerned as to whom he sells his wares."

"I'm sure that he will be pleased to meet you." Aerik smiled at his friend as he worriedly watched his mate continue to pace the room deep in her own personal thought. He did not want to intrude and allowed her the space she needed. He did however send her a command that would take the edge off. He knew she needed nourishment. He had stalled, wanting the need to feed to be fully upon her knowing it would help her to take that drastic life-changing step. If she failed to be able to feed on her own then he would as Tray put it "force" her. He would not allow her to starve herself.

"The pleasure will be all mine. Twelve children under sixteen died from his most recent activities." Tray crossed his arms over his chest then added, "His punishment will be most severe and will consist of twelve things that I have devised, one for each of their deaths, before he ceases to breathe."

Aerik knew that whatever Tray had planned for the arms dealer was going to involve extreme torture. His friend had an incredible soft spot for children. Although he would never admit to such, Aerik saw evidence over the centuries of Tray's generous kindness to children in need. "I'll see you upon your return then. I intend on taking Jamie home to my estate in Chichester. I may even take her to the highlands perhaps castle Bearach would be a good place for her to adjust without the pressures of society bearing down on her."

"Remember, if you need anything at all do not hesitate to call me." Tray grinned. He knew his words weren't necessary, they would always have each other's backs.

Aerik nodded knowing that if anything, Tray would always be there for him. He glided to Jamie's side slipping his corded arms securely around her. He felt her relax as she leaned into his comforting hold. "Mia, it is time for us to go back to the cavern. Close your eyes and let me take us there."

CHAPTER 19

Jamie did as he asked because it was easier than objecting. She was feeling shaky inside which kindled a fear that there maybe something wrong with her. She had no sooner closed her eyes then they were back in the safety of the mountain cavern. The natural formations and gems glistened off the soft glow of the numerous candles. It was so beautiful here. She didn't think she would ever get used to the prisms of colors the lights and gems created. She didn't want to let go of Aerik so she didn't. He continued to cradle her in his arms as if she were a babe. Jamie laid her head against the padding of his upper chest and listened to his heart beating. It was so loud, so strong. She could feel each beat as if it were a drum playing for her own pleasure. She swore she could actually hear his blood rushing through his veins. She felt tingly all over as if her body had been delicately stoked with a hundred feathers. His heart beat louder in her sensitive ears as if it were calling to her. She tried to look up at Aerik's face but his pulse beating in his neck drew her attention instead. She tried to look away, to look past it but the shear effort made not just her insides shake, but her whole body trembled. What was happening to her? Her gums felt tingly, her teeth…she stuck her finger in her mouth and something sharp pricked her fingertip. As she pulled her finger back she watched as a bright red ball of blood welled up. "Aerik, what's happening to me?" She was on the verge of panic. She used her tongue and felt that her eyeteeth had grown to pointed fangs.

"Jamie, you need to feed. You need blood. This is your body's way of saying that it is hungry," he explained as he tenderly took the end of her pricked finger to his lips. "You must take from me," he told her calmly. In her mind he whispered as well as spoke aloud, "Your body knows what to do, my blood is calling to you. Can you feel it?

Can you hear it?"

Jamie nodded yes her mind in turmoil at the thought of what he was asking her do. She couldn't stick her teeth in his skin, she just couldn't. But the thought of doing just that became so overwhelming she literally shook in his arms.

"*Jeta- me*," he cooed as he lifted her so that her head cradled his neck, "I want you to take from me. You must feed. It is our way of survival and you must survive for us, for me."

"I can't," she cried out weekly. "Just hold me please."

Aerik wanted desperately to send her into submission and command her to take his blood but he would not. He needed to hold out and see if she could do it on her own. It was possible that there may be a time in the future that would require her to feed without his assistance. If she were unable to feed herself then she would go mad or starve. Of course there was always Trayvon, he would see that Jamie fed, but that was not an option he was willing to settle for. Aerik never thought of himself as a jealous man but he learned differently when he watched Trayvon giving to Jamie as she lay dying for the second time in the short duration that he had known her.

He decided that if she could not take from him while the unrelenting desire to supply nourishment to her new body was upon her full force, then perhaps if he combined the desire of a vampire's driving sexual appetite to that which she was already afflicted with. When he was in the throws of passion his desire to take from his partner was at its greatest. He began by slowly stroking her legs. "You will be more comfortable without these clothes binding you," Aerik whispered as he made her clothes dissolve. He moved them to the bed in the middle of the cavern and laid her gently into the pile of supple furs. He stared hard at what was his, for she was his...and his alone, she was perfection at its finest. Every limb, every curve, every hair...perfect. There were no flaws, no imperfections no matter how slight they may be. There were none. The reality of her beauty was so intense, so stark that an overwhelming need, a desire to protect, to love, to possess her was so profound it encompassed his soul. He not only wanted her he needed her. Her inner light wrapped around his darkness and together they created vibrant colors. He gently rolled her onto her stomach and began to massage her muscles. He then kneaded with his fingers and followed that with his lips and tongue. His mind melded with hers and in the midst of her disarray he built a fire of growing passion. He rubbed a natural vanilla scented oil into her back, and marveled at the way her skin glistened from the glow of the candles that surrounded them. As the enticing scent filled the air he thought he would go mad with desire, his thoughts a shower of lust and he shared them with her.

Jamie felt as if she were losing her mind. All her senses were on fire and she was surely going to hell. Nothing had prepared her for the onslaught of sensations that she was feeling. She could smell, taste, see, hear and feel ten times that of which she could previously. It was really almost too much to handle as her mind tried to comprehend the very power of it all. Aerik was rubbing oil into her skin that she could actually feel seeping into her pores. His hands felt like silk as they glided smoothly over her oiled skin. He missed nothing, rubbing the entire length of her arms, then without missing a beat moved to her legs. She moaned as he began to rub the soothing oil into her small rounded bottom. She not only smelled the scent of vanilla, she could smell his blood. The two mixed together with the constant pounding of his heartbeat nearly driving her mad. She rolled over unable to stand another minute and she twined her fingers into his thick hair. She pulled him up wanting to kiss him but he stopped to kiss her breasts instead. She moaned again as he suckled one then the other. His fingers slick with oil teased the tip of one breast as his tongue laved the other. Jamie arched her back pushing up to meet his mouth as he tormented her with his lips. "I can't take this, I feel so good." She breathed roughly gasping for air as she squirmed on the bed furs beneath him. She nearly came undone when he began flashing erotic images of himself making wild animalistic love to her in her fevered mind. She felt his need as well, for he was bombarding her with it. The waves of need were so intense she could feel it throbbing between her legs. Aerik pushed her thighs apart and nipped her where her legs met her body. He sent her an image of his taking her blood from the vein that fed her womanly desire at the junction where her leg met her body. He stroked her once, twice. He used his finger and entered her moist heated core. She wanted him. She wanted him now and she didn't want to wait. As if he were reading her thoughts his tongue flicked at the red bud that was her pleasure. He licked sucked and nibbled till she begged him for release. Still he would not give it. She wrapped her legs around him and fisted her hands in his dark hair.

Aerik didn't know how much more he could take himself. He was rock hard with need and her begging was almost his undoing. He gave into her need, which she made his own, and he replaced his fingers with his thick shaft. He briefly teased her, playing at her hot wet entry. He would give her a little then withdraw, then a little more then withdraw again. Jamie wasn't having any of this. She wrapped her legs around him and pulled him into her, not letting go till he was buried deep inside her. She was like putting on a glove. She was hot, tight, a liquid fire that squeezed and engulfed his swollen rod. He sunk into her depths with a moan that vibrated through them both. Again and again he entered her. Over and over building friction so erotic it threatened to burn them both. He was the fury of the storm that raged between them, passion that was a tornado out of control consuming them both. Jamie's nails dug into his back creating small drops of blood that beaded and ran down his skin to mix with the vanilla oil that now cover them both. He knew the minute that Jamie smelt his blood. He could feel her insides roll with not only unbridled passion but hunger, the unholy hunger that was the hunger of the vampire. He raised his head up and looked in her face. Her green eyes shined with an iridescent light that made them glow. Her fangs though long, appeared delicate which enhanced her beauty as she held onto him as she was hit with repeated waves of lust and desire. Her long golden hair fanned out on the bed beneath then, a golden halo so shiny so silky, it demanded to be touched. As he filled her from below he lowered his head to her so that her fangs scraped gently against his neck making him grow even larger, harder. "Do it," he whispered. "Make me come as you take from me." He sent her more images of what he wanted. What he wanted of her.

Jamie couldn't stand it a moment longer. She could feel his empowering love for her, his passion, his need, his desires. She could see in her mind what he wanted her to do. Her own body cried out with a need of its own in an all-consuming unholy desire to sink her teeth in his neck and satisfy the demon that took control of her mind. She kissed his neck as he encouraged her silently in her thoughts as well as whispering heavily, seductively into her ear. His breath was hot with his vampire demands. She could taste the saltiness of his skin, smell the copper scent of his blood, hear it rush and pulse with every beat of his heart. It beckoned to her. Her one tooth pricked his skin and she heard his sharp intake of breath, his moan of pleasure as it escaped his lips. Though she wouldn't have believed it possible she felt him swell within her, stretching her filling her as he rode her harder still. Giving in to all that she was, to all that she had become she sank her teeth into his waiting neck, latching on as she was assailed by more feelings and emotions than she could possibly fathom. His blood was not what she expected; it was raw energy in every sense of the word. It filled her craving body with a satisfaction unlike anything she had ever known. It was undeniably intoxicating like a fine liqueur that teased the pallet. Her spirit cried out from fulfillment as Aerik rocked her to the very core of her being. Her physical body shook with the tremors of a heated climatic passion; so right, so needed, so perfect she was totally satisfied. Fed as well as sexually sated. She purred into Aerik's neck as she nuzzled him there. She was amazed at how the pinprick holes closed on their own as her fangs retracted. Something inside her told her that the incisors dripped a liquid that healed the skin. She continued to suckle at his neck as she twisted her fingers in the hair at the back of his head.

"Will it always be like this?" she asked softly as she rubbed her leg up and down the side of him just to feel their skin sliding together as one.

"For all eternity," he whispered back.

"I did it." She smiled up at him seeking his approval.

"I knew you would." He would never admit to her that he had

harbored that small shadow of doubt.

Three weeks later Aerik told Jamie to stand still for the third time as he carefully tied a blindfold, which covered her beautiful emerald eyes. "No peeking."

"I promise."

He pulled her into his arms and they dissolved into a shower of mist. When they materialized Aerik took her small hands in his. "Before I remove the blind I want you to know that everything you see is yours. It is my gift to you."

Jamie took a deep breath in anticipation. Aerik had been way too secretive, not giving up even the slightest of a hint as to the gift he was about to bestow upon her. He would only admit that it was to be a small gift, a token of his love for her. "Hurry up and get this blind from my eyes. I can't stand it a moment longer." She was literally bouncing up and down on the balls of her feet, her long hair bounced and swished as she tried to contain her excitement. This was the first gift that Aerik had ever given her, besides eternal life, and she wanted to experience it now.

"Not yet." He took her gently by the arms and turned her to the left slightly. He bent down and brushed his lips across hers.

"Aerik! I'm going to take this blind off myself."

"You don't want to kiss your husband?"

Jamie stamped her right foot on the ground inpatient at his ploy to stall. "I'm about to kick you."

"Your tenaciousness is going to get you into trouble one of these days, little girl." His voice was husky, seductive, hot against her ear. He grinned when he heard her heartbeat quicken as it did whenever she was aroused. He waved his hand and the blind disappeared.

Jamie sucked in her breath in a gasp of disbelief. "Oh Aerik." She turned slowly taking it all in. "It's my garden of stones," she whispered. "It's real...oh look Aerik it's all here." She didn't look back at him but walked along the very path she had painted on the studio wall of her home. She went straight to Aerik's stone, where not he but Gavin Kintour was buried. She ran her fingers over the weathered etching. Lord Aerik Bearach. "I know I saw it all in my mind but – this is so much more beautiful than I ever imagined it to be."

Aerik took a seat on the old stone bench beneath the aged willow tree that stood over the marker like a sentinel. He watched Jamie's shocked expression of delight light up her already perfect features. "I'm glad you like it because it's yours."

"You can't give someone a cemetery." Jamie wrinkled her brow. "Can you?"

"Well," he shrugged, "the cemetery does comes with the castle." He shrugged. "I never thought about separating the two."

Jamie looked at the tall stone and rough brick wall that flanked the ancient cemetery. She had just assumed the wall belonged to an old church. "Castle?"

"Of course if you don't want the castle." Aerik cocked his eyebrow as if in thought. The next moment he was pushed off the bench by an invisible hand, landing on his back in the grass. An instant beyond that Jamie materialized sitting astride his torso laughing. "Are you kidding me!" She leaned down covering him with numerous butterfly kisses.

"It is yours." He loved the way her eyes sparkled like emeralds in the moonlight. The way her honey gold hair swirled around her as she moved. "I thought that it was sad that you only had but one cemetery. All girls should have at least two."

"Oh Aerik, I'm so happy this is the best gift ever." She scrambled to her feet pulling his hand to follow her. "Come on."

"Where are you going?"

"I want you to show me everything, walk through the cemetery with me."

Aerik took her small delicate hand in his and they walked down the path. They stopped at each grave marker and he would give her a brief history of whom the stone immortalized.

"There has always been something so peaceful, so calming to me about being in a cemetery. When I was little I was always playing in the one back home."

Aerik raised his eyebrow and looked at her as if she were strange. He faked a wince for her benefit when she smacked his arm.

"I used to take my Barbie dolls out there. I imagined that the ghosts of those buried there would come and play with me." She smiled. "It drove Jimmy crazy when he would see me talking to my family members as if they were there. He called me Creepy Casper for a long time." She laughed softly. "He was even grounded for it once." She stopped dead in her tracks and turned to Aerik. "Ya know I think I will collect them."

"Collect what?"

"Cemeteries."

Aerik tossed his head back and laughed. "Oh you're too perfect."

"And what's that supposed to mean?"

Aerik couldn't quit laughing. "A vampire that collects cemeteries. That's classic."

"Hey, what can I say, I'm a classic kind of vampire." She looped her arm through his and they continued walking through her garden of stones.

The end

Printed in the United States
45428LVS00002B/22

9 781413 721157